UNHOLY YEARNING

SINFUL NATURES 2

LYNN BURKE

Copyright © 2022 by Lynn Burke

All rights reserved.

Editor: Kat McIntyre

Cover Artist: Golden Czermak/FuriousFotog

Model Photographer: Christopher John/CJC Photography

This is a work of fiction. Names, characters, places, and incidents are the product of the author's imagination or are used fictitiously, and any resemblance to actual persons, living or dead, business establishments, events, or locales is entirely coincidental.

No part of this book may be reproduced in any form, except for the inclusion of brief quotations in a review or article, without written permission from the author.

Visit my website at authorlynnburke.com

***Warning: this MM title contains multiple partners/multiple pairings including MF and also infidelity**

UNHOLY YEARNING

As a Christian counselor, I strive for integrity in helping guide others in God's will for their lives.

Until a young man walks into my office for premarital counseling—the stranger who ensnared my soul eight months earlier with his bewitching green eyes.

Levi Townson.

The one whose addictive, luscious mouth I can't cleanse from my memory.

My hunger for another taste of him should assure me of my need for a savior, not shepherd me down the rabbit hole toward depravity.

Levi's yearnings mirror mine, the kind that dominates my will. Incinerates and leaves me powerless against my sinful nature.

But if we fall from grace, neither of us will escape unscathed.

1

ZEKE

"We no longer have to be slaves to sin!"

Hundreds of the people packed around me in the mega church, shouting out amens at Pastor Welker's words from where he stood on stage.

"We are new creations!" he continued, jumping onto his toes with excitement, his voice booming from speakers in surround sound.

More affirmatives rose along with hands and fists, repeated by the church leaders seated behind where he paced back and forth delivering God's words for the day. Like a pep rally, the crowd rolled with their spiritual leader's preaching. Emotionalism at its best, drawing everyone to their feet.

I stood like an easily led lamb, but I didn't get caught up in the high as I'd done all those months ago at the rock concert I never should've attended.

Memories hit me like flashing stage lights, taking me back to that night.

Sensual bass.

Writhing bodies.

The stranger with bewitching green eyes.

His ass in my hands...our groins grinding together, the yearning I'd seen on his face mirroring my own—

Don't go there.

Teeth clenched, I reminded myself of where I was—in a damn church—and *what* I stood for: God, His word, and living a holy life.

The Spirit moved through the congregation, but my hands rested on the back of the seat in front of me while I fought off my desire to accept the bisexual label I'd felt on a deep level for as long as I could remember.

I'd chosen to be a man of God, and that life didn't include sexual perversion.

If only I experienced what the rest of Pastor Welker's flock did.

Not so different from the mega church I'd attended as a kid once my heathen parents found God, Simply Grace Church's attendance reached upwards of a thousand. And thousands more supported the nonprofit community by monetarily providing for dozens of missionaries and paying for Christian schooling and Bible-based counseling. I'd been hired for the latter to labor alongside others wishing to help souls struggling to find God's will for their lives.

My good friend Aaron stood beside me, also quiet and still as our pastor stirred up his flock. He, too, appeared unmoved, blue eyes hazed over while staring ahead, but the burden of being the sole care provider for an invalid parent sometimes overwhelmed him to a brain fog mode where nothing broke through.

Not even an amped up sermon about accepting and living in the "new man" in Christ and choosing His way in one's daily walk of life could lift Aaron's shoulders to straighten him to his full six-foot height.

The praise and worship team hurried on stage at the pastor's bidding at the end of the seemingly rousing sermon. Voices rose along with various instruments, deafening to the point I cringed rather than rejoiced in the salvation freely given that everyone sang about.

I believed in God and got on my knees before His throne countless times a day, but I never felt the Spirit move like the church's attendees did.

My dedication, my determination to live the way I did stemmed from heartache and the stubbornness Mom claimed I had always carried like a badge of honor.

Said stubbornness had helped me escape the type of trial almost two years earlier a counselor would hope against and pray to avoid during his career. I'd dug my heels in, determined to advise the couple I'd counseled when I should've handed over the reins at the first red flag.

But in my desire to help the troubled couple, I'd pushed.

And the wife's true colors had shone through when she'd snuck into my office unannounced and shed her trench coat, revealing nothing but flesh and curves beneath.

Declining her suggestion of a hard fuck over my desk had come easy since nothing about the woman had tempted me. But she didn't understand the meaning of the word no and continued in her pursuit.

I'd filed for a restraining order the following week and ended up pressing charges when she wouldn't relent in her stalking.

Denise Foster had landed in the psych ward, and her husband filed for divorce.

A fucked-up mess God had allowed—for His glory. I accepted that truth shortly after the entire affair quieted.

I had accomplished what my old pastor should've done when I'd been a teenager. Stood firm in his faith.

Pastor Hardy had fallen in love with a woman he'd counseled, and his transgressions broke up two marriages. His son Braden, my then best friend, suffered the worst, and the fallout also included a split in the Boston church we'd grown up in.

While hurt and disappointment in the one man I'd placed on a pedestal would've sent most teenagers into a spiral of sin like it did his son, the incident had settled my future in my heart.

I would prove that a man, regardless of his sinful nature, could say no in the face of temptation. I would be the role model that youngsters needed to look to for spiritual leadership. I would stand strong and choose right so that people like Braden wouldn't pay the price of other's sins.

That stubbornness led me to Bible college and additional classes to get my master's in Christian counseling.

And less than one year into a practice my parents had financially supported, I faced what my old pastor had—and proved what I'd set out to do. But my sense of pride churned my guts as much as the fact a marriage had still been ruined.

At least no children had been emotionally damaged.

Braden had spiraled into drugs and alcohol, but God had intervened five years earlier. We'd spoken right before his first semester in seminary began, and I couldn't have been happier to hear he'd turned his life around. Braden had finally found peace and happiness after the trauma his asshole of a father had caused.

Like me, he'd chosen to dedicate his life to God, and we'd made a pact that day, setting our paths in stone.

However, the second time I'd been faced with a life-changing decision, I'd been powerless to the dominating force of *him* while hundreds of people danced around us. My stranger who'd ensnared me with one glance. The one who continued to haunt my dreams and left me aching.

Addictive...luscious on my tongue, his fine ass beneath my hands...

Aaron nudged me with an elbow, pulling me from my musings that stirred my blood in a way no message from the pulpit ever had.

Shame had me lowering my head along with the church's dimming lights, and Pastor Welker prayed God's blessing over his quieted congregation until we met again.

Another praise song began as the crowd began to disperse around us, their murmurs a buzz of background noise in my ears.

"See you at the gym tomorrow?" Aaron glanced over his shoulder at me as we waited our turn to file into the aisle, his eyes downturned at the corners as always.

"Definitely." We'd been meeting at five-thirty, five days a week since I'd moved to the Philadelphia area eight months earlier.

"Push day," Aaron reminded me, and I grimaced.

My damn quads still ached from our Friday workout.

"Getting old sucks," I muttered my complaint, even though I hadn't yet hit thirty.

"As if I need the reminder." He rubbed a hand down over his face and closely clipped beard, blinking slowly.

"How's your dad doing?" I asked, knowing right where his mind had gone—same as it always did whenever we discussed age.

"It's Sunday," Aaron said with a shrug.

The one day his dad enjoyed still being alive since he could livestream the church service.

"I'm picking up KFC for lunch, so that'll keep his good mood around longer," Aaron continued, his focus flitting over a group of young women—single and glancing his way. He ignored them as though his libido had shit the bed years ago.

But I didn't look a second time either.

I followed him up the main aisle behind the women, our progress slow while we waited for those in front of us to exit into the church's massive foyer.

Sunlight shone through the glass wall along the building's front, blinding me before we even stepped foot into the lobby. The second a blast of fresh spring air from the propped open doors hit my face, I breathed deep. A good, long run would loosen my stiff muscles I hadn't spent enough time stretching and rolling after abusing them at the gym.

A lesson learned the hard way, and not for the first time.

We escaped the crowd, and Aaron clasped my hand with his calloused, firm grip. "Have a good one."

I bid him the same and watched him go, his broad shoulders hunched, head down. He carried burdens I couldn't begin to imagine, but one, at least, I figured we had in common.

Attraction to men.

We'd never discussed it, and I sure as fuck hadn't uncovered my sins from that night in Nashville, but I'd never once seen Aaron show interest in the female form. And there were a fuck ton of women at the gym who liked to prance around with more skin showing than covered.

Like me, he hid his sexual proclivities well. Our lusts of the flesh were best left to rot in the grave with the "old man", our inherent sinful natures Pastor Welker had preached about that morning.

I am a new creation in Christ, I told myself, lifting my face toward the sun, soaking in the warmth of her life-giving energy and the reminder of my truth. *And nothing and no one will ever make me believe otherwise.*

Stubbornness was good for something, even when my heart and body yearned for more. *Riches and crowns await me in glory*, I reminded myself, *a mansion for my faithfulness to God's calling.*

A burst of light laughter drew my focus off my affirmations and the promises of God's word. Mr. Astbury, another member on the church's counseling staff, headed my way, his wife on his arm—and a beautiful, younger version of her a step behind them.

Obviously their daughter, she leaned in to the brunette beside her as they trailed the older couple, the two younger women caught up in whatever they whispered about. Hair like a sheaf of wheat shone with golden tints in the sunshine beaming over her head. Tucked waist and perfect sized breasts...just enough cleavage my mouth watered to mark the smooth skin purple from sucking and biting.

My dick took interest in a woman for the first time in ages—the first person at all since *him*.

Mr. Astbury called to me, pulling me into the present.

Smiling, I tore my focus off the young woman on his heels. "How are you, sir? Mrs. Astbury," I greeted, shaking both of their hands.

A few pleasantries along with praise for the uplifting message were exchanged between us.

I could feel their daughter's eyes on me the whole time and preened just the slightest bit, making sure to keep good posture and show off the pecs I'd been working at alongside Aaron.

Her steady focus tingled the side of my face, and I finally gave her mine, holding out my hand when I realized my co-worker had forgotten introductions. "Zeke Sipe," I told her.

Eyes like dark chocolate and just as delicious looking flitted down over me, quickly returning to my face. "Lily Astbury." Husky and low, her voice hit like a shot of adrenaline to my groin.

She slid her palm along mine—and the coolness of metal on her ring finger brought a silent curse to my brain. Turning our clasped hands the slightest bit revealed what I'd assumed.

A small diamond ring sparkled back at me, mocking my dick and the excitement of finding a woman who turned me on.

It figured. After that night in Nashville, a godly woman had finally caught my eye and she was off limits.

My smile stayed fixed in place as I quickly released her hand and took a step back.

"You haven't met?" her father asked, giving me a reason to remove my attention from the young woman I would have pursued wholeheartedly if she'd been available.

"We haven't," I replied.

"Lily just graduated from college," her mother said, and I remembered her dad telling me about their youngest daughter.

She'd gotten engaged to her childhood sweetheart over Christmas break when I'd been up in Boston visiting my parents.

With the size of our church and the amount of people I'd met since moving to Philly, I wasn't surprised I'd forgotten all about her.

"Well, welcome home and congratulations," I told Lily.

She looked me over again, her eyes twinkling with the kind of interest from a taken woman that made my skin crawl—and dick twitch, even though her petite curves weren't meant for my hands.

The little vixen was too damn young, too damn wild with unsown oats to have a tiny rock on her ring finger. I wondered if her fiancé knew that truth or if her beauty just dazzled him into not caring she liked to flirt with other men.

"She and Levi will be coming into the office for marriage counseling," Mr. Astbury said, "and since I'm her father, I thought it best if you sat down with them."

Fucking hell.

Red flags, an ignored libido, and the type of suggestive eyes any red-blooded man would respond to?

Pure trouble.

"Perhaps Pastor Jameson would be better suited for marriage counseling?" I suggested the older gentleman in the third and final office of our hallway who I'd only come across a dozen or so times in my months of working at Simply Grace.

"His biopsy came back, and it's not good news. They're only giving him six months."

My lips thinned, and I shook my head.

"Such a shame," Mrs. Astbury murmured, both her husband and I nodding in agreement.

The two younger girls whispered quietly, not giving a rat's ass about the counselor who had been with our church decades longer than Pastor Welker.

"I already had Mrs. Vale check your availability," Mr. Astbury said about our shared secretary, his smile returning. "I had her pencil Lily and Levi in for Thursday at four."

Annoyance prickled at the liberty he'd taken without speaking to me first.

But if I hadn't laid eyes on his daughter prior to his suggesting I meet with the young couple, would I have refused to counsel them?

No. I wouldn't have.

That truth had me nodding as I submitted to the fact God had allowed the events to transpire that put me in a possibly compromising situation.

He'd given me yet another chance to prove myself, but I knew greater temptation lay in wait. Because Lily Astbury called out to my sinful nature, and unlike with Denise the psycho stalker, my desire ran on the *fuck, yes* side of wanting to bury my dick in her wet warmth.

"Levi will be home this afternoon," Lily said,

drawing my attention back on her blushing cheeks and smiling, glossed lips.

I remembered her father saying she'd been in Florida while her fiancé had studied at a Christian college in Tennessee.

"You must be anxious for September," I said, watching her eyes closely.

Her smile widened as she winked. "Terribly."

I'd meant for her nuptials, but her saucy smirk suggested she meant her wedding night.

Minutes later, I climbed into my car, my head in a constant state of prayer.

Father above, I'm going to need your help with this one.

I hoped her fiancé was better equipped to deal with her, because the temptation to touch, to taste, was very real. Even strong enough to weaken my stubbornness to live a godly life, blameless in the sight of God.

2

———

LEVI

Made it here safe & sound, I texted my mom the second I parked into my new apartment complex's lot. Not that she cared. They hadn't supported my love of all things numbers and geeking over becoming an accountant because they thought I should've gone into ministry.

No card, no appearance at the ceremony Friday night. Not even a phone call to congratulate me on graduating with high honors.

Mom: **Okay**

I waited, wondering if she'd say anything more—like invite me over for dinner. We hadn't seen each other since I'd returned to Philadelphia for spring break, and we'd spoken on the phone once since then—when Dad had been looking for the screwdriver I'd used and forgot to put back where it belonged.

I'd never been a priority. Their first and only love was Simply Grace Church and Pastor Welker, and when I decided on a different future than they wanted for me, I got called my least favorite word.

Disappointment.

So much for that grace and mercy Pastor Welker preached from the pulpit.

The apartment I would live in alone until my wedding night lay a half hour away from the church I expected Lil and I would continue to visit on a regular basis after marrying. That left us a solid twenty from both of our parents—fine by me.

I looked forward to being my own man.

To breathe.

To make choices not influenced by the church, the pastor, the Christian college I'd attended, or parents who insisted on seeking out God's will in every aspect of daily living.

The freedom to marry the one person who had always accepted me regardless of my awkward social abilities and insecurities.

Lil had been the person to defend me back in sixth grade when I got called a fag for ogling a boy in our class. She'd told me to ignore the liars who she said were just jealous of how smart I was. Still, I'd never told her my secret. I found boys attractive and always had, but I guarded my truth since liking boys was a sin.

She'd become my girlfriend not long after

sticking up for me, and we had been together ever since. Middle school sweethearts—the good girl and the secretly closeted-for-life gay boy.

But I loved her dearly, enough that things...well, *worked* as God intended between a man and woman.

Or maybe it was the thrill of doing wrong that got me hard enough to make love to her on the two times we'd transgressed. Not that I'd truly enjoyed it.

My heart sped as I sat in my old Honda in front of our first-floor apartment door at the thought of having another chance. A quick glance around didn't reveal her car, and a knock on the locked door left me standing under the overcast afternoon sky, my scuffed-up duffle bag in hand.

Alone.

I pulled my cell from my back pocket and put through a call.

She didn't answer.

Lil had only let me down once before, with something less trivial than not meeting me after being away from each other for a few months, but she knew such actions triggered my insecurities.

"What the hell, Lil?" I muttered, touching the screen to call again, praying nothing had happened to her. What would I do without her? She'd become my other half, as familiar as the air I needed to survive—

"Hey, boo!" she answered, breathless and laughing. "I'm so sorry! Mom, Sabrina, and I are still at the mall's bridal store. Time got away from us."

My heart went heavy in my chest.

Same as a few other times, I wondered if Lil looked forward to the wedding and freedom more than she did actually marrying her best friend.

I smiled because I ought to even though she couldn't see me. "That's okay. I can just go hang at my parents' house until you're done."

The thought made me want to puke.

"I left a key under the fake rock there on the right." Lil's voice muffled like she continued trying on gowns while speaking to me—almost as though I wasn't worthy of her time.

My eyes stung.

I glanced over to find a clearly fake rock on the stoop. A little obvious, but when had Lil ever been anything but? "Found it," I told her, bending to retrieve the plastic key holder.

"Make yourself at home. I'll be there in a few."

I forced another smile, pushing against the emotional letdown sagging my shoulders. "Okay. I can't wait to see you."

"Love you, boo." Her reminder didn't lighten the heaviness in my heart.

"Love you too, Lil."

A slow sigh released from my lungs as I shoved my cell back in my pocket and let myself into my new home.

The living room greeted me with the second-hand furniture she and Sabrina had shopped for: one decent couch, a coffee table, and two end tables. We didn't have a TV, but my parents had an extra in the basement I expected I could pilfer.

I set my bag on the entryway's tile that appeared new, dragging lemon-scented cleaning products into my lungs. A hint of vanilla lay beneath, and my lips curved upward on their own, reminding me of all the good, of the blessings in my life I didn't deserve.

Nothing smelled better than my Lil slathered in her favorite vanilla bean lotion.

Well, one thing had months earlier when I'd made the biggest mistake of my life...but I couldn't think about that night.

Doing so left my groin and chest aching in a way far beyond disappointment, drawing depression over me like a smothering shroud.

Lil and I hadn't been engaged at the time, but I still felt as though I'd cheated on her. One kiss with a man at the concert I'd snuck out from my strict dorm room to attend had ingrained the truth of my nature in the deepest parts of me.

The parts I'd wanted to lay at the man's feet, beg him to fill...

Just stop.

Swallowing hard, I focused on the present, my future with Lil whose acceptance and affection would have to be enough.

Teeth clenched, I thanked God for gifting me something else to give my attention to rather than the memories of where I'd felt alive for the first time in my life. With quick strides, I checked out the rest of our apartment. A single bedroom crowded with the queen-sized bed Lil's parents had bought for us as an early wedding present, a tiny kitchen, and an even smaller bathroom made up the whole of our new space. Two dressers were stuffed in at the foot of the bed, both of which I expected Lil would claim once we married in early September.

But in the meantime, the place was all mine for the next three months, two weeks, and six days.

It took less than a half-hour to unpack all my belongings from my car. Meager, mostly cast-off items and second-hand store clothing filled the boxes and bins.

My parents never had much money, but they made sure to tithe no matter if it left us with dented cans of soup and Saltines for dinner.

God first, church second had been ingrained in my head for as long as I could remember.

And their only son? A gift from God, they'd called me, but not enough of a blessing to be a priority like I was to Lil who reminded me all the time how much I meant to her.

I glanced at my watch.

Well, most of the time.

My lips thinned over her taking so long to come see me.

I put all of my clothes into one dresser while waiting for her to show up. Reassembled my rickety computer desk in a corner of the living room to create an office of sorts. We didn't yet have internet, so I used my cell to check out local listings.

Landing a job was my number one priority. Without it, I couldn't support my soon-to-be wife.

An hour later, I realized my stomach growled, but the kitchen cabinets were bare except for six plates, matching glasses, and flatware. A box of old pots and pans sat in the corner, and I rifled through the items, hoping like hell Lil had plans to get more stuff for cooking.

I'd bought Lil a pack of the Andes mints she adored, and they called to me from the table where I'd left them.

Instead of digging into her gift, I decided to use the last five bucks I had on me to grab a couple of cheeseburgers and large fry at the McDonalds around the corner. I headed back to our apartment, warm bag in hand, and the door stood open when I returned.

My smile appeared as I heard Lil calling out my name. Only an hour and twenty-three minutes late. I ran the last couple of steps anyway and stopped in the entryway as she exited the bedroom, our gazes catching.

"Hey," I breathed out, my heart rate picking up pace at her beautiful smile and dark, twinkling eyes.

She squealed and launched herself at me, slamming into me hard enough I stumbled back against the door. Her soft lips landed on mine, tasting like chocolate mint, and I waited for more than a sense of comfort to hit me with the same force her tiny body had.

Nothing swept through me like that night in Nashville.

No jolt to my dick, no insane craving for *more*...or to settle between her slender thighs.

Still, I kissed her hungry mouth, being so bold as to drop my bagged dinner and grab her backside. At five-ten and a half, holding her slight body was no hardship. With the first flick of her tongue along mine, my dick woke up a bit, enough to take interest, and I groaned.

"Missed you," she whispered against my lips. "So damn much."

"Same."

"Thanks for the Andes."

"Of course."

She pulled back, her pupils widened and her breath thready as she slid her hands over the sides of my shortly clipped hair to lace her fingers behind my head. "Guess what?" Her eyes shone with more than just happiness over seeing me.

"What?"

"I found my dress!" She squealed again, jiggling in my arms, and I tightened my grip to keep her from falling.

Her excitement affected me like it always did, and I found myself grinning. Things were going well, the wedding plans smooth from what I'd heard. No bumps in the road, no struggles to hinder our moving forward.

Lil's eyes grew hooded while peering at my lips. "Mom's not here."

My girl was obvious, as always.

"Sabrina?" I asked, my semi swelling enough I felt sure I would be able to perform.

"Nope." Lil popped the P, and I set her onto her feet.

She grabbed my hand and tugged me toward the bedroom.

We didn't speak another word, but we rarely needed to. After being boyfriend and girlfriend for most of our lives, communicating without a sound came naturally. Like an old married couple gone gray together.

The last time we'd had sex was over spring break in the back seat of my car and had been a complete failure for me. And the one before that had been our first on the night of our engagement which had ended good for both of us on her parents' living room floor, long after they'd gone to bed.

Originally we had talked about waiting for our

wedding night, remaining pure in the eyes of God, but my girl was persuasive. Voracious too, I'd learned. Sex was all she'd talked about since spring break when we went our separate ways to finish up college. Every phone call centered on sex once we got caught up, and one night, she'd even gone so far as to tell me her shameful fantasy.

Lil's cousin from California had been in a three-some—and her boy-crazed head had latched on with a strong hold, giving her a fantasy she often thought about. And talked about.

I'd been horrified by her admission, my insecurities rising up like a killer whale after a poor, hopeless seal.

But I had a secret one of my own.

Swallowing my hurt hadn't come easy, but I'd managed to assure her I loved her regardless while fearing I would never be enough.

To make matters worse, when we FaceTimed Lil wanted to talk dirty and see each other get off. If she knew what it took for me to ejaculate over my abs while she watched on her cell, she would be horrified. Call me names—a cheater, a liar.

Damnit. Focus on pleasing the love of your life, you jerk.

I pulled back our comforter before laying her down on the bed, unable to hold her gaze due to the twisting of my stomach.

Completely naked, skin covered with goosebumps, Lil held out her hand to me. I shoved off my jeans and stretched out on top of her, careful to keep my weight from her. My chubbed dick rested between her thighs, and the wet heat of her core gliding along the back of my length while kissing her eventually made me hard enough to get the job done.

She'd gone on the pill a few months earlier, so I didn't waste any time since who the heck knew how long my dick would stay erect. Our mouths came together again, and I swallowed her whimper as I sank into her body.

Tight. So tight—wet enough her body took my length without resistance like our first night together.

Better every time...

But not quite enough. Something lacked between us—or rather, lay between us.

My old sinful nature, my shame, that I couldn't ignore no matter how hard I tried to tell myself I wasn't trapped in our engagement, that God had gifted me so much more than I deserved.

I struggled to stay hard with every withdraw and thrust. The fight to focus on how we fit together thankfully took my mind off *him,* even though lingering on the memory of his hands on my body would've made me capable of satisfying her completely, in a way we both would've enjoyed.

She slid a hand between us, and I lifted up in a

plank to watch Lil get herself off. Perhaps once I learned more of her body, her needs, our sex life would become fulfilling in the way I hoped and prayed for.

Like it would be with him.

My erection flagged as the unwanted thought warred with the whispers of guilt in the back of my head.

"Don't stop," Lil whispered, and I clenched my jaw, eyes closed and brow furrowed in determination to give her what she wanted. "Yes...Levi...please..."

I humped against her with my semi like a damn dog, thinking it would help my situation.

At least it did hers. Lil's insides clamped around my flagging erection, pulsing with every breathless whine filling our bedroom as she came around me.

Hopeless in chasing my own orgasm, I slowed and eventually stopped once she quieted and went lax beneath me.

"You didn't come again."

I hated the pity in her eyes and quickly climbed off her, my flaccid dick wetly smacking against my thigh.

"I'm sorry," I muttered, shifting to perch on the edge of the bed, my head in my hands.

She trailed her fingertips down my spine while sitting beside me. "It's okay. I'm sure once we're married and you don't feel bad about the whole premarital sex thing, we'll be fine."

Fine. Not great, certainly not passionate or consuming, like I'd dreamed about.

"You're probably right." I entwined my fingers through hers, forcing a smile.

Lil tilted her head onto my shoulder. "Dad set us up with the new counselor at church. Maybe we can talk to him about it."

We'd agreed to the premarital counseling her parents cared enough about to encourage—mine couldn't be bothered with our wedding plans—but the thought of sitting beneath Pastor Jameson's watery, drooping eyes hadn't sounded appealing at the time.

"New counselor?" I asked, excited for that at least.

"The one hired right before we got engaged. Zeke Sipe. I met him after church this morning. He's young for a marriage counselor, but Dad said he's certified and more than capable from what other couples in the church have said. You're going to like him."

"Okay." I agreed same as I usually did with whatever Lil suggested.

She squeezed me tight, her breath hot against my ear. "You're a good man, Levi."

The same thing she'd said the last time I couldn't perform that night in the back of my car. I'd blamed the location, the lack of comfort.

If only she knew the truth.

I kept my lips clamped shut, knowing I would never find another woman who would love me like she did, who'd accept me wholly. Revealing the sin I had committed would definitely rip us apart.

"He's easy on the eyes," she murmured.

"Who?" I asked, clasping my hand over hers trailing across my chest.

"The young counselor."

I chuckled, shaking my head. "You think every guy under thirty is hot."

"No, seriously. Zeke is...I don't have the words for what he is, but you'll see. We're meeting him Thursday at four."

I pulled back a bit and kissed her forehead. "Should I feel threatened by this Zeke?" I asked with a joking tone, same as I always did whenever my girl talked about other guys—something she'd done since day one, something that hadn't ever bothered me one bit.

Because I could thoroughly understand the draw to men.

She gave me a quick kiss. "Of course not, boo. You know I love you most."

"Mmm hmm," I offered with an exaggerated tone while smiling.

"Was that McDonalds you had? And did you get me anything?"

"I only had five bucks."

Lil let out a sigh and snuggled against me again.

"I'll have some extra money this month after getting our internet set up, and you know my mom. She would feed you every night if you showed up on our doorstep like a lost puppy. But if it's that bad, I'm sure Dad would help you out since your parents can't."

I shifted on the mattress, grimacing. While I hated her family supporting me until I found a job, I didn't have much of a choice.

"Thank you," I choked out, hating how easily my emotions got the best of me. Lily Astbury certainly wasn't getting a strong, confident man for a husband.

Letting her down had become my greatest fear, and the secret shame of having done so without her knowing twisted my insides.

"Want to share my cheeseburgers and fries?" I asked, pushing from the bed in an attempt to soothe the sudden restlessness inside me.

"Sure."

"In three months, we'll be married," Lil said once we sat clothed at our small table, her contentment and happiness not having its usual effect on me. "I'll be working at the church's school, and you'll be buried in a mountain of numbers and paperwork I'll have to drag you away from." She squeezed my hand tight with her promise.

I wished I had her positive outlook, but doubt sent a shiver snaking down my spine.

3

ZEKE

At the gym on Thursday morning, I asked Aaron what he knew about Lily Astbury and her fiancé. He said they'd been together since middle school—and that Lily had flirted with him relentlessly the summer before she and Levi got engaged.

Yet another red flag to churn my guts and haunt me long after stopping by Clyde's Cafe for my black eye coffee. The double espresso jolted me exactly as I needed but also amped up my unease.

I'm just going to trust You since I don't know what the fuck to do.

Mom would have laughed at the prayers riddled with curses continuing to fall from my lips as I sat in traffic, but I blamed her and Dad for their sailor mouths they'd never disposed of when becoming new creatures in Christ.

Cursing hadn't been a sin in our home, and I continued on with that bit of truth instilled in me from childhood. It felt good to drop an F-bomb whenever the mood struck.

Somewhat calmed by the time I reached the church, I greeted our secretary Mrs. Vale and escaped into my office.

I set my half-full coffee on the edge of my desk and accidentally bumped it with my bag, sloshing it across the carpet.

"Fuck," I muttered under my breath, knowing I didn't have time to drive back for another.

The day didn't get any better from there.

I met with a fifty-something widow whose only child no longer spoke to her, but had I been the son she constantly badmouthed no matter how much I reminded her of God's grace and mercy, I would have split from the controlling bitch too.

Why couldn't so-called Christians choose to love as God commanded? Showing acceptance and grace would lead people to Christ long before judgement and Bible thumping like I'd come to recognize about Pastor Welker's flock.

Then came the private school's bully who'd been entrusted to my spiritual leadership and wanted nothing to do with me. At least I didn't face the same temptations with him that my best friend Malachi had with Isaac, his pastor's son.

He'd given in to his lusts of the flesh—but had

found a love any hot-blooded human would envy. Their connection came through in the words of their co-written songs, in the way they crooned at one another on stage, how they touched, kissed, in front of thousands of screaming fans.

A long lunch break offered the chance to hit the church's cafeteria/cafe for a chicken Caesar wrap and shit cup of coffee, and I hid away in a corner where I pretended to be busy with a few files so I wouldn't have to force small talk I didn't feel up for.

Thoughts of Malachi and Isaac left me feeling like a ship lost at sea. Jealous. Lingering too long always took me back to that night...

"Enough," I muttered what I did whenever my emotions got caught up in wanting what my sinful nature craved.

The taste of a man on my tongue—my stranger.

Goddamnitalltofuckinghell. I left the café, jaw clenched in determination to move forward down the path I'd laid for myself. Counseling God's children.

Lily Astbury.

My insides jittered with every passing hour once I returned to my office, and by the time four rolled around, a heavy boulder sat lodged in my gut that had nothing to do with the lunch I'd forced down.

The clock above my desk ran slow compared to my heart rate, and I eyed it, every click of turning minutes loud in my ears.

At least the church had soundproofed the rooms to give privacy to those needing to unload to listening counselors.

A soft knock sounded, sending a swoosh of adrenaline through my arteries, and I stood, smoothing down my tie.

Every inch of my skin stretched tight as I strolled across my small office, in no rush to greet Lily and her fiancé Levi.

Grasping the door knob, I paused.

God help me. Give me the strength to deal with this little vixen.

I pulled the door inward, and the scent of vanilla swept over me, turning on my drool factory along with the rest of my body.

Dark, flashing eyes, a sexy smirk—

"Hi," she purred, popping her jean-clad hip out and toying with the ends of her long, dirty-blonde locks falling over her shoulder.

I cleared my throat and stepped back, motioning her in even though I wished I could yank her into my arms and devour her mouth instead. "Good afternoon, Lily."

She moved into my office on a cloud of sweet-scented temptation, holding my gaze. "Zeke, this is Levi, my fiancé," she said, her husky voice making my semi twitch. "Levi, Zeke."

I'd forgotten all about the damn man coming along with her.

Forcing a pleasant smile, I tore my focus off her for the man approaching in my periphery to fill the doorway.

Pale green eyes stared at me as though caught in a goddamn spotlight, snagging my breath like a kick to the groin.

Him.

My stranger from Nashville.

A rush of blood pounded in my head, drowning out the curses ringing between my ears. I fought to exhale, to make it sound steady lest my staggered insides' reaction rose across my face for Lily to see.

Levi stood unmoved in front of me at almost eye level, frozen, his face void of expression.

Stunned as fuck just like me.

Every inch of me buzzed like a live wire ready to explode—the exact same energy that had zapped between us as real as the sooty lashes around his gorgeous eyes. My fingers stretched at my sides, tingling to reach out to grab hold of his wide shoulders and yank him against me, but I didn't move.

Should I admit to knowing him or pretend we'd never met?

Was Lily aware he'd kissed a stranger eight months earlier? Had Levi—the man who'd flooded my entire body with a deep yearning to sin—admitted to his fiancée his lust for the same sex?

Even if he had, she couldn't have known I'd been

the one since he and I hadn't exchanged a single word let alone names on that night.

Levi blinked first, dropping his focus to the floor in such an act of submission I wanted to tip his clean-shaven chin up, and...I didn't know. Kiss him? Fucking devour his luscious mouth, his beautiful fiancée be damned?

Fuck.

With no answers to my dilemma brightening above my head like a cartoon light bulb, I did the only thing I could in the situation.

"Come on in," I rasped out and forced myself to take my focus off his clean-shaven jaw to shut the door. My hands shook, and every breath I drew remained shallow as fuck.

The sound of feet shuffling on carpet met my ears, and I quickly closed my eyes, shooting off a silent prayer along with a half-dozen more curses before turning to face the affianced couple I was to counsel before they married.

The only man I had ever kissed but couldn't bear to look at.

The young woman my body wanted to feast on as I once more took in her crossed legs where she sat on the couch.

Lily glanced down over my front while Levi faced my desk beside her, his back straight as he perched on the edge of a cushion. She smiled a suggestive smirk once her gaze returned to my face.

Fuck, she had a banging body, and her blatant offer roused hunger—but I wanted *him*. The object of my fantasies, the one who'd enticed me to come in my sleep, making a mess of my sheets.

Her man, the one who'd put a rock on her finger even though he'd gotten hard as fuck against my body months before asking her to marry him.

My guts churned, and I swallowed with difficulty while numbly finding my way to my chair. I forced a smile like I did countless times a day when talking to the people God brought into my life—but I couldn't turn my focus on Levi.

I feared the addiction of losing myself in his bewitching eyes.

Rather than diving right in and starting to ask questions, I gave the two of them what I always did when meeting people in my office for the first time.

"I know it's not easy opening up to strangers," I said, my voice surprisingly steady as I propped one ankle over the opposite knee, acting calm as shit while my heart tried to burst from my chest, "so I always break the ice of a first session with offering to answer whatever questions you might have for me."

Lily glanced at my left hand before flicking her tongue over her lower lip.

My dick twitched again.

"Dad said you've been here since last fall?"

"I moved to Philly in October, right before

Halloween," I replied, refusing to look away from her steady gaze.

Her head cocked to the side. "I'm surprised we haven't seen each other before last Sunday."

Oh, I'd seen her fiancé before...and I wondered again if she knew what he'd done in a Nashville auditorium at a very gay, sin-filled pop concert.

My smile stayed firmly fixed in place even as my skin continued to tingle from Levi's stare I could feel as tangibly as my fingers clenching on my lap. "I was in Boston visiting my folks over Christmas when your dad told me you got engaged, and I was out of town when you were home over spring break too."

"Hmm." Her lips continued to smile, the upper curve generous and glistening with gloss. "Well, welcome to Simply Grace a little late."

"Thank you." Knowing I had to acknowledge the other person in the room wreaking havoc on my nerves and body, I took a steeling breath, scared as hell over the words about to exchange between us. "Levi—" I faced him, his pale eyes staring into my soul and fucking ensnaring every inch of my mind. I cleared my throat at the sight of his widened pupils, the raw desire no longer hidden by the surprise of being faced with a man he never expected to see again. "Do you have any questions for me?"

"No," he whispered—and I saw it. The fear I'd noted in Nashville after he'd taken my mouth as though desperate for a taste of the man he'd ground against while dancing to the sensual beat that had matched my thrumming pulse.

Lily didn't know.

And his eyes begged me to keep my silence.

Fucking hell.

"So what made you decide to be a counselor?" Lily asked, and I tore my attention off Levi, my heart thudding heavily in my ears. "Usually counselors are gray haired, boring old men," she continued.

Grasping onto the gift Lily gave me, something more to focus on, I took my time answering her question. I uncovered the sins of my childhood pastor, how he'd taken advantage of his position, led a woman astray, broke up two marriages, and ruined his son's life for years. Spilling his poor choices came as easily as it always did. While some in the church would frown upon my sharing a man's sins, I did so to remind myself why I'd chosen that path, for honesty's sake—and the asshole deserved to be outed for all the damage he'd done.

I never shared his name but let those sitting down with me know that I had reasons for being there, that they would never get anything but a man of integrity, striving to prove God's way could be followed above sinful cravings.

Lily's eyes dimmed a little at my firm statement of holding myself to higher standards, and Levi stared at his lap when I faced him to gauge his reaction to my declarations.

I had failed with him, terribly so. Levi was my one fall from grace I refused to repeat.

But could never regret.

I would carry the memory of his taste and the feel of his hard body and his fine ass beneath my hands to the grave. The only man I'd ever touched in a sexual way, the secret I wouldn't ever speak of again.

Thank fuck he seemed to feel the same about leaving our past sins buried with the "old man" Pastor Welker had been harping on about for weeks.

"Any other questions?" I returned my gaze back on Lily, my insides and mind somewhat more settled while my chest continued to ache.

"You're so young," she said, flicking her tongue over her lower lip, the action drawing my focus. "Have you even *lived*?"

"I've had close to thirty years on this earth, most of that time pleasant. Fulfilling in my chosen work. But if you're asking if I've gone out and experienced what this world has to offer, I have."

Not fully satisfying the lusts of my flesh—with a man—but my past lay buried beneath the blood of the Lamb. My sins weren't any of her business.

"The two of *you* are kind of young," I said, ready to take the focus off me before she pried even further.

She rolled her eyes, proving my words. "Not you too."

"Your parents think you're too immature to marry?"

"It's better to marry than burn," she murmured what the Apostle Paul had written in a letter to the Corinthians, her gaze on my mouth.

Lily Astbury was a sexual creature, and had Levi not been sitting beside her, she would have tempted me too.

I angled toward Levi. "And what are your thoughts on that statement?" I asked, knowing I turned down a path that probably wasn't where any pastor or counselor should go.

Sex—since compatibility would be an issue from what I knew about Levi.

I told myself I did so for both their sakes.

But more than caring prompted my question. My flesh yearned to flirt with sin, and the possibilities of "what if" spurred me forward.

4

LEVI

"We're both graduated from college," I found my voice to say something to him. *Zeke.*

Holy hell, I loved the sound of his name echoing in my head along with the memory of how his hands felt on my body, his tongue in my mouth.

"Not much younger than you," I added, trying to stay focused on why Lil and I sat in his office rather than what I'd done with him eight months and one day ago.

Lily had told me Zeke was hot, and how I wished I'd known who he was, that I'd caught a glimpse of him prior to walking in for our counseling session.

Even though he'd checked out Lily, his focus caught on her beauty when he'd answered to her knock, the sight of him had stolen my breath and damn near taken me to my knees.

I had shuffled forward on autopilot, my heart in my throat, my insides twisting like a tornado—and he'd turned his dark blue eyes on me at Lily's introduction.

His attention pulled me up short in his doorway, my feet frozen as every emotion I'd felt all those months ago once again slammed into me.

Lust for the flesh.

Need to be understood and accepted by someone like me.

Desire to taste his mouth, breathe in his exhales.

I'd wanted to lose myself beneath his wide shoulders and powerful body, the heart that had raced under my palm while we had danced.

Energy had shivered down my spine that night, tingling my backside that he'd grabbed so damn hard I'd bruised for five days, and I shifted on the couch beneath his stare at the memory.

I'd felt...*alive* and couldn't regret sneaking off campus to attend a concert any god-fearing person would frown upon.

"Not so much younger," Zeke agreed quietly with the statement I'd made what seemed like hours ago.

Did Lil notice how time seemed to stand still while he and I looked at one another?

I tore my attention off Zeke to find her watching him, namely his mouth. What went through her brain? Did she wonder what it would feel like to kiss those lips?

Heat flooded my face as a strange sensation turned my stomach.

I knew—remembered all too well—and I didn't want Lil touching him.

The truth my jealousy didn't go the other way around had me sinking back into my seat, guilt warring over my continued lust for him.

"But what about the marrying so you don't burn?" Zeke asked me, pushing for an answer to the question I had avoided.

I studied my hands, rubbing over my jean-clad thighs.

"If you're suggesting we're marrying just so we won't sin," Lil answered for me, "we already have and nothing has burned us yet."

Oh, holy hell.

My eyelids slammed shut. "Lil," I whispered harshly, my insides tightening.

"He's our counselor, Levi. Honesty is the best policy," she stated quietly, patting the back of my hand in a motherly way like always. But it wasn't insecurities making me want to sink into the couch. She'd embarrassed the hell out of me—and flooded me with shame for not being totally honest with *her*.

"Dad said whatever we share in this office is covered by the same non-disclosure thingy that all psychology people have to abide by," Lil went on. "Isn't that right, Zeke?"

I couldn't bear to open my eyes to see if he

watched me or stared at her with raised eyebrows. She'd proven her maturity with the usual little-to-no filter on her mouth. Surely he saw how she looked at him too, where her mind went, even though she was engaged to be married.

Had she not assured me at least once a day how much she loved me, would always choose me, I would have attempted to give her freedom and tried to move on myself. But as needy as I was for acceptance and assurance, I clung to her the same as I had since sixth grade.

Lily Astbury had always been my comfort, my safe place—and my emotional and mental health couldn't afford losing her forever.

"Anything shared inside this office stays here," Zeke said.

I let out a breath I hadn't realized I held and dared to open my eyes. Zeke's gaze rested on where Lil's hand still pressed against mine. My other hand moved on autopilot, lightly clasping atop hers to let her know I appreciated the physical comfort.

A slight furrow appeared between his brow, and a muscle ticked beneath his scruffy jaw.

Shoots of...*something*...raced through me. A thrill over the fact he didn't want me touching her? Satisfaction in having my thoughts confirmed he didn't like that I was off limits?

"Are the two of you sexually compatible?" he

asked, and I cringed again, withdrawing both of my hands from Lil.

"We've only had sex three times," Lily continued, her voice on the quieter side for a change. "The first time was fantastic, but the second time and the last one on Sunday afternoon..."

My throat tightened at her pause, and I dug my fingers into my thighs. *Go ahead, Lil, tell him how I can't climax.*

She patted my hand again, but I kept mine to myself. "I'm sure things will get better once we're married and Levi's guilt doesn't get the best of him."

I feared it wouldn't—because of the man sitting across from me.

"You don't feel guilty for having sex before marriage?" Zeke asked her.

I dared another glance at his face. A glint lit his eyes as he studied Lil, an emotion I couldn't name. He seemed relaxed where he sat lounged in his chair across from us while I longed to swipe at the imagined million ants skittering across my skin.

"Nope." She popped the P like always when sure of herself. "We're getting married in a few months—"

"Three months and sixteen days," I whispered.

"—so what's the harm in enjoying ourselves now?"

"I don't usually share my unpopular opinion on this topic," Zeke said, keeping his voice low as well, "but premarital sex is seen as a sin when in reality, partaking early would reveal vital areas where a couple might not be a good match."

He met my stare, and I felt his words clear to the tips of my toes while struggling to breathe. Was he suggesting in a roundabout way that it wasn't guilt that kept me from performing? Did he mean I ought to take a long look at what made me hard like I'd been that night while grinding against him?

Did he still think of our stolen moment, remembering how we fit together, how our bodies had moved as one with the same mind, the same need?

My dick swelled beneath his lingering gaze as I rubbed at the tingling along my forearm.

I flicked my tongue over my lower lip, scrambling for something to say that wouldn't out me and ruin the future Lil and I had planned together.

"I think we'll be a perfect match." Lil stated brightly what her parents assured us of, her voice betraying a fake tone I'd heard countless times.

I sagged again, knowing her brain as well as my own. She worried I wouldn't be able to keep it up once we were married.

My throat tightened, but my groin remained swollen beneath Zeke's dark blue-eyed stare.

"Isn't that right, boo?" She laced her fingers through mine to stop me from rubbing at my skin.

The muscle tic in Zeke's jaw made another appearance at our clasped hands, and the sudden lightness in my chest filled me with warmth, twitching my length in its jeans prison.

"But in the meantime," Lil continued, "we're going to continue exploring, learning, and finding ways to make things enjoyable for both of us."

More heat flooded my face as Zeke cleared his throat and deliberately looked away from us.

His jealousy hit my tongue like the sweetest caramel, but the ache in my groin, the skittering ants over my skin...it became too much.

I glanced up at the clock above the door. Fifteen more minutes.

"Eight-hundred and ninety-seven more seconds," I muttered under my breath without meaning to, but Lil kept on talking as though she hadn't heard.

Focus on something else...

My eyes took in the rest of his office with a quick glance I hadn't managed earlier but forced at that point in order to ease the crashing needs and emotions in my head. A big desk sat in front of a tan wall, its chair on wheels rolled back. A few files scattered atop, as well as a cell and a pencil holder.

A name plate reading *Zeke Sipe*.

And a box of Milk Duds, the only personal item outside a couple of framed diplomas hanging on the wall.

The corner of my lips twitched at our shared love of chocolate and caramel.

"So, tell me how you two met," Zeke said.

Lil filled him in on how her best friend's parents had sold their house and left the state, and she'd been on her knees asking God for a replacement when our moving truck had pulled into the vacant house beside hers. She'd run from the swing set in her back yard to greet the new family.

Mine.

And she told Zeke how on the first day of school I'd been bullied and she stood up for me—the gift she'd been given from God.

And we had been together ever since.

I shifted beneath the stare I could feel on my downturned head while Lil continued to prattle on about our families, sharing all my insecurities and triggers from my parents' focus on the church that heated my face.

"They're heavily involved in ministry?" Zeke asked me, and I gave him a quick glance—but couldn't handle more than that. My focus dropped back to my hands.

"His mom—"

"I'd like Levi to answer, if you don't mind, Lily." His admonishment came out with a bit of a bite to it.

"Sunday school," I stated quietly when Lily didn't sputter over being told what to do or try answering for me a second time. "Choir too. Dad is a deacon, and Mom runs the church's small library."

"And how do they feel about your marriage to Lily?"

"They're too busy serving God to pay any attention to me or my future since it doesn't align with what they would have me do." I blurted the truth without thought and instantly cursed my stupidity.

"Ministry?"

I nodded, horrified I'd told a man who worked at the same church as my parents such personal information.

Lily crossed her arms beneath her breasts rather than taking my hand like she usually did when upset for me. "Their loss," she said with a huff, one that always came out when we spoke about my parents' lack of involvement in my life.

She'd had an easier upbringing full of affection and love, even though her parents were overly protective which caused issues of her own.

The wrong decisions and disappointing them had her wanting to make better choices when they'd thought it was my positive influence. She'd become a people pleaser to the extreme, and I was the timid shy guy.

Polar opposites, a perfect match.

Lil told Zeke that her parents *saw* me, proclaiming how good I was for her, keeping her wild side in check with my quiet suggestions to counter her impulses.

They didn't know their daughter that well—she rarely listened to me.

She went on about our plans for the future, the

job she got at the Grace School, and how she expected God would help me find work soon.

I'd searched every day once she'd had the internet connected at the apartment, but I hadn't found a hint of anyone hiring a numbers guy fresh out of college.

Maybe God withholding an answer to our prayers is payment for our transgressions—or my sins.

"A math guy, huh?" Zeke asked, but I couldn't look at his face.

"I love numbers. They're a constant," I said. "They'll never let you down."

Silence settled for a moment, my face hot from what had to be his stare.

"Are there any books you'd recommend to help our sex life?" Lily asked, giving my brain whiplash.

I bit back my groan, shifting on the couch.

Holy hell. Kill me now.

5

ZEKE

Lily was way too fucking immature to get married. What was Levi thinking?

She felt safe in my office to uncover their sins without hesitation, much to his embarrassment. His cheeks had gone from pale to pink and back again while rolling with the tide of Lily's every sentence.

The young woman was gorgeous, but Lily's discernment lacked to the point that if I hadn't exercised self-control, I would've told her to shut the fuck up and let the man speak. Twice I bit my tongue to keep from sticking up for Levi, my hands itching to pull him tight to my chest to ease his humiliation.

And her hands on him? I fucking hated it.

Hated he'd automatically laid his over hers—an outward claiming? Or trying to make me jealous?

If the latter, it worked like a fucking charm.

But I had no right. Lust alone couldn't trump what they shared.

And my unholy yearning was wrong.

At least she appeared oblivious to the fact inevitable sexual energy radiated between me and her fiancé. Stolen glances full of enough heat to make me hot under the collar wouldn't have gone unnoticed by most.

Lily didn't know the man she agreed to marry had a secret, one that I feared would cause serious issues in their future.

Longing to assure him that he wasn't alone, that I understood and cared about what he felt and thought occupied my mind, but I couldn't go there.

Refused.

He had to find his truth and make the right decision for himself without any external prompting.

I had already probed with my questions and dropped enough hints of things he needed to think on before their wedding day arrived.

So what could I recommend to help a non-heterosexual Christian man decide if he could please a woman, be content with a woman, for the rest of his life? Hell knew I'd dragged my feet on dating for that very reason.

"There are a few Christian based books I know of, Lily," I said, my heart breaking for how much Levi seemed to want to sink into the couch and disappear.

She beamed at Levi. "Everything is going to be just fine, boo."

He cringed at her words, and fuck, how my arms ached to take away his unease and bring him comfort.

But it wasn't my place.

I put both feet on the ground and leaned forward, elbows on my knees, giving Levi my attention. As though my gaze physically caressed his face, he lifted his head, revealing a deep pain I empathized with.

Same as the first time our eyes connected through the crowd in Nashville, I could feel the draw, the weakness of my flesh that wanted to dominate my stubborn will hellbent on pleasing God.

"Levi," I said his name quietly as a prayer, tasting him again in my memory. Chocolate and caramel as though he'd been eating my favorite candy before plastering his mouth to mine.

My dick swelled, trapped by the way I sat, but I didn't shift to ease the ache. The discomfort kept me grounded, kept me focused on the fact I wanted to sin with the man in front of me regardless of the young woman holding his hand.

He's off limits. Forbidden.

Reminding myself of those truths didn't lessen the consuming need inside my soul to know him in a deeply intimate way, that according to God's word, only a man and woman should enjoy.

But fuck, how my dick leaked to partake in that sin.

A slide of my gaze down his chest which stretched his black T-shirt made my groin throb, and the bulge in his jeans...

Christ, he was turned on like I was, regardless of his embarrassment.

I make Levi hard as fuck.

Clearing my throat, I glanced down at my hands clasped between my knees, focusing on the throb in my balls, the need to release...inside him—his ass, his mouth—wherever he would let me.

Fuck.

I blew out a heavy breath, keeping my attention off the two I was supposed to be counseling. "Time is about up."

"Thanks for today, Zeke," Lily said, her voice revealing she hadn't picked up on the sexual tension stealing the oxygen from the room. "So, next week?" she asked, hopping to her feet and grabbing her purse off the floor where she'd set it beside the couch.

"Check with Mrs. Vale on your way out," I said, knowing even while saying the words that I would cancel whatever session they scheduled.

No fucking way could I sit in a room with Lily and Levi again without losing my sanity.

"Will do. Thanks!" Lily offered a flirty smile and a wave before turning away.

At least she hadn't stepped in close to shake my hand. That would mean I'd have to do the same with her fiancé, and I didn't think I could touch him without yanking him against me and having another taste of living.

Levi stood to follow her from my office—slow as fuck, discretely adjusting himself as she started for the door, her back toward us.

He muttered something about ending three minutes before the hour, which made my lips twitch. A cute numbers tic I'd noticed he had.

As if I need another reason to find him fascinating.

I lifted my head, our gazes clashing once more, and my control slipped, losing to the desire I felt for him. Straightening in my chair, I gave my dick some breathing room. A quick tug on my balls drew his focus to my swollen length on purpose—fuck my old sinful nature to hell for taking over in that moment.

His lips parted as I grasped my length, moving it slightly to ease the ache.

Levi's rushed inhale caused precum to seep from my slit, and I bit back a groan as he spun and hurried after Lily, his ass flexing with every step.

The man sure as hell knew how to wear a pair of jeans. On the tight side, tempting and itching my hands for another grope.

Goddamnitalltofuckinghell, I'm fucked.

6

LEVI

I was too hard, too damn turned on to think about anything but the release that had been brewing in my groin for...how long? I couldn't remember the last time I'd gotten off.

For once, my brain didn't focus on numbers—days, minutes, or seconds.

And I lusted for relief to the point I couldn't bother thinking on the humiliation Lily had caused me in front of Zeke. At the annoyance of how she'd revealed so much personal information, regardless of it being a private session specifically meant for such things. Total embarrassment couldn't even flag my erection.

Being in close proximity with Zeke had created an ache I grew desperate to ease, especially having gotten the confirmation he felt something for me.

The lust that had exploded between us in Nashville hadn't lessened in the slightest.

But we didn't have the freedom to seek fulfillment.

I would have to find it elsewhere.

Lily didn't say much on our drive to the apartment, and she didn't argue when I grabbed hold of her hand and pulled her inside rather than walking her to her car she'd brought so we could go to counseling together.

I kicked the apartment door shut, my focus on one thing only—getting inside her and taking what I'd never been selfish enough to before.

She giggled when I spun her in our bedroom and pulled her shirt off over her head. She didn't complain when I dropped to my knees to yank her skintight jeans down over her legs.

No panties—but that thought didn't pulse need through my dick.

It was the memory of dark blue eyes searing my skin, strong fingers digging into my ass that had me fumbling with excitement.

I turned Lily around, pushing her chest onto the bed.

"Levi," she breathed out my name, lifting her backside like my desperation turned her on.

Round ass—a puckered hole...and dripping pussy. Yep. My lust made her hot.

My hands shook, but I managed to open my jeans and shove them mid-thigh.

Without a word, I grabbed hold of her hips and sank into her tight sheath with one harsh thrust. Regardless of her being a woman or the fact a wet vagina clasped at my throbbing length, I stayed hard as hell while gladly accepting what she offered. Leaking and aching.

Forgive me...

Eyes closing, I gave over to my sins and took advantage of the best friend I loved more than anyone.

My throat tightened. Eyes stung. And still I rammed into her, chasing the tingling rising from the base of my spine at imagining fucking into Zeke like I did my fiancée.

Guilt clogged my chest, and I rasped for breath.

Fornicator. Liar. Cheater. The words repeated in my head with every snap of my hips, but I was too far gone in my lust to acknowledge the guilt.

Levi, I imagined him groaning my name—and I came with a hard grunt, spunk shooting through my length with spasming shocks that weakened my knees.

"Fuck," I whimpered through clenched teeth, my head thrown back as euphoria, hot and sweet, rolled over me.

Lily shuddered and cried out, her core clamping

down on me as I dribbled the last of my climax inside her. "Oh God...Levi. Shit, shit, shit..."

I continued to thrust even though I'd finished, giving her everything I could with my softening dick since I'd been so selfish in using her body.

Once she relaxed, I stopped moving except for my heaving chest.

"God, that was so damn good, boo." She let out a sigh and giggled. "What got into you?"

More like who I wanted inside of—and the other way around too. My backside clenched at the thought.

Zeke Sipe. His heart, his mind, his dick. I lusted for all three with a desperation I didn't understand when I had the sweetest, most loving, willing woman in front of me.

I soothed my hand across her lower back, my eyes stinging again. Damn remorse swamped me with staggering effect, and I pulled out, watching copious globs of white ooze from her pink, swollen hole.

"Sorry," I whispered, aware of cool air on my wet dick hanging between my thighs. Spent because of a man. Not Lily. *Sorry* would never be enough, the word souring in my mind.

"Mmm." She shifted, revealing the hand she'd had beneath her, probably strumming her clit like she needed in order to get off. A fact I'd learned over

FaceTime chats since spring break but hadn't bothered with the Sunday before.

Selfish jerk.

Two of her fingers trailed through the mess I'd left behind, and she shoved it back inside her with a small moan.

My dick didn't so much as twitch at what I expected other men would find hot as anything, and I swallowed hard, turning away to get her a towel.

I couldn't look at myself in the mirror while washing and pulling my jeans back up. Lily curled on her side when I returned to the bedroom, a smile on her lips.

"Roll onto your back," I told her quietly, focusing on her legs rather than her face.

She obeyed and sighed while I wiped the evidence of my sin from between her thighs. "Love you, boo."

"Love you too, Lil," I choked out, still unable to meet her gaze.

"Come here." She held out her hand when I finished, so I tossed the soiled towel into the laundry basket and stretched out beside her, my eyes clenched shut. She moved in close, snuggling against my chest, one of her legs sliding between mine. "Are you okay?"

"Yeah," I breathed out my answer, holding onto her for dear life.

"That was hot as hell."

I nodded, bumping my chin against the top of her head, unable to voice anything past the guilt tightening the throat she nuzzled.

"You ought to fuck me from behind more often. Maybe that's the answer—being faced with my ass rather than my front." She laughed lightly, but I didn't find her observance funny.

"Your front is just as beautiful," I muttered, wishing I had the balls to tell her the truth.

"Zeke is hot as hell," Lil stated with more than a suggestion in her voice while trailing a fingertip over my nipple.

I stilled, breath held at the thought she'd known what I'd been fantasizing about while fucking her.

Had I been too obvious and she guessed? Did she love me regardless?

She flicked my hardening nub when I didn't respond, and a shot of lust actually sped to my groin.

"You like him," I said instead of focusing on my dick's attempt to thicken again.

"Mmm."

I grasped her hand to keep her from flicking a second time. "He likes *you*."

"You think so?"

I laced my fingers through hers, holding our hands over my chest. "When you walked past him into his office, he couldn't take his eyes off you."

Lil propped up onto her elbow.

Forcing myself to hold her steady gaze didn't

come easily, but I managed, hoping like hell she couldn't read the guilt eating at my stomach.

"Were you jealous?" she asked

Yes—that Zeke had looked at her like he thought about stripping her down and taking her right there on his desk...when I'd wished it was me on the receiving end of his attentions.

But then his focus had found my face, and all thoughts had been obliterated by the energy connecting us together like it had in Nashville.

I'd lusted after Zeke Sipe in that moment, same as I had eight months earlier.

And he wanted us both.

The jealousy swirled in my stomach again, but I had no right to be upset he found Lil attractive. I'd lied to her. Cheated.

A sudden thought lit my brain—a way to even the secret score in my head, to make things right. Guilt would dissolve on my end, and Lil and I could have our happily ever after. Allowing her to taste the sin that I partook of in Nashville would lessen my shame.

I'm certain of it.

"The wheels in your head are turning, boo." She smiled softly, cradling my cheek in her smooth palm. "What are you thinking?"

Tossing my idea out there could possibly make one hell of a mess—but it could also help my girl sow her wild oats. And Zeke and I could have the opportunity to share an intimate moment without her knowing.

Fuck it.

"Your number one fantasy," I whispered and held my breath, half hoping Lil wouldn't listen to my suggestion like usual.

Lil's eyes widened—and pupils swelled. "Are you...seriously? You would do that? For me?"

"There's nothing I wouldn't do for you, Lil." I damn near choked getting the words out, but from fluttering butterflies rather than jealousy.

Better choices, my ass. Shit, her parents would hate me if they found out what path I just suggested we travel together.

"You would share me with Zeke."

Because I would have the chance to see him stripped bare. Vulnerable. Masturbation fodder for the future where I knew I would need to please her on my own.

"Yes," I said quietly, realizing as I did that I'd hid even more truth from her. Perhaps there wouldn't ever be an even playing field between us.

Excitement sparked in her dark orbs even though she nibbled her lower lip while searching my eyes as I tried to keep closed off. "You think he's hot for me?"

"Definitely," I didn't hesitate to assure her.

"I caught him checking you out too, you know,"

Lil said with a smirk, rubbing her thumb over my lower lip.

I snorted a forced laugh, taking my focus off her face. "Whatever."

"I'm serious."

"Well I'm not interested," I lied, still unable to meet her gaze.

"I wonder if he's bi."

I had no doubt in my mind. "Don't care," I stated instead of the truth.

"If he agrees—and he's into you, would you..."

I fought off the need to swallow. "Would I what?" I rasped out, closing my eyes as though relaxing on the bed when every inch of me wanted to shiver at the thought of that *what*.

"Let him touch you? Because that would be really, *really* hot." Lil's voice took on a breathless quality that should have jolted life back to my groin.

I imagined his hands on me, his tongue tracing over my torso, my abs...

It would be hotter than hot—and would without a doubt lead us down a slippery slope I couldn't allow, no matter how much I yearned for that very thing.

"You're it for me, Lil," I told her while opening my eyes. Her hair looked like a rat's nest, and I tucked some strands behind her ear. "But this could be your chance to make your fantasy come true before we get married—if you want."

She let out a heavy exhale. "You heard that story about his pastor. How he looked up to that man so high on a pedestal that the fall wounded Zeke on a deep level."

I realized what she was getting at, and I found my eyebrows raising at a level of intuition I'd never seen manifested before in her. "He would see a threesome as a failure, wouldn't he?"

"How could he not?"

I tucked Lily back against my side, her cheek on my chest, my brain once more calculating, but I wasn't sure we would persuade him.

"You know I love you more than anyone, right, Levi?"

My heartbeat stuttered. Lil rarely called me by my name. "Yeah," I forced out, even though I'd often wondered if she loved herself more with how much I got left on the back burner of her priorities.

"I want us to make it together until we're old and gray," she continued, her voice soft. "Best friends side by side, holding hands through life. You've always been my rock, boo, my gift from God."

"Same."

"But..."

I waited, breath held like I stood on the edge of cliff, teetering on an unstable foundation I'd once upon a time been so sure of.

"Yes." Lil rushed an exhale. "I would love to have

my fantasies fulfilled before we settle down. Just to get it out of my system, like you said."

My chest fluttered over tasting the forbidden— even if he and I didn't do anything more than watch one another while pleasuring her. "Do you want me to ask him?"

Lil snorted. "Can you pull up your big boy panties high enough?"

"Shut up," I muttered, forgetting for a moment how well she knew me. I hated making myself vulnerable, going out on a limb where I could be left disappointed.

"I'm just kidding." Lil snuggled against my side. "I'll ask him for us. In fact, I think I have the perfect idea," she stated with her usual confidence.

I hoped she did, even though I feared the possible outcomes—both good and bad.

Too many truths fluttered about unknown in the wind, ones that could bring our dreams for a future together to ruin.

7
____

ZEKE

I found my usual place beside Aaron as the praise and worship team rocked the house on Sunday morning.

Once my roaming eyes located Lily and Levi sitting down near the front of the auditorium with her parents, I wasn't able to look elsewhere. Twice, she leaned into him, shoulders brushing with his as she whispered something in his ear.

They stood every time the rest of the congregation did, hands clasped between them.

Jealousy kept my stomach clenched for the full hour of the service, and trying to focus on Pastor Welker's message was an absolute joke. The need to flee from where God had led me only to test me had me shifting on my feet.

"Everything alright?" Aaron asked me as soon as

the final song drew to an end and the lights rose to full force for the congregation to exit.

Tearing my gaze off my stranger and his fiancée, I nodded. "Yeah." My haggard voice revealed my lack of sleep since Thursday's meeting.

All I saw when I closed my eyes was Levi's face. Those green orbs enticing me to touch and enjoy a taste of sin again. My balls ached from denying myself release even though I went through each day more hard than flaccid.

Damn dick, damn sex drive...I'd admit to anger simmering in my gut over what God allowed His children to endure all with the purpose of bringing Him glory.

How did abstaining bring Him praise if no one knew about our steadfastness?

The fallout of partaking in that sin would bring the opposite, so the right choice *would* be pleasing in His sight, I told myself.

That was what I clung to while following Aaron up the aisle toward the lobby.

"We on for tomorrow?" he asked what he always did when we exited the church on Sunday mornings.

I'd skipped Friday, using the excuse of over-sleeping even though I'd lied. I hadn't been able to get my hard dick to relent even after a cold as fuck shower. Heading to the gym with a goddamn boner tenting my shorts wasn't an option.

And I refused to jerk off when I knew it would be

Levi in my mind, his name on my lips as I spent myself.

The monotony of the church service had kept my dick relaxed, but it twitched with life at the thought of finally getting release.

We stepped outdoors into the warm summer morning, and I loosened my tie with a quick yank.

"Tomorrow?" Aaron asked again, and I realized I'd never answered him.

"Yeah."

"You okay, man?"

"Yeah," I repeated, my feet itching to cross the parking lot and get the hell away from the church before the Astbury family exited.

Too fucking late.

Goddamnit. Lily and Levi trailed her parents through the church's glass doors, their hands clasped, bodies bumping against each other's with each step.

Jealousy flared to life inside my gut again. I wished I could've been beside him rather than her. Jaw tight, I tore my focus off them.

Aaron clasped my shoulder. "Call me if you need to talk."

I nodded, unable to say a goddamn thing.

"Zeke." Mr. Astbury lifted his voice, and Aaron caught the grimace I couldn't help.

"I'm a call away," he said, and I nodded. "Mr. Astbury," Aaron greeted the folks approaching us and walked off, his shoulders hunched and head down like usual.

I inhaled and straightened before turning toward my co-worker. No point in feigning a smile that would dissolve faster than I could force it. My gaze flicked to Levi first even though I told myself to not look at him.

Damn self-control lost out to lust for Levi every time.

He watched me and glanced away quick as fuck, focusing on Lily's face, but that heated second was all it took.

My skin buzzed, and my dick swelled, trapped thank fuck in the tight briefs I'd worn just in case.

Mr. Astbury started talking to me after a round of greetings—I didn't know what the fuck about, but I nodded anyway, pretending interest. Something along the lines of lunch at the church's cafe in the next couple of weeks, thanking me for my time spent with the kids.

Kids. Yeah...but not that much younger than me.

The fuck was I doing agreeing to marriage counseling? A young single man who didn't know jack shit about relationships because he couldn't decide if he wanted a woman or a man? The fuck had I been thinking focusing on those studies specifically?

Fuck the path I'd bent my will toward.

And fuck Pastor Hardy for being the catalyst that led me here.

I would prove myself. Every goddamn time.

Mr. Astbury held out his hand, and I paused a second before accepting, my brain still caught up in stubbornness.

"I'll see you tomorrow in the office." He smiled and collected his wife's elbow once more.

They moved off, and I went to turn away before I said something stupid, but Lily touched my bare forearm right below where my rolled dress shirt's sleeve lay, halting me dead in my damn tracks.

The gentle, teasing caress as she slowly removed her hand only made the ache in my groin worse.

"We wanted to thank you for Thursday," she said, breathless, her cheeks pink and her dark eyes shining.

Levi shifted beside her, his gaze flitting to mine. Fucking ensnaring me. Emptying my mind. Making my goddamn dick leak.

"We're having a small dinner party and would love for you to come."

I cleared my throat while studying the unease in Levi's eyes. "I'm busy," I managed, scoring one for the self-control.

Lily giggled. "I haven't even told you when, silly."

My forced smile wobbled as I tore my focus off green eyes to face dark, twinkling ones.

"Do you make it a practice to not meet outside the church with those you see for counseling?" she asked.

"No," I gave her the truth.

"Then you'll come." Lily face lit up, her beaming face breathtaking enough my dick oozed precum again.

Fuck. My. Life.

I needed to get off.

I glanced at Levi, trying to get a read on him and his thoughts. He seemed stoic in his desire to keep our past a secret, and although his hard dick on Thursday suggested he still wanted me, I expected he'd keep his hands to himself come hell or high water.

What smart, bisexual man wouldn't when promised to a beautiful woman like Lily?

"Zeke?" Lily pushed, and I tore my focus off Levi, the kryptonite to my stubbornness.

I'd already cancelled the Thursday appointment she'd made with Mrs. Vale—perhaps I shouldn't have done so. Maybe God had plans I needed to allow Him to unveil.

Should I stay or should I go?

A beam of sunlight broke through the clouds, glinting gold over Lily's dirty blonde hair like a blessing from heaven. She was His child and required direction from one who had studied in order to give it to her.

"Okay," I croaked, sure I put myself in a place of danger even while believing the Holy Spirit led me there. I would stand firm.

Lily's face lit up.

Fucking beautiful...but Levi.

Giving him my attention had me biting back a groan. Fear and excitement, the emotions I always found in his pale eyes shone back at me.

"Tuesday at six?" Lily suggested, breathless once more.

"Two days and five hours," Levi's whisper barely reached my ears.

I would have to jerk off a dozen times before then in order to keep on the straight and narrow.

"Sounds good," I rasped out.

She rattled off the apartment's address, took Levi's hand, and sashayed away with a flounce of her hair and a flutter of her fingertips.

Levi and I hadn't exchanged words, but it was the memory of his expressive eyes that stayed with me on my ride home, straight to my bathroom where I shoved down my dress pants and took my aching dick in hand.

Precum smeared down my length, easing my harsh tugs. Teeth gritted, I allowed myself a moment of secret sin since no one would be hurt in my finding release. I recalled the chocolate and caramel taste of Levi's mouth, the reason for my Milk Dud obsession since Nashville—remembered the hardness of his body against mine.

I closed my eyes and gave over to the fantasy it was his ass clenching around my dick rather than my fingers. I imagined his moans and gasps mingling in the air with mine. Tingles grew to life in the base of my spine, and I leaned over the toilet, hand on the wall to keep myself steady.

"Fuck." I blew with the force of a goddamn tsunami, shots of spunk ripping through my length and pulling grunts from my lungs. "Hell..." I opened my eyes and watched my balls empty into the bowl. Too damn much. I'd waited so long out of sheer stubbornness, and my knees went weak from the release.

Shaky as fuck, I sucked oxygen into my lungs while wiping my thumb over my slit. One last shudder and I slumped forward.

Cursing Levi.

Cursing Lily.

Cursing my "old man" and the fact God wouldn't just eradicate sinful natures once a person gave his life over to Him.

———

Two days later, I bit back those exact same curses when Lily opened the door and invited me into their apartment in a too-short sundress that showcased her tanned legs.

Damnit.

I tore my focus off her slight but curvy form to glance around.

A tiny one-bedroom rental, the kitchen and small dining table was directly ahead through a small hallway. Set with three plates.

Three.

"I'm your only guest this evening?" I asked, hating the unease in my voice.

She shut the door behind me, the click one of finality, the kind of subtle noise that raises hairs on the back of your neck and jackknifes your heartbeat.

"Yep." She popped the P, her tone revealing all I needed to know.

Devious little minx.

I should have turned and walked out, but Levi appeared in an open doorway in the hallway, a green T-shirt making his eyes and pecs pop.

I'd jerked off ten minutes before leaving my condo, but my libido didn't understand the meaning of the words *wrung out* when it came to my stranger.

No longer a stranger.

His unsure smile stole my damn breath. "Hey."

I swallowed hard. "Hey."

Lily flounced toward the kitchen. "Hope you're hungry," she called without glancing over her shoulder to see how Levi and I continued to stare at one another. "I baked my first chicken. There's only boxed stuffing and canned cranberry sauce, but I make some mean mashed potatoes."

"She does," Levi agreed quietly, his gaze slipping down over me, his face flushing.

My entire body seemed to swell beneath his quick glance—dick, chest, and heart.

Fucking hell. Should have worn those damn briefs again.

I let him fill his eyes, fighting the desire to do the same. I failed as usual when it came to him. Levi wasn't much shorter than my six foot, his jaw clean shaven like a baby's behind. I wanted him to turn around and give me an eyeful of his fine ass.

"Come on in," he rasped once our gazes found one another again, tilting his head toward the kitchen.

"Lead the way," I croaked out, hands fisted at my sides to stop myself from reaching for him. Where the self-control came from, I had no fucking clue because he looked so damn good I would've been more than satisfied feasting on him for dinner.

He turned toward where Lily had gone. Dark blue jeans hugged his backside like they were meant to rather than sagging like other guys his age wore them.

"Goddamnit," I muttered, my hands twitching at the memory of how his ass cheeks had fit them perfectly.

Levi glanced over his shoulder, catching me adjusting myself. The flush on his face intensified, his lips parting.

I bit back a groan and shook my head, begging him with my eyes to not say a word. To keep his hands to himself since one whisper of encouragement from him would ruin us both.

He shuddered—and moved toward the kitchen with resolute steps.

Thank fuck.

Unable to pray for guidance, I unrooted my feet from the entryway's tile and followed Levi into the bowels of temptation.

8

LEVI

Zeke sat tense at our small table, shoulders straight, his focus on his plate. He'd gulped an entire glass of ice water before Lil placed the food in front of us, and I wondered if he'd gone for brain freeze to do away with the erection he'd grown right inside our door.

Hard and long along his left thigh.

My mouth watered more for a taste of him than the mashed red potatoes Lil had made for me.

She'd come over earlier in the day to prepare our meal, so focused on the task she hadn't tried to jump me for another good time like we'd been having every day ever since I gave in to the fantasies in my head while pleasuring her.

Or maybe she saved it that night just in case Zeke actually said yes to what she planned on asking him for after dinner. And thank goodness she'd decided to take the lead. I never would've been able to.

I'm having a hard enough time not puking my guts up.

I shifted on my chair, my stomach twisted to the point I didn't eat more than a few bites. Tension strung me tight, and I couldn't even join in the light conversation Lily and Zeke carried on over dinner.

What he did for fun—jogging and hitting the gym with his friend Aaron who I'd known forever since we'd grown up in the same church. A few years ahead of us in school, Aaron hadn't ever been in youth group with Lil and me, but I saw him around all the time.

It'd been the sight of Aaron's transformed athletic body a couple years earlier that led me to start working out at home since I couldn't afford a gym. Sit ups, push-ups, using my body weight to mimic movements done with bars and dumbbells. Without an actual weight set, I wouldn't ever achieve his muscle mass, but I'd toned myself the best I could.

I glanced over Zeke's broad shoulders to the obvious swell of muscle beneath his button-down shirt.

Goals, but where Aaron had only drawn my envious gaze, I also wanted to touch and taste Zeke.

"Dad told me Aaron's father isn't doing well,"

Lily said as though picking up on the man in my thoughts.

Zeke shook his head.

"Parkinson's, right?"

"Yes. He's unable to move around without assistance, and he's showing signs of dementia. Aaron said he's seriously depressed."

"That's so sad," Lily said, her tone implying she cared about Mr. Weston's emotions rather than where my mind once more lodged.

On Zeke.

Her plan to invite him into our bed.

"He was such a sweet man," she went on, setting her fork upside down on her plate. "He always had chocolate mints in a basket to hand out after church when I was a kid. That's where my love of Andes comes from. What's your favorite candy?"

"Milk Duds," I answered for Zeke without a thought, remembering the box on his desk.

He caught my eye, and I swallowed with an audible gulp at the heat flaring to life in his gaze.

"Those are your favorites," Lily said, nudging me beneath the table with her knee.

"Yeah," I choked out. I'd devoured a box from nerves during that concert I'd snuck out to the year before...had Zeke tasted them on my tongue that night?

His focus slipped to my mouth, but he jerked it

away as Lily stood to clear the table. "Let me help," he offered, his voice strained.

"You'll do no such thing," Lily told him with a bossy tone I knew to obey. "Why don't the two of you go to the living room, and I'll clean up in here."

I inhaled until it hurt, slowly letting my breath out while pushing back my chair.

Zeke followed me, and same as when I'd led him into the kitchen and caught him growing hard over my backside, tingles raced through me, but I couldn't find the guts to glance over my shoulder.

We sat at either end of the couch, leaving room in the middle for Lil for when she joined us. My leg bounced, and I wiped my damp palms down my jeans. The sounds of plates clinking together and running water from the kitchen filled the tense silence between us.

I couldn't look at him. Couldn't swallow against the arid desert of my mouth.

"Does she know?" Zeke broke the quietness, his question twisting my stomach up tighter than my shoulders. "About that night in Nashville?"

"No."

"You should tell her."

"And ruin the best thing I'll ever have?" I forced myself to face him, my leg still going at it while my stomach twisted up tight. "The gift of a woman's love I don't deserve and will never be worthy of?"

Zeke kept his focus on my eyes, and the silence

returned between us until I shifted, needing to move beyond the nervous twitch jumping my knee while ants seemed to skitter cross my skin.

"I admire you, Levi," he stated quietly. "You're a good man and more than worthy of love."

A good man. I wanted to snort at his misjudgment. If only he knew the depths of my depravity.

I recalled his reason for becoming a counselor, how he'd dedicated his life to showing how people could make right choices. The idea I'd implanted in Lil's mind, what she planned, swirled my stomach like a tornado.

What had I been thinking?

About myself. I'm a selfish jerk.

But I couldn't—wouldn't—take it back. I yearned for Zeke.

He won't ever agree—

"I should leave," he murmured as though he felt the war of emotions inside my head.

"Please don't," I quickly said, even though he probably had the better thought. Lily's imminent arrival into the living room would bring embarrassment, I didn't doubt, and would definitely place him in a position he shouldn't have to face with how mature and professional he'd been over my fiancée's flirting.

But this...*thing*...between us needed to be put to rest. He would either agree, and I could get my fill of him to be content with Lil alone, or he would refuse, drawing a final line between us I would have no choice but to respect.

"Bathroom?" he asked, pushing to stand.

I pointed, staring at his back as he moved off with sure footsteps.

Broad shoulders I wanted to grasp, trim waist I wanted my legs wrapped around, a flexing ass I wanted to bite...

Heat flooded my face, and I tore my focus off him by slamming my eyelids shut. *What is wrong with me?*

I couldn't find the strength to pray away the lust coursing through every cell of my body. Shame for my desire should've filled my mind, my heart, but the memory of Zeke overrode my better sense.

"You okay, boo?" Lily asked, flopping down onto the couch beside me unexpectedly, and I jumped. She giggled. "Your mind has you all tensed up, doesn't it?"

My voice refused to work, and she grasped my knee, stilling my twitch. "Calm down or you're going to make yourself sick," she whispered as the sound of the flushing toilet reached us.

I closed my eyes again, inhaling through my nose and exhaling through my parted lips.

"Hey." Lily squeezed my knee, but I couldn't look at her. "It's going to be okay. He'll either stay and fuck around or leave."

"Lil," I gasped out, *fucking around* playing like a scene in my head.

I'm going to puke...or pass out. Keel over in three point three seconds, flat on the floor—

"We shouldn't do this," I rushed to say, desperate to escape. "He'll never agree, and it's not right of us to put him in this situation."

The bathroom door clicked open, shutting my mouth, and Zeke approached, his gaze coming to rest on Lil's hand on my knee. A frown flitted over his face fast enough I wondered if I imagined it— wishful thinking. "I should get going."

Yes.

"Not yet." She patted the couch beside her while angling toward the empty cushion and taking her touch away from me. "I—*we*—have something we'd like to talk about."

Zeke glanced at me before eyeing Lily like a coiled snake ready to strike. He perched on the couch's edge, even though I knew a sixth sense itched his feet to leave. "We can reschedule for an office meeting," he offered, but she shook her head.

"This is better." Lily released a heavy exhale— and climbed onto his lap in a flash, swarming my nose with vanilla.

Oh God...here we go.

Zeke's hands found her hips while he pushed back into the couch as though trying to escape her. "What are you doing?" he asked, his tone haggard while glancing at me.

He didn't push her away, his grasp on her

seeming more like an involuntary reaction—one that held.

Lily let out a nervous giggle, probably from not immediately getting set back in her seat like I'd expected Zeke to do. "I'm just going to lay it all out on the table and figured this would be the best way of keeping you in place until I'm done."

Zeke turned his attention on her, still as a marble statue. The pulse thrummed in his neck, and I licked moisture onto my lower lip.

"See," Lily started, her voice breathless while laying her hands on his shoulders, "there's this fantasy that I have, some wild oats that really should be sown before Levi and I marry, and since I'm wildly attracted to you, Levi thought you could be the one to ask."

Zeke stared as though processing, and I silently counted the slow-moving seconds in my head while my heart raced.

He's going to say no. He has to. Say no. Scratch that. Please say yes.

His eyes and thin lips stated his will leaned toward denying us.

But the bulge in the ten-inch space between his groin and Lily's core was on board with fucking around.

He turned his face toward me, and I bit the inside of my lip.

"Levi."

Like a damn prayer, he whispered my name, and as if he'd put a spell on me, I scooted closer while he sat frozen like I'd been at the concert. Had his heart rate sped up like mine? Had his body gone numb, his mind emptied beyond the need to touch? Had the throb in his sack begged for a release only a fall from grace would bring?

My knee brushed his thigh.

Zeke hissed at the contact, and the pupils of his eyes swelled fully, eating away at the dark blue.

"We want you in our bed, Zeke," Lil said, her voice barely reaching me through the pulse thumping in my ears.

"Sinning," Zeke rasped, his attention still trained on me.

"No one has to know," Lily pushed, scooting closer along his thighs toward his torso. "Just the three of us." Her hands went to the back of his head like she often did to me whenever we kissed.

She's going to put her mouth on Zeke's.

My guts churned, but getting whatever taste of him I could meant sharing with her.

"Goddamnit." A muscle ticked in Zeke's jaw, and he released one hand from Lil's hip to grasp at her hair. "We're going to burn."

Please.

9

———

ZEKE

I'd gone to the bathroom and dropped to my knees, begging God for the strength to leave. Why I hadn't just gone straight for the door when I'd stood, I couldn't figure out.

Weakness.

For Levi. All Levi.

Lily saddled up close to my aching dick, but Levi's green eyes reeled me in more than her sweet scent as her panted exhales came closer to my mouth.

"Goddamnit," I muttered, losing the fucking battle same as I had in Nashville.

The one situation I wanted to avoid, keep clear of, and I'd landed in the pool of lust neck deep. Hopeless. Powerless.

Unbidden, my hand found her hair—and my focus stayed on Levi's face, needing to keep that connection between us while I damned myself to hell. I muttered something about burning and allowed Lily's lips to ghost over mine. She tasted sweet like chocolate mint. Delicious, but not Levi delicious. Angling my head allowed me to hold his gaze while his fiancée kissed me all soft and gentle when I wanted hungry and rough.

She moaned as our tongues met, the noise doing nothing to rile me up like Levi's nearness did. Just the brush of his knee against my thigh made me hard as granite.

He whimpered and pressed in closer, his eyes wide, lips parted, and my dick leaked.

For him.

My conscience screamed at me to toss Lily to the floor and get the hell out of there. My body ached to bury in tight heat—his, hers, in that moment, I didn't give a shit which. I just *needed*.

Stubborn self-restraint? Fucking gone from the searing heat of his thigh alone. I sat powerless against the energy feeding between us and the rolling train of lust simmering in my balls.

"Touch me, boo," Lily pleaded against my mouth, and Levi obeyed, sliding his palm up her bare leg beneath her short dress.

Fuck—I didn't want his hands anywhere but on me.

I pulled my head back, escaping Lily's mouth, and watched as he worked his shaking fingers beneath her panties. A growl longed to rise and rumble my chest—I wanted to rip his hands off from her body.

Mine.

No. Not mine.

He belonged to Lily, and the fire in my guts, the raging jealousy had me clasping her waist tighter to push her away—

She fucked herself onto his fingers, bumping the back of his hand along my dick.

"Fucking hell," I muttered between clenched teeth, all thoughts of taking off and ridding myself of the jealousy long gone.

The urge to thrust against him knifed at my control, and I clenched my jaw tight.

"Yes," Lily hissed, moving herself back and forth on his hand, her body trembling.

Every time Levi brushed over my aching length, groans rose past my lips. I swore his actions weren't accidental. He kept silent as a mouse, glancing at me more than her—when he touched me. Like he needed to see my reaction, soak in every grunt his soft touch enticed from my lungs.

I grabbed hold of her ass, yanking her nearer, making it so the back of his hand stayed put right where I wanted it. On my throbbing dick.

"Oh God," Lily whispered, gyrating on Levi, her eyelids fluttering shut as the sounds of wet finger fucking heightened around us. "So good. More. So close..."

I tightened my hold on her flesh and helped her fuck Levi's hand into my leaking length—but my focus stayed on his face, same as he did with me.

Pupils dilated.

Panting lips.

Pulsing need thrumming between us.

Lily trembled and cried out with her climax, pressing forward, trapping Levi's hand between her core and my groin.

I thrust against him, biting the inside of my lip to keep from blowing like a dry humping teenager.

Levi's breath caught, eyes wide and hazed, and a hiss escaped his lips I wanted to bite, fucking devour.

He shuddered—came with a soft grunt.

Fucking came without being touched while holding my gaze with lust-hazed eyes.

Sexiest fucking climax I'd ever seen, the kind of foundation rocking that changed a man's life. I wanted to watch the same thing time and again while I buried inside his body, claiming and owning with every thrust of my hips, sating him in ways Lily would never be able to.

My balls tightened, and I gritted my teeth to keep from filling my pants with spunk.

His soon-to-be wife shivered, draping herself

against my chest, her mouth nuzzling in my neck while I continued to fight off the throb in my balls.

A frown flitted over Levi's face as he studied her.

He's jealous...Christ, what have I done?

I gently pushed at Lily, and she slid off my lap onto her knees and between mine.

Fuck...no, no, no...

Her fingers fumbled with my jeans, and I glanced at Levi.

The furrow on his brow returned. Deepened like he longed to yank his woman away from me.

If it had been him desperate to get to my dick, I wouldn't have thought twice, but Lily?

Levi didn't want her hands and mouth on another man.

"Stop." I grabbed hold of her wrists, and she peered up at me, her dark eyes blown black by lust.

"Let me take care of you," she whispered, and Levi shifted beside me, pulling back so our thighs no longer touched. Coolness slid over my pants where I'd been burned by his body heat.

"No." I scooted to the side, trying to stand and escape from Lily without knocking her off kilter. "I have to go. Now. I'm sorry—thank you for dinner." I couldn't bear to look at either of them and quickly left, my legs weak, ears straining for a hint of noise in the silence behind me.

Guilt crashed into me the second I stood on their stoop, and I dragged a lungful of warm, humid air into my lungs, feeling as though I couldn't get enough oxygen.

Moron. Fucking idiot.

I'd acknowledged the red flags, but fuck!

Jaw clenched, I strode across the parking lot the best I could with my stiff dick trapped inside my pants. Once in my car, I popped the button and slid my zipper down, giving me some breathing room. But I didn't take myself in hand.

I drove home, prayers and curses on my lips while precum continued to dribble down the length jutting from my jeans. Once I arrived home, I knew I had to give myself relief.

Keys in one hand, I halted right inside the kitchen door, unable to stumble to the bathroom, the shower, or my bed.

Jerking myself right there in darkness to forced thoughts of bench pressing a new max made me want to laugh, but it worked. Or maybe I was just too far gone in the need to bust a nut that keeping my mind off *him* came easily.

Until the tingles rose in the base of my spine.

The image of Levi's parted lips and hooded eyes slammed into my brain.

"Fuck," I gasped. "Levi."

I watched as I shot wet ribbons of white across my tile floor, every downward slam of my fist jerking my length, spraying spunk everywhere.

I gave zero fucks.

The release felt too damn good, the fantasy of coating Levi's smooth-shaven face, his tongue with my cum—ball-tingling perfection.

But once my high wore off and I returned to earth, my hand soaked in cum, the shame came back tenfold. The regret, the guilt that ripped at my guts like Wolverine's claws, and my head sagged between my shoulders as I gasped for breath.

Another fall from grace...had I ruined Levi and Lily before they'd even exchanged vows?

I'm no better than him.

My throat tightened at the thought of Pastor Hardy, and I knew what I had to do.

I cleaned the mess up before hitting my knees and prostrating myself before the throne of God.

Right there. In my goddamn kitchen where I'd come with another man's name on my lips, I begged God's forgiveness, pleading with him to make me strong, to give me back my stubbornness, my self-control.

No peace stole into my chest to soothe the guilt.

No quietness settled my mind.

And no sleep came when I finally pulled myself off the floor, stiff as fuck, and collapsed onto my bed.

10

———

LEVI

The door clicked shut behind Zeke, and Lily and I sat in silence, every second ticking past making the cooling mess inside my jeans uncomfortable as hell.

Heat rose to my face at how easily I'd come, how quickly.

Because I'd been looking at him, touching him, feeling the hard evidence of how much he wanted me.

Me.

Not Lily. No doubt rested in my head over what had enticed him to stay, to drop his shields for a taste.

But Lily had gotten his mouth, not me.

Ugliness rolled in my stomach, same as when she'd kissed him, same as when she'd gotten on her knees, ready to blow him. I'd wished it had been me, not her, touching him.

"That was so damn hot," she let out a sigh, pulling herself back up onto the couch, all sprawled limbs, messy hair, and swollen lips.

Beautiful enough I couldn't help but smile even though I wanted to puke over how we'd forced Zeke to stray from the path he'd set for himself, how I'd mentally cheated on her.

"I've never been so wet. It's a bummer he didn't let me touch him. I would have loved to go further." Lily slid a hand between her thighs and shifted like she needed more. "Want to fuck?"

"I'm...uh..." I rubbed a hand over my head, my face heating as I glanced away.

"It wasn't hot for you?"

"*You* were," I burst out, avoiding her gaze lest she see the truth in my eyes. "The noises you made, coming all over my hand like that...you were so hot, Lily...I, um..."

"Oh my God." She giggled. "You got off? Like, in your jeans?"

My head jerked up and down, and I wanted to sink into the couch cushion and never return, but from shame over my lie rather than embarrassment.

"Holy shit, that's sexy." She slid her fingers beneath the edge of her panties. "So hot."

I'd never gone down on Lily before...the thought of doing that to any woman churned my stomach in a different way than jealousy did, but hell knew I would never get it up after what I'd just experienced with Zeke.

Not for Lily, anyway.

Ignoring the sticky mess in my pants, I slid to the floor, steeling myself to give my girl release again. Pleasuring her had to be the top of my to-do list.

"Levi?" she whispered as I tugged her thighs, bringing her toward the edge of the couch.

"Lay back," I managed to rasp out while sliding her panties off her smooth legs.

She did as told, letting her thighs fall open.

I didn't want anything to do with the musky-sweet pussy in front of my face, even if the swollen folds were a pretty shade of pink. I wondered over the color of Zeke's dick. What he would taste like. The noises he would make while I took him into my mouth.

Ignoring the squeezing in my chest, I flicked my tongue over Lily's slit. She gasped, so I did it again, delving in deeper and getting a full-on taste of a female's body. Tangy, but not totally unpleasant.

"Oh...Levi, holy shit, that feels good."

"Yeah?" I still couldn't look at her face.

I can do this.

"Put your fingers in me again."

That I could do too, no problem. Soaked and silken, her core pulled me in, and I felt along the soft, satiny skin inside her.

Did an asshole feel the same? Smooth and hot? Tighter, maybe?

My dick twitched in its cold, wet prison, and I shut my eyes, fighting against the replay with Zeke crowding my mind. I wished I could regret our stolen moment enough to want to go back eight months and change it. To turn away as he'd stalked toward me beneath the flashing lights.

I wouldn't have grown a pair for the first time in my life and been the one to initiate the kiss that had left me shaking, an absolute mess.

Enough.

I leaned in, seeking out Lily's clit she needed to play with to come. I'd seen her do it countless times on video calls and sorta had an idea of what to do.

She gasped and jerked as my lips closed over the erect nub at the top of her slit—clit found.

I grabbed hold of her hip to keep her in place and gave her my fingers, my mouth suckling beneath her soft curls she liked to play with.

Lily grasped at my hair, her thighs coming up alongside my head. "Oh my God, Levi...yes, right there." She continued to rain praise on my ears, my chest swelling with pride.

I focused on the noises leaking from her lips, the way her body twitched and shivered in pleasure.

Maybe this will be enough—

"Yes...shit, Levi. I'm going to come." Lily propped up on her elbows, and I forced myself to meet her gaze. Nothing stood between us physically, but a boatload emotionally, the secret yearnings that could tear us apart...

Leaving me alone, desolate and desperate without her support, her affection.

"Don't stop," she whispered, panting, her breasts heaving.

Lily Astbury had been my life for ages, and there wasn't anything I wouldn't do for her.

Focusing on my work, I scraped my teeth over her clit, rotated my fingers deep inside her—and she cried out, falling back and arching. Her core spasmed around me, cum dripping onto my palm.

Sitting on my haunches, I watched wetness continue to dribble from her, leaking around my thrusting fingers until she went lax and grabbed hold of my hand to stop me from overstimulating her.

"Good?" I asked, wiping my hand on my pants that needed a turn in the wash anyway.

"Better than good." Lily sighed.

I pushed up from the floor, my legs cramping a bit. "I'll get you a towel."

She stayed put, and I stepped into the bathroom, avoiding the mirror like I'd become fond of doing whenever Lil and I had an intimate moment. Chest tight, I ignored the cold, sticky mess in my pants and dampened a face towel, my eyes stinging.

Lily first—always.

I returned to the living room, dropping to my knees once more.

"You don't have to clean me up."

"I do," I whispered, not knowing how else to show her how much I cared about her and the future ahead of us.

Even if I desired a man waking up beside me every morning rather than her.

I'm a horrible person.

Zeke had said he admired me for making the right choice, but if he knew my heart...I was rotten to the core.

"Do you think he's upset?" Lil asked as I wiped between her thighs.

"He seemed it."

"I wonder if we can get him to come over again."

"I doubt it." But I wanted it. More. Tons more.

Cum dried inside my jeans, but I felt like a piece of shit and deserved to wallow in my filth. I sagged on the couch, and Lil cuddled close, smoothing back my hair with her fingertips.

"It wouldn't hurt to ask," I found myself saying, my eyelids clenching shut. "If you feel the need for...more." I cringed with how that word chanted in my head.

"You wouldn't mind?"

That I didn't care another man touched and kissed who I planned to marry? "No."

I'm a jerk.

That truth rang in my ears when Lil had gone and I showered a short time later, scrubbing the damning evidence from my groin. Tears dripped down my cheeks, off my nose.

If my parents had loved me, given me the time of day, I wouldn't be so desperate for attention. If Lily hadn't latched onto me, clung to me, and occupied my thoughts as a kid, I probably would've seen more personal growth in my awkward life. If I'd gone with my gut more, like that night I'd snuck off campus and went to a concert by my secret favorite artists, Malachi and Isaac...

The dynamic duo whose lyrics spoke to me on such a deep level I always felt as though my insides wanted to burst from my skin when listening to their harmony.

Remade.

A second life.

Sprout wings to fly, to be free.

A sob wracked through me, and I sank down, curling into a ball on the bottom of the tub, the spray hitting my shaking body.

I'm broken. It's like emotions bleed from my pores. And no water, no Holy Spirit can wash the pain away.

God knows I had tried—but nothing had given me the sense of life like I'd felt at that concert the first time I'd laid eyes on Zeke Sipe and allowed myself the freedom to just *be*.

Energy had zapped between us, the kind that jumpstarted a dead heart.

I'd lost my desire to pray, and all thoughts of submitting myself to God and His word since that night had ripped away from my conscience as though I'd never even believed in an omniscient, omnipresent being.

Everything I'd done since Nashville had been for Lil, not God.

But I began to fear I wouldn't be enough for either of us.

I needed counsel to escape the twisting in my soul that whipped me in circles like a tornado.

And there was only one man I trusted to understand exactly what I faced. The emptiness. The constant war. The inescapable wound that refused to heal.

But would he even talk to me again?

11

———

ZEKE

I cut out of work early on Thursday since I'd cancelled Lily and Levi's four o'clock appointment. Although exhaustion hung on me like an oxen's yoke since Tuesday night, I pulled on shorts and my running shoes, hoping to tire my body to the point I would pass the fuck out.

I ran on empty. Literally. My feet pounded the pavement, my breaths rasped in my ears, and still my brain refused to shut up.

I'd given in to temptation. Kissed Lily. Enjoyed the fuck out of Levi's hand pressed against my dick. Acted on the lusts of the flesh when I should've stood firm in my determination to prove myself a man of integrity.

Of faith.

My failures should have assured me of my need for a savior, but my focus honed in on the battle between the old and the new me rather than just accepting what God's word said about my spirit. I traversed the same unlit path as Malachi had done before being led astray by Isaac's wily ways.

My faith wasn't nearly as strong as his had been —but I would stand firm.

I recognized my own truth—I had a lot to prove, and not because of dogmatism. Even though I'd grown up in a church and had been force fed a Christian lifestyle, I always walked the line when it came to religion. My life's passion had been to prove a man could make good decisions.

Even if he didn't feel "new" and pretended to be a godly man.

And I'd fucked up by submitting to what Lily had wanted—because of my desire for Levi.

Guilt had poured over me like a tidal wave of cold as fuck water, shriveling up the heat and dissolving the demand for release in my balls when reality had settled in.

And I couldn't rid my mind of the shame.

Heaving for breath, I let myself into my condo and walked around the small space, hands atop my head, trying to slow my heart rate. My legs resembled Jell-O, rubbery as hell.

My temples throbbed.

The easiest way to escape temptation? Stay away from compromising situations. Avoid people and places that caused weakness to rise and choke off my ability to keep God's armor firmly in place.

My flesh longed for sin, but I was stronger than lust, I told myself over and over.

I managed to finally catch some sleep, dreamless and restful.

But the knot in my gut, the unease tensing my shoulders worsened as Sunday drew near. While I would've loved nothing better than to skip church and avoid them altogether, I had an image to uphold.

I arrived after praise and worship began, sliding into the seat Aaron had saved for me in our usual row closer to the back of the sanctuary.

Dark circles clung beneath his eyes, and I leaned toward him. "How's your dad?"

"Not good." His lips thinned out, and I clasped his shoulder, squeezing and offering support in the only way I could.

Inhaling slowly to steel myself, I turned my focus on the stage, refusing to let my gaze wander toward the pew the Astburys always occupied nearer the front to the left of the center aisle. That stubbornness lasted all of two minutes.

As though Levi could feel my stare on the back of his head, he shifted, glancing over his shoulder.

Fucking fireworks.

Zaps of electrical current through my chest that woke every nerve ending in my body.

The need to suck oxygen like I'd run 5k at a full-on sprint.

Christ, just the beauty of his smooth face, remembering the yearning I'd seen in his eyes that night—thank fuck I couldn't make out his features perfectly. I would have drowned in his green orbs, my soul lost.

Found.

The word whispered in my head, echoing long after Levi turned back toward stage, his shoulders hitched.

Found what, though? The truth of my flesh, my bisexual nature I'd already known about since childhood? That I'd found the person who made my heart soar and my mouth dry out with a mere look?

Or perhaps the kind of passion I'd hoped to find with a woman someday so I could be a godly husband, be seen as an inspiration.

I wanted a man.

One affianced to a young woman.

Pastor Welker continued on with his month-long sermons on being a new creation in Christ, but I couldn't focus on the words given to him by God. I didn't want to be there—in church, around other believers with the joy of the Lord on their faces.

My ass shifted on the chair more often than not, earning me a few glances from Aaron.

"You okay?" he finally whispered.

I lied with a nod, knowing I couldn't share my

struggles because I'd be roasted alive like Pastor Hardy had been back in Boston.

In that moment, I realized something about myself: I feared failure more than I feared hell.

What did that say about me as a man? Pride always came before a fall...was God allowing the trial I faced to humble me? To bring Him glory?

Rather than grow contrite in my heart, my forehead furrowed with a deep groove. Why would a proclaimed God of love continuously try to break down His creation—in order to make Him look better?

Sure, said creation had to submit and choose right in order for that to happen, but the truth of that just felt...off.

Unkind.

Sounded a hell of a lot like pride on *His* end.

My heart thumped heavy, spreading heat through my body. Sweat dampened my back, and I clenched my fist at my side as the desire to punch something coursed through me.

I'd always been told to trust God whenever life got hard or I had too many questions without answers. Things would be made clear once we arrived in glory, I'd been assured by both my parents and various pastors over the years.

The fact that the truth of living by faith sucked had always crossed my mind, but even more so with the consuming obsession I'd been plagued with.

My legs itched to flee, and I bounced with nervous energy once the service ended, desperate to escape the crowd. The murmurs of people smiling in their Sunday best. Washed up, dressed to the nines, hair and makeup done...like they'd donned the new man and left the tired, stressed-out *real* person back home beside the coffee pot.

Aaron got snagged by one of his dad's friends in the foyer, and I told him I'd catch him in the morning at the gym. He nodded my way, and I scurried out the door, my focus on hightailing it across the parking lot toward my car around the right of the building.

People spilled from the exit on that side, and my feet stumbled as my car came into view—Levi had already escaped the sanctuary and stood by my driver's door.

Hands shoved in his pockets and shoulders slouched, he eyed me like a wild animal. Cagey and wary.

As well he should've been. If we'd been in another state away from people who knew us, far from a church parking lot, I'd have shoved him face down across the hood of my car and given him what we both yearned for. The fulfillment of our lust, the complete connection of two souls that had somehow entwined with wire after one kiss.

I couldn't find my voice, so I offered a nod as I approached.

"Hey." His gaze flitted away from me as he wet his lower lip with the tip of his tongue.

My teeth clenched over the tightening in my groin.

"I'm wondering if we can meet again?" he whispered.

"No."

"N-not for dinner or anything like that," he hastened to correct, studying my dress shoes. "In the office. Your office. A counseling session."

His voice wavered, and part of my stubbornness softened over how he loved her enough to ask for more—enough to make himself vulnerable and face possible embarrassment.

"No," I repeated, not able to stomach the thought of having that vixen behind closed doors ever again. I didn't trust her. Couldn't for all three of our sakes.

"Zeke..." Levi glanced at my face, and our gazes ensnared. Caught as usual. "I—I'm so damn twisted up inside," he whispered. "I need someone to talk to, and my parents haven't ever been emotionally available. Lil is too close to the situation, and her parents...well..."

Ah. So a session *without* Lily, then. I understood, but I couldn't be the one to counsel. No fucking way could I be alone with him behind closed doors. "I'm sorry, but—"

"Please." He cut me off, his eyes wide and welling with tears. "Something is broken inside me, and I feel like I'm bleeding out. Maybe if we just sat down and discussed what happened, this unrest eating at me would ease."

It wouldn't. My desire for Levi wouldn't wane after some shared words over what we'd allowed to happen between us. Reliving, dissecting what we'd done and how we felt would only make me want him more—and same for him if he experienced the connection between us as strongly as I did.

"I'm not looking to sow my own wild oats," Levi said when I didn't respond. "Just...needing answers. I don't think I'm going to be enough for Lil—"

In her current frame of mind, she wouldn't be satisfied with his sweet, giving nature.

"—and I feel like I can talk to you because you know what I'm going through. At least I think you do."

A deep inhale filled my lungs, the leaked exhale easing the tension in my shoulders. "Yeah, I do," I admitted, my voice low, and fuck, there was release in being honest. "But I can't tell you what decisions you need to make, Levi. You need to do what you believe is right in the eyes of God."

Fuck, those canned words churned my guts.

"And what if I'm questioning my faith, *forcing* myself to submit to Him rather than *gladly* because of His sacrifice to save my soul from hell?"

We stared at one another long enough that we both shifted, glancing away as though afraid someone would feel the shimmering tension that always snapped to attention whenever we were in close proximity.

Lily stood nearer to the church with a group of girls, but she caught my gaze and waved, a flirty smirk on her lips.

While I didn't know the two of them all that well, I felt sure Levi had made a mistake in continuing on his path toward marriage with her.

Lily was far from ready to settle down.

And Levi had to decide where his heart, his faith rested before he could become a godly husband.

Fuck knew his parents couldn't be bothered, the assholes. He couldn't talk to Mr. Astbury either, and Mr. Jameson was still out of the office on medical leave. Levi required counsel.

And I'd dedicated my life to helping those in need. Thrived off it.

Whether meeting with him ended up glorifying God or not, I had a job to do.

"Thursday," I forced out, turning back toward him, fucking butterflies of all things attempting to steal the oxygen from my lungs. "Four o'clock."

He let out a quick exhale. "Thank you."

Don't thank me yet.

Lips in a line, I nodded, and he stepped out of the way of my driver's door, allowing me access to my car.

I escaped his gaze, the energy ghosting currents

over my skin from being near him...but the effects he had on my body lingered long after I pulled out of the parking lot and lost sight of him in my rearview mirror.

Mistake or the right choice?

I lusted for Thursday so hard my hands shook. Feared its arrival to the point my stomach threatened to heave.

No prayer passed my lips, and all I had to blame was myself, the old man who refused to remain buried in my past.

12

LEVI

I puked up my lunch an hour before my planned appointment with Zeke. I'd lied to Lily about why we couldn't hang out, not wanting her to know that I was meeting with our marriage counselor she had kissed while riding my hand.

Twice since that night, I'd brought her pleasure with my mouth and fingers, but nothing she did, nothing she said got my dick hard enough to give her what she begged for shoved between her thighs even though I'd had *him* in mind while we made out.

I felt sure I was broken beyond repair because I'd made an awful decision to push the threesome idea in order to cover my shame.

She'd left in exasperation after my last failed attempt, her annoyance at my inability to get it up creating even more anxiety to twist my insides.

Add in the fact I hadn't found any job openings

in my field, and the demons of insecurity and depression hit hard.

I clenched my steering wheel with white knuckles, my heart in my throat while driving the thirty minutes to the church. No amount of counting inhales and slowly releasing exhales calmed the twitchy muscles beneath my skin or eased the vise-like pressure clasping at my head.

The heavy metal door at the church's back leading into the office area squeaked loud enough I flinched when pulling it open. Mrs. Vale offered me a quick smile even though she was on the phone.

I stood inside the door, glancing at Zeke's closed one, unsure if I should go right in or wait for Mrs. Vale to finish up her call. Did she even know Zeke had told me to come? Had she booked him another appointment?

My palms grew damp, and I rubbed them over my jeans, thinking maybe I ought to just leave and forget about talking to Zeke. Maybe it would be better to just live in denial, to set aside my fears about my future and trust God.

But I no longer knew how to do that.

"Levi, what can I do for you?" Mrs. Vale asked, bringing my thoughts back to the office.

"I'm here to see Zeke," I rasped out and cleared my throat.

She glanced down at what was probably a planner. "I don't see you on the schedule."

"Oh. Well, I spoke with him after church on Sunday, and he said I could stop by."

"There's no four o'clock listed, so why don't you go on in." A kind smile lifted her wrinkled lips.

"Thanks." I shuffled toward his door but hesitated, taking too long to decide what to do.

"You can knock if that makes you more comfortable," Mrs. Vale said from behind me.

I did as she suggested, Zeke's muffled, "Come in," reaching my ears.

One last fortifying breath and I pushed into Zeke's office. He sat behind his desk, focused on some papers in front of him, and awareness of his presence sent a shiver over my skin. I shut the door quietly, but he still didn't acknowledge me, didn't lift his dark head and pin me in place with the hungry gaze I lusted to see on his face.

"Hey," I squeaked out, shoving my hands in my pockets.

"Be right with you, Levi," he said without glancing up, his tone formal, as stiff as the set of his shoulders. "Why don't you have a seat?"

I eyed the couch then the chair in front of his desk. The latter would be easier to hide behind if need be, but I'd gone to his office for honesty's sake.

The couch's soft cushion welcomed me, but I couldn't sit back and relax. Like the first time I'd gone with Lil for counseling, I perched close to the edge, probably appearing like I wanted to jet out of there rather than spill my guts.

Zeke hadn't shaved the dark stubble lining his jawline. Rugged was a good look on him.

My dick agreed.

I shifted, unable to take my attention off him. His suit coat hung over the back of his chair, a light blue dress shirt stretching tight across his broad shoulders. Forearms flexed as he wrote with a pen, the soft scratch against the paper barely reaching me past the pounding pulse in my ears.

He forced me to wait.

Made me squirm.

Did he do so on purpose, or was he trying to clear up the work on his desk before getting pulled into a conversation I had a feeling he'd rather not have? My insecurities focused on the former, causing my feet to grow restless. I wanted to hide from every emotion his nearness alone watered to life inside my aching heart.

Finally, he clicked his pen and set it aside. Clearing his throat, he smoothed down his tie—and lifted his head.

I held my breath as that connection between us flared to life, lighting up my skin. Even emotionally closed off, the perfection of his facial features warmed every cell in my body, settling in my groin. Strong forehead and nose. Dark eyebrows. Higher cheek bones and a plump lower lip I wanted to suckle.

Why did a man turn me on when God had gifted me Lil? Why did the lust for Zeke's hard body make me wish for things the Bible and the church preached against?

Not that I really cared any longer on that last part. I believed a person ought to love the one life led them to without prejudice, without hatred. Love should be freely given, freely received. The world would be a better place if more people believed the same.

"What can I do for you today, Levi?"

Oh, how I would have loved to flirt with a man for the first time, to tell him all I wanted him to do for me—what I could do for him. But I didn't have the guts. It had taken every ounce of will I had to drive to the church and enter Zeke's office.

"Nashville," I croaked out the only word I could.

Zeke exhaled heavily as though resigned.

"Something took hold of me that night," I spewed out, needing to keep him from apologizing or calling our kiss a lapse in judgement. "I snuck off campus to go to the concert even though every single person in my life wouldn't have approved. And I saw you... I-I'm not usually that bold."

"You kissed like you are."

Holy hell. The heat in his gaze shivered over my skin, and I licked my lower lip.

"What we did was a mistake."

"No! How can you call it that?" I shot out, surprising myself, my chest tight. "I've never felt anything so right. You made me come alive."

His gaze flicked over my mouth before he turned his focus to the certificates framed on his office wall as though reminding himself of why he sat at a desk in a church office. "Regardless of our feelings, Levi, I've decided on a life of servitude, just as you've chosen a future with a woman."

"I'm questioning myself."

There. I stated the truth in the back of my mind I hadn't even fully entertained. While the words eased some tension from my shoulders, the sexual energy thickening the office's air didn't relent.

Zeke angled back toward me, studying my face long enough that I shifted to ease the growing ache in my balls. Having his attention was everything— even though being the center of his focus made my face warm and my throat dry out.

Nothing compared, and I realized in that moment I didn't want to live the rest of my life without it. My expectations of a relationship with Lily were doomed to fall flat no matter how much I hoped to please her.

"You would let the sins of the flesh come between you and the woman you love?" Zeke asked quietly.

"I've loved Lily since sixth grade—and I always

will—but not in a sexual or passionate way. I've tried." I huffed a non-funny laugh while shaking my head. "God knows I've tried, and I can't get there—" I cut off the words ready to pour from my lips, clamping them shut.

"Unless?"

Shit. He somehow knew my next word. What would he think of the full truth? Would he be ashamed of me like I was? Would he finally see I really *wasn't* the good man he'd claimed me to be?

Both questions in my head tempted bile to bubble in my stomach.

I've come for honesty's sake...

"Unless I'm thinking about you," I whispered, my eyes clenched shut, my face hot as hell and insides tight.

"Levi."

"I know it's sinful," I spewed, my hands grabbing my thighs hard enough I might leave marks. "But it's the truth, Zeke. It's my truth, and no amount of prayer or changing my focus has made a difference. I don't want Lily like I want you. Ever since that night we danced together, since I felt your hard body against mine...your delicious bruising grip on my ass—"

"Stop."

I shut up, finally opening my eyes.

He stared at my mouth as though replaying what ran through my mind on a daily basis. The warmth of his lips, surprise making him hesitate before taking control over what I'd initiated. Getting lost in the flavor of him, the masculinity I'd dreamed of. Silken tongue mimicking what I wanted more than anything in the world.

Zeke had felt right in ways Lil never would.

"I believe God brought me and Lil together, and she's been nothing but a blessing," I whispered, "but I'm left experiencing emptiness more often than not. I can't be everything she needs."

He swiped along his scruff, glancing away again. "She's a...very sexual creature."

"She's always been boy crazy."

He quirked an eyebrow at me. "And that never bothered you?"

"No." My lips twisted in an attempted smirk while I shrugged. "I could understand the draw."

Zeke nodded as though he did too.

"I'm gay," I blurted out and bit my lip.

I finally spoke the words of who I was to the one man I wanted more than anything. Giddiness rose inside my chest, a relief of sorts, but my lips refused to show my inner emotion.

He eyed me, studying my face while I shifted on the couch. "You aren't attracted to Lily?"

"No. I mean, yes—but to her as a person, not in a sexual way. I just...never acted on any of my urges before. Never watched porn, never thought of kissing a man until that moment time froze while

Malachi and Isaac sang to one another and I first saw you."

The tension thickened between us, but I focused on the final truth I had come to admit.

"I'll never be man enough for Lil," I choked out, hating that fact even though I felt the words down in the depths of my soul.

"Is she aware of your attraction to men?" Zeke's dark blue eyes grew so intense my dick throbbed inside my jeans.

"No." I swallowed hard. "Lil and I know each other so well...sometimes we don't even need to talk about things and can still state what the other is thinking, but this part of me is something I've kept hidden, haven't once uttered into the air—until now."

Zeke nodded, taking time before responding. "What happened when I left after dinner the other night?"

I considered lying, but hadn't I sought him out for honesty, for answers?

"She wanted to fuck," I whispered, choosing the curse because she hadn't been interested in making love.

"And did you?"

Heat flooded my face, and I slid my palms down my thighs again. "No. I, uh...came inside my jeans when she did."

"*Because* she did?"

I shook my head. "No, but I lied and told her that was why I couldn't perform."

"Fuck." Zeke rubbed at his jaw again, the muscle clenching beneath his fingers. "I seriously need to find another line of work. First her, now this." He shook his head and took a deep inhale as though seeking answers inside his head.

"I used my mouth to pleasure her," I forced out, wanting my counselor to know how hard I'd tried to make things work for the two of us. "And twice more since then because my dick refuses to participate."

"Maybe it's because of what Lily said in our first session together—it's the thought of sinning that hinders you."

I huffed another snort. "Have you listened to a word I said?" I motioned toward my groin, the obvious ridge etched along the top part of my thigh. "Shame has nothing to do with it. I. Am. Gay. I like men—specifically *you*."

Zeke's gaze dropped to my throbbing dick, lingering for five seconds, just long enough to make my swollen length jerk beneath his stare. He ripped his focus off what he refused to let himself have. "This can't happen, Levi. Those stolen moments of living in our flesh all those months ago are going to remain buried in our past."

"I can't stop them from resurrecting," I whispered, my chest aching again. "I've tried, Zeke. Fuck, how I've tried. Maybe Lil was right about the wild oats thing. What if we did, Zeke? What if you came over and the three of us spent the night together, doing whatever it is we needed to in order to move on?" I held my breath even while part of me rejoiced over having the balls to toss what I yearned for out there.

Vulnerability didn't come easy, and the tension rising between us only made me squirm more. My stomach fluttered when he didn't deny me immediately.

Zeke stood, sending a thrill shooting through me —until he started toward the door. "I'm sorry, Levi, but our time is up."

I glanced at the clock above him, noting only twenty-eight minutes had passed. He didn't desire what I did—he dismissed me without putting anything to rest between us.

Goddamn him.

My throat tightened, but I got up, ready to walk past him, out of his life like he obviously wanted me to.

But he didn't open the door for me, and I stopped two feet from his personal space, giving him all my attention, allowing all of my emotions to show in my eyes while breathing in the subtle hint of a woodsy, clean scent I remembered too well.

Putting myself out there sucked ass, and my stomach churned over it, but I needed to try one last time, otherwise I would forever question what could have been.

Our gazes locked, the yearning to touch him, taste him again stronger than any force on this earth.

"I can't *not* want you," I whispered, lightly caressing his chest with shaking fingertips.

"Christ," he whispered harshly—prayer or curse, I couldn't tell. "Fuck."

Zeke grabbed the back of my neck and yanked me in, his mouth bruising mine from the rough contact.

Heat erupted like bursting fireworks, sizzling my skin and lighting my chest up with life like I'd only known once before. I clutched at his tie, my other hand finding the back of his head to keep him against me, his mouth on mine—licking, tasting... tongues fucking.

Zeke's passion was everything I remembered and more. Hungry and urgent, consuming my mind, my heart, bringing back that feeling of being reborn, of finding myself—my true self.

Heat licked along every inch of my tongue as he stroked mine.

My knees went weak, and he swallowed every whimper I emitted while sagging against his hard body. Muscle. Bone. A wall to prop me up, sturdiness I could trust to carry me.

Zeke grasped my ass with one hand, his other sliding between us to grab hold of my leaking dick.

"Ung," I grunted against his mouth, jerking in a sharp breath of his exhale. "Oh...oh God."

He squeezed, clutched at my length, my balls, his teeth nipping at my lower lip before he licked the pain away.

"You taste so good...so *fucking* good," he groaned into my mouth and speared his tongue over mine.

This is life. This is living. What I've always wanted...fuck.

The base of my spine tingled, but I was too far gone in my need to break away before I embarrassed myself. I thrust into his hold—

"Yes," he hissed, his breath hot on my lips. "Levi."

—and my climax erupted up through my dick like a geyser, soaking the insides of my jeans with wet heat.

Zeke swallowed my soft grunts with greedy kisses, his low groan seeming to draw more cum from my balls.

Holy hell...holy fucking *hell.*

One last shudder rippled through my body, and he lightened his grasp on me—but didn't let go even though our mouths separated.

I forced my exhausted eyelids open while sucking down oxygen, and my dick gave one last attempt to twitch at the lust in Zeke's eyes. Black ate at the blue of his irises. Pink stained his cheeks, redness on his lips from devouring mine.

Both of our chests heaved, tingles racing over my

skin like a livewire even though I'd come so hard I could barely stand.

Our gazes remained locked, and time paused like it did in all the happily ever after movies when souls connected. No way he could deny us—instead, he could give me the out I suddenly realized I wanted more than to marry my best friend—

His cell phone dinged on his desk, and he stepped back, causing a chill to run over my front and sending me sagging against his door.

Reality settled over his face as a droplet of cum snaked its way down between my balls.

"Don't," I whispered, not sure what all I meant with that one word. *Don't walk away. Don't choose your cell over me. Don't leave me trapped in an engagement I shouldn't have initiated...*

But he did all three, turning to pick up the phone. A quick swipe and his entire body tensed, the muscle in his jaw popping. "You need to leave." His voice sounded like sandpaper, rough and abrasive to my ears and damn heart that had gotten too caught up in him.

"Zeke..."

"Leave. Now."

I swallowed hard—and did as told, barely managing to rasp out a goodbye to Mrs. Vale while stumbling through the church's exit. Heart shrinking inside my chest, I stepped into bright sunlight, blinking away the sting of tears. Hitched breaths allowed hot air into starved lungs as my dragging footsteps took me across the sweltering blacktop.

My soul should have been levitating, riding a high of having tasted my obsession again, but the shroud of depression closed over me, riddling my mind with darkness.

13

ZEKE

I know what you're doing.

I read the text again, my heart in my throat, my ears barely catching the door closing behind Levi.

A random number I didn't recognize. One no person had texted me from before.

My hands shook as I clutched my cell, my focus glued to the screen. My stomach heaved, acid burning the back of my throat over the lust I couldn't control. Sin had risen like a roaring lion, dominating my will—and I'd submitted like a lamb led to the slaughter, desperate to taste him again.

Were there cameras in the church offices? Had Pastor Welker caught us in the act of fornicating?

My head jerked up, my focus combing every inch of the ceiling...the light fixtures...the heat vent. Nothing suggested eyes watched my every move.

So what the fuck?

I sank into my chair, my heart still racing as I thought up reasons for the text. It could've been a wrong number. Had to be.

And fuck, my aching dick...even faced with the possibility of being caught eating at Levi's face like a starved man, my balls continued to throb. Precum smeared inside my slacks to the point a wet spot darkened my groin area.

"Fucking hell." I grabbed hold of my balls and tugged them down, forcing memories of Levi's whimpers while coming from my mind. "Focus, you dipshit."

I scrolled through my contacts—and I dialed Malachi while glancing at the clock, my mind racing to the date and where he might be. What city, which arena preparing for a concert.

"What's up, Ezekiel?"

"Asshole," I muttered over his use of my full name.

Malachi laughed, and envy coiled around my heart. How had my best friend, youth pastor turned openly gay musician, found such peace outside God?

But he had, the evidence I'd seen while in Nashville so pure, so real, my soul craved the same.

"Remember how I said marriage counseling isn't all it's cracked up to be?" I nearly whispered, reminding him of a conversation we'd had almost two years ago.

"Yeah." His tone lost all sense of jollity with that one word. "What's going on, Zeke?"

I scrubbed a hand down over my face, letting out a ragged groan, thankful as fuck my dick relented the slightest bit.

"Another stalker in the making?" he pressed.

"No." I swallowed hard. "This time it's the guy in the relationship."

"Fuck."

I huffed a laugh, tugging on my ball sack again. "Oh, it gets worse. It's him. The man from your concert, and I'm finding it extremely difficult keeping him at arm's length."

Silence reigned in my ear long enough I glanced at my cell to make sure the call hadn't gotten lost.

"Are you shitting me?" Malachi finally asked.

"No." I slumped in my chair, tipping my head back and closing my eyes. "He's engaged to one of my co-worker's daughters. They're getting married in September, and I got pulled into premarital counseling."

"Fuck."

"Yeah."

"Does his fiancée know?"

"No—and she's not going to, either."

"Fuck, Zeke." Malachi let out a few more curses. "You refused to meet with them again, right?"

"I cancelled their last session, but he...he came in today, begging for help. He's lost and broken. Loves her since they've been best friends since middle school but wants me."

"Shit."

"Yeah."

"And what do *you* want?"

My dick balls deep in his ass, his cum smeared between us. His cries in my ears, his fingers grasping at my shoulders. My name whispered from his goddamn delicious mouth.

"What I shouldn't," I muttered the truth in a lot less words. "The last couple of weeks, Pastor Welker has been talking about being a new man in Christ—but I don't feel new. There's nothing inside me that is restful."

"Maybe you're living the wrong life."

"I'm on a dark path, same as you were. Can't see shit. Can't figure out what's true and what's not outside my damn stubbornness."

"The whole 'gotta prove godly men exist, that man can make right decisions?'" Malachi knew me too well. "You're saying I'm not godly?"

I snickered at memories of him and Isaac plastered to each other on stage while thousands of fans screamed, egging them on. Hips grinding, tongues appearing between their lips...pure, unadulterated sin.

Love.

Malachi laughed when I didn't answer. "I know I'm a godless heathen. Proud of that damn fact."

"You made the right decision for you," I stated quietly, unable to deny the beauty of him and his other half.

"I would choose Isaac all over again." Malachi sobered. "I would live through that hell of our beginning a million times over if it meant I got to spend my life with him. He's my everything, and I'm going to soak up every second I can."

Envy once more coiled around my heart at the assurance, the peace in Malachi's voice. My dick finally gave up hope of feeling flesh wrapped around its length.

I'd pushed away my covetousness of their happiness once I'd left Nashville. Started over in another city due to that mess I'd left behind in Pittsburgh—

But after meeting Levi, the want inside me, the unholy yearning for more, had intensified.

I questioned what I was doing with my life. And wondered if I would be able to escape unscathed.

14

LEVI

Funny thing, darkness. Some types thickened to the point that even the sun couldn't pierce its gloom.

Lil used to be my light, the calmness I could follow through any storm, but Zeke had ripped that joy from me, made it impossible for her to settle my insides and mood again.

She'd invited me to her parents for dinner on Saturday night, bubbly as always, seeming to have forgotten how I'd blundered up our attempts to have sex on Wednesday and how annoyed she'd been with me.

Maybe she understood my dismal tone over the phone and had taken pity on me. It wouldn't have been the first time her motherly instincts extended to my poor soul since my own mom seemed to forget more about her son than remember.

I sat at her parent's dining room table, unable to smile. Her usual laughter and smirks didn't bring a spark of life to my barely beating heart.

I'd made myself vulnerable, took a chance on my own, and I resented myself for it. Resented Zeke for denying what we had—what we *could* have. His God and his calling were more important than the one his body obviously craved.

I wasn't enough.

Again.

Not that I truly wanted him. I had my best friend already at my side, ready to pledge her life to me.

At least, that's what I assured myself of countless times even though it didn't help to drag me from the depths of mental hell.

I'm well and truly trapped.

At least my future lay with my first love, and as she gushed with excitement over the raspberry cream cake she and her mom had ordered, I whispered in my head that everything would work out in the end.

"What's wrong, boo?" Lily murmured against my ear while reaching for her glass of water.

"Long day," I muttered. I didn't lie. Hours spent searching online didn't find me a single possible place of employment. It was like fate toyed with me, pushed me into making another decision.

If only I knew what it was.

"Dad told me that you had a meeting with Zeke on Thursday. I thought he'd cancelled?"

Shit.

My face had to pale since I literally felt the blood drain from beneath my skin. "Um...yeah. I asked to meet with him privately for...things I needed to talk about."

"Secret husband-type stuff?" she whispered with a giggle.

The blood rushed back to my cheeks. "Kind of?"

She leaned in close, her lips brushing over my ear. "There's nothing I don't know about you, Levi. We could have gone together."

Yeah...no.

"Next time." Yet another lie.

"Dad set up an appointment for us next week."

I jerked my head toward her. "With Zeke?"

"Yes." She winked, and my stomach twisted.

"He agreed to another session?" I asked, my voice nothing more than a squeak.

"Of course, silly. That's his job."

His job. The life he'd dedicated himself to. Helping those in need.

I was in need...desperate need.

Bad enough to skip church the next morning because no way in hell could I sit through a service without thinking about Zeke's mouth, his hands while Pastor Welker preached God's supposed infallible word.

I lounged on my bed, scrolling the internet for job opportunities same as every morning and actually found something. Not exactly what I'd hoped for, but I sent along my resume as requested.

Anything would be better than sitting on my ass and counting down the day's minutes.

I spent the next half hour searching for a job more in line with number crunching while Lil sat beside her parents in church, worshiping a God who didn't have His children's best interests at heart.

Thou shalt not...

Thou shalt not...

Internally, screamed out in rebellion, longing to own who and what I was like a living, breathing entity dwelled deep inside my soul.

Zeke sexually aroused me when my fiancée did not. And it wasn't just lust for hard muscles and a dick. Or was it?

No other woman had turned me on, so I'd always considered myself to be a closet gay. But no other guy I'd ever seen made me hard like Zeke did. Was there something wrong with me?

Fifteen clicks of my clock sounded while I stared at the wall and considered my body might be broken.

One way to find out for sure...

Biting the inside of my lip, I turned off my laptop's safe search—and allowed my fingers to type out what I wanted to see, something I'd never been tempted to do before.

Image after image flooded my screen.

Flaccid lengths.

Hard ones.

Leaking slits.

Hands shaking, I did another search...and groaned at the perversion filling my eyes.

Blow jobs. Ass licking...rimming, it read.

Anal sex.

A two-second looped GIF showed a man on his hands and knees, his dick dripping pre-cum as another man thrust into his asshole—and I envisioned myself beneath Zeke, gladly receiving what he gave me.

"Oh God." I grabbed hold of my balls, hissing to find them tight against my groin while my backside clenched.

I clicked on the teaser, and dozens more GIFs popped up, filling my mind with all things gay sex in looping form. Staring wide eyed, I scrolled, tugging on my balls and sliding my hand up over my sweats tented by the biggest hard on I'd ever had.

Okay, maybe not biggest—Zeke caused those, but still.

Videos...I needed videos.

Heart thrumming, I closed out that search and typed in another.

Full-on porn video teasers.

"Shit."

I clicked on one of two men fucking face to face, my dick jerking in its confines.

Easing my laptop closer to my knees, I exhaled slowly, so far gone in my lust I made the decision to take it all the way I could while on my own.

I pushed my sweats down beneath my balls, allowing my aching dick some room. Wetness smeared over the tip, and I rubbed the pad of my thumb over the swollen head, smearing it in circles around my sensitive skin.

Definitely gay. No doubt.

The hungry kisses, the grasping hands, the masculine grunts and groans that filled my ears with every thrust onscreen...

I moved my hand over my length in time with the man fucking his lover like I wanted Zeke to do to me, my hips rising like the one on the bottom. My insides clenched up, and I bit my lip, breathing hard through my nose.

My hazy fantasies took on shockingly clear form. Zeke above me, holding my gaze with hooded eyes while laying claim—waste—to my body.

The laptop slid to the side, tilting onto the mattress from all my shifting, but I couldn't stop fucking into my hand.

"Oh fuck," I whispered, my eyelids falling closed.

Zeke panting over my lips.

Sweat slickening our bodies.

Hearts racing, moans spilling from our lungs.

I exploded, ropes of cum splattering up over my chest. "Fuuuuuck," I groaned, shuddering with every dribble coaxed out by my tight fist until overstimulated and I had to stop...satisfied in a way I'd never felt before.

"Shit." I sank back, fighting to fill my lungs, my pulse pounding.

The guys in the video continued to groan, their "Fuck, yeahs" icing on the cake of my sated bliss.

They both came with deep grunts, and still I laid there, lax, cum cooling on my skin.

I peeled my eyelids up, glancing at the copious amount of ejaculate my body had shot out to fantasies of Zeke fucking my ass. The guy on top in the video pulled out and leaned down, licking his lover's cum off his stomach.

I glanced at the mess splattered across my abdomen again, curious. Wetness coated the hand still holding my spent dick, so I lifted a cum-covered fingertip to my mouth. A flick of my tongue hit my taste buds with bitterness and salt.

Not pleasant but not disgusting either.

Better than pussy, that was for damn sure.

What does Zeke's taste like?

"Fuck." I let out a heavy sigh, throwing an arm over my forehead, my sticky hand resting on my messy stomach.

More fantasies flashed behind my eyelids.

Me on top, sliding my length into Zeke's welcoming body. His hands clutching at my head, him devouring my mouth while I gave him everything I had. Zeke begging me to fuck him harder, deeper, like the guy in the video.

So hot.

Swallowing, I grabbed my laptop and put it back onto my lap with my clean hand before clicking on another video left-handed.

A beefy man holding a much smaller guy in his arms rutted up into him like a wild animal.

Fucking hell.

My dick twitched to life, and I rubbed another one out even though Zeke and I were too close to the same height for that exact fantasy.

Two hours later, my balls drained dry, my length chafed from too much rubbing, and I exited the porn site.

Gay as night is dark.

I'd made a mistake in asking Lil to marry me, but I loved her too much to break her heart.

I stood in the shower, my forehead against the tile, shoulders sagging as hot water beat down over my muscles. My desire for Zeke, to experience what I'd flooded my eyes and mind with rather than go to church, was going to wreck me.

The man hell bent on helping me and Lil lay a solid foundation for our impending marriage had captured my heart and body in a way she never had.

But he didn't want me.

And I had no other choice but to accept the bed I'd made—even if that meant imagining someone other than my future wife beneath me while I buried my dick inside her soft body.

15

ZEKE

I skipped church on Sunday since I couldn't bear the thought of seeing Levi—or Lily again for that matter. But her father had asked me for one last counseling session for the two of them that week. Unable to give a reason to deny his request, I agreed.

Running didn't empty my mind or exhaust my body, and by Wednesday morning, I crawled out of bed, bleary-eyed.

No fucking coffee grounds sat in the container.

"Goddamnitalltofuckinghell," I muttered, slamming cabinets and scowling. I showered quick as fuck and headed to Clyde's Cafe in dire need of a fucking triple shot of espresso.

The last thing I felt like doing was going to church early and hanging in my office until my first appointment. I sat at a small table beside the cafe's front windows instead, sipping and sighing, ignoring the chatter around me while waking up.

The hairs on the back of my neck rose, and I glanced around the cafe, not recognizing a single person or finding anyone looking at me.

What the fuck ever.

I went back to my coffee, rubbing the hairs on my nape down with my free hand.

A different sort of sixth sense tingled awareness over my face, and I lifted my focus toward the front door, knowing who I'd see.

Levi shuffled in, his head down, glancing around. Shoulders slumped. Dressed in slacks and a short sleeve button-down. And tie.

I watched him get into line, noting how he tapped his fingers against his thigh.

Insecure.

Nervous.

Timid.

And I wanted nothing more than to give him all my attention, wrap him up in my arms, and soothe him. Fill him with peace—and my dick.

Grimacing over the sudden tightness in my slacks, I shifted on my seat, unable to tear my attention off him as he took one step at a time, slowly approaching the counter until it was his turn to order.

I couldn't hear his voice.

His hand shook while paying cash for his order.

The woman gave him his coffee, and he turned my way.

Our gazes clashed and held, and he stumbled to a stop.

I had to meet with him the next afternoon with Lily. Maybe it would be better to lay all my shit on the table so he understood my inability to explore the lust between us before the three of us got shut inside my office together.

I didn't want to be the one responsible for breaking an engagement even if I knew the truth about his sexual preferences.

I motioned him over, and he hesitated before approaching, his gaze wary, his body seemingly closing in on itself. "Have a few minutes?"

He glanced at his watch. "Seven minutes and thirteen seconds."

I bit back my grin at his tic I still found cute as fuck. "Want to join me?"

Levi slid onto the chair across from me, focusing on the coffee he wrapped his hands around.

"You look dressed for a day job."

"An interview," he said.

"That's great," I said, smiling, "Congrats."

"It isn't exactly what I was hoping for, but I'm getting desperate. Supporting a wife requires a job, you know?"

The thought of him going home every night to Lily...fuck, that stung.

"Nervous?" I asked the obvious rather than considering my jealousy.

"If I don't puke up this coffee before the interview, it'll be a miracle," he mumbled. "But I need to pull up my big boy panties as Lil would say. I've got this."

The green pallor on his face suggested otherwise, so I decided to dive in with the few minutes I had left.

"One of my first marriage counseling sessions ended in disaster."

Levi lifted those life-giving green eyes to my face, stealing all thoughts from my head for a few seconds.

"Five minutes," he stated quietly as though he'd been counting those seconds in his head, but I knew he didn't let his tic out to be an asshole in telling me to hurry up.

I filled my lungs full and dove in.

"The wife had commitment issues. She cheated, but her husband loved her and wanted to work things out. She came onto me with words and actions enough times I finally broke down and got a restraining order after months of her stalking my every move."

I sipped my coffee, and Levi stayed quiet, his attention still on my face, waiting patiently.

"When I returned home from Nashville, I found her in my bed. I called the cops, and it only got uglier. She landed in the psych ward where she defi-nitely needed to be. Her husband divorced her—and blamed me for their ruined marriage."

"Sounds like it would've happened even if you weren't in the picture."

"She wasn't stable, and I *know* I wasn't responsi-ble, but a part of me felt like I didn't help matters, or her, one bit. She spiraled out of control because of me, because I wouldn't give her what she wanted." I met Levi's gaze even though I'd rather have stuck my head in the sand. "So you know why I can't do this—even though I already feel like I've gone too far in fucking the two of you up." Shame dug her claws into me like she attempted to shred my clenched gut, and I tightened my hold on my coffee cup.

"We all have our own issues," Levi stated quietly, his eyes flickering over my face as though trying to read every micro-expression, every line etched into my skin. "But we're responsible for our actions. Whether thoughts are prompted by another, what we do isn't involuntary."

"Sometimes I feel like it is," I admitted quietly, my focus dropping to his mouth. "And sometimes, I find myself powerless to fight the lusts of the flesh."

"Lusts of the flesh." Levi's lips pursed, and he shook his head. "You do realize it's just instinctive desire, right? We humans are nothing more than animals with the ability to think outside natural tendencies. We're all striving for companionship, finding a mate, even if it isn't for procreation. That's a part of life."

"But we've chosen to live beyond that by accepting God's sacrifice and His word as truth," I reminded him.

Levi's chin raised slightly, the hint of rebellion and sass in his eyes making my dick twitch. *Brat* looked good on Levi. "*You've* chosen that route."

I lifted an eyebrow. "And you haven't?"

He tilted his head to the side, still studying my face, but his gaze narrowed slightly. "I've chosen to live for the woman who wants me by her side—even if we're not sexually compatible."

They definitely weren't. And their marriage was going to end in heartache eventually. While the thought of Levi attempting to make love to his wife time and again without success twisted my guts up with jealousy as nasty as a bitchy wolverine, an idea fluttered through my head on how to save him some of the pain he would face.

I didn't dismiss the wayward path weaving to life inside my brain even if it wasn't the high road. Perhaps a bit of selfishness prompted my consideration, but I couldn't dismiss its possible powerful impact.

An erroneous decision, something a godless heathen would do, but it could work—and save them both a ton of hurt in their future.

I would choose wrong, but for the right reason—

Levi—and guard my heart because I would never give up my calling no matter how much I hated the idea of him eventually finding a man who could love him freely.

The idea solidified in my head, and the lack of shame baffled me. I'd been ready to beg forgiveness for the sins I was about to commit for the purpose of opening their eyes, but a strange calm descended over me. I didn't feel as if I ought to prostrate myself before any throne.

"So, Thursday?" I asked, wondering if he caught the hint of excitement in my voice I hadn't expected.

Levi nodded, glancing at his watch. "Unless you cancel on us again."

No chance in hell.

"I'll see you then," I told him with a brief nod of assurance, realizing selfishness definitely factored in more than I'd thought.

But I'd stepped forward and couldn't find the strength to turn away.

He stood, discretely adjusting himself before straightening. Pink fused his cheeks when I lifted my focus off his groin to his face. "You do things to me she never will," he stated quietly, the lack of remorse in his tone a double dose of assurance that I made a good choice.

I know. And I'm going to make it obvious you weren't meant for one another.

"Good luck at your interview," I said.

He turned and fled, his flexing ass holding my attention until my cell vibrated in my pocket. The second Levi passed from sight, I pulled it out and swiped my messages open.

You're a lying cunt.

Cold rushed through me, furrowing my brow. Same goddamn number as before. *What the ever-loving fuck?* I typed out a response rather than ignoring it like the first time: **I think you've got the wrong number.**

A reply came through before I could sip my coffee. **Ezekiel Sipe, I'm never wrong when it comes to you.**

What. The. Fuck.

I stared at my name typed out in stark black, my mind racing.

I know what you do in the dark, the sins you commit in your mind.

Shit continued to pop up while I stared, frozen and fucking baffled.

I've seen your heart. I know what makes you tick.

My hands shook as I finally typed back. **Who the fuck is this?**

Another came through fast enough I knew they used speech to text. **The one you denied, the one who would lay down her life to make you happy.**

"Fucking *hell*!" I whispered harshly and powered

off my cell. Denise Foster had found my new number. Goddamn psychotic *bitch*!

I hopped up from my chair and stepped outside, my neck hairs rising again. A slow scan of my surroundings while striding toward my car didn't reveal a blonde-haired raving lunatic with wild eyes, but I fucking felt her like I'd done countless times in Pittsburgh before realizing she had stalked me.

How the fuck had she located me clear across the state? And what was it going to take to make her disappear for good?

"She fucking found me." I told Malachi the second he answered after I climbed into my car.

"What?"

"Denise *fucking* Foster—the psycho bitch from Pittsburgh!"

"Fuck. Hold on." Something rustled in my ear— blankets, I realized with a glance at my watch. I must have woken him up. "What's going on?" he asked a few seconds later after I'd gotten onto the road.

"She's texting me all sorts of shit like she's watching my every goddamn move."

"I thought she was in a psych ward?"

"She was last I'd heard." I glanced in my rearview while making a few turns, telling Malachi what she'd said. No one seemed to follow me, so I headed toward the church.

But if she'd been stalking me, she already knew where I worked. Where I lived.

"Goddamnit," I punched my steering wheel, my skin prickling like jabs of icy needles.

"You need to call the local cops and tell them what's going on. Get another restraining order—then get her ass tossed in jail because she won't stay away."

Malachi was right. There was no other option unless I made it easy for her to break into my place one night and beat the shit out of her in self-defense.

As if I could do such a thing. The clench in my gut made me rethink my self-control. It had gotten shot to shit with ideas of helping Levi and Lily recognize they weren't right for each other.

"Fuck my life," I muttered, realizing I really had that sort of animal inside me.

"Maybe it's time for a new path, my friend."

I snorted a sarcastic laugh. "What? Head out on tour with you as a groupie, partaking in tasting the flesh I've never allowed myself?"

"That *flesh* tastes mighty fine," Malachi stated with a chuckle.

"Asshole."

"You'd like those too."

"Goddamnit, man, I'm trying to be good over here."

"You *are* good, Zeke. One of the best men I've ever met. Kind and accepting. Helpful and support-ive. You've been nothing but a friend to me even though we believe differently. No one has stood by Isaac like you have with me."

"That's all the new man," I claimed, even though loving Malachi through his trials and beyond came as easy as breathing. He was like a blood brother to me. I would never turn my back on him.

"Bullshit. I've been around you long enough to know who you are inside, and your desire to help others is naturally ingrained—just like your parents."

They loved all, no matter their gender, their sexual preferences and always had. Although rough around the edges, *they* were true Christians—if there were such things.

And I needed to prove myself to be the same.

I pulled into the church's parking lot, my tension lessened by Malachi's words. "I've got to get to work."

"Do me a favor?"

"Anything," I promised him, the one man who knew the secret urges I'd never acted on until Levi.

"*Live*, Zeke," Malachi said, "because we aren't promised tomorrow. The things you love the most can be ripped from you by one leg cramp."

It had taken him almost losing Isaac from drowning for him to decide what he wanted in life.

Love.

Peace.

Joy I envied when seeing it on his face.

"I'll try," I whispered, turning off my car.

But living didn't mean tossing all caution to the wind. I wouldn't be impulsive in my decisions, allowing instinct to rule. Yes, I would choose wrong, but I planned to do so in order for the better good.

I strode into my office, thankful for the lack of raising hairs on my neck, and put through a call to the local precinct before my first client of the day arrived.

16

———

LEVI

I couldn't tear my brain waves off Zeke mode, and I bombed the interview. Horribly so. The CPA looking for basically an errand boy didn't have me in his office for more than eight minutes and twenty-six seconds before offering a tight smile and sending me on my way—because I'd puked up my coffee in his trash can seconds after sitting down across from him.

He said he'd let me know, but I pushed for an answer.

A big fat no.

Welcome back, depression.

At least I had our Thursday session with Zeke to look forward to, and until Lily climbed into my Honda and we headed to the church, my heart raced and my palms sweated.

"So, you'll never guess what!" she said, breathless while buckling herself in.

I didn't bother asking since I knew she'd launch into her tale whether I responded or not.

"Sabrina's dad might have an opening in their accounting department."

My ears perked up. "Seriously?"

"Yep." She popped the P and went about applying a generous amount of gloss to her lips in the mirror hidden in the sun visor.

Her dad owned a manufacturing company that made industrial-sized dishwashers for restaurants, and last I'd seen, he drove a new Mercedes.

"Any idea what he's looking for or how much he'll pay?"

"I'm heading over to Sabrina's tonight to pick her up, so I'll ask him before she and I take off."

"You're a doll." I smiled, some of the tension leaving my shoulders.

"That guy you met with yesterday morning just wasn't meant to be, boo. When one door closes, another one opens."

I nodded at her canned thoughts, ones both our parents shared. Such shit came with the religious territory, I supposed, since I wasn't a big believer in karma or fate either.

But with how I met Zeke, how he ended up back in my life...

Maybe there was more—but no way it could be a God of love allowing temptation like that.

The church came into view ahead, and my heart rate kicked back up. I pulled into the parking lot, palms once more damp.

"Nervous?" Lily asked when I rubbed them down my thighs after turning off the car.

"A little."

"I promise I won't embarrass you today."

I smiled. "I wouldn't care if you did."

Zeke Sipe already knew more about me than she did.

"Just...use tact when propositioning him again, okay?" I suggested past the pulse thrumming to the point it wanted to close off my throat.

She laughed lightly. "I was kind of in his face, wasn't I?"

"Yeah," I forced a chuckle. My seven minutes of shared coffee with Zeke had me thinking Lily and I couldn't get our hopes up. "Prepare yourself for a no, Lil, and if you need more in the future, after we're married..." I let out a heavy exhale. "I won't say no to whoever he is."

I glanced her way to find her studying my face, a sense of seriousness there I hadn't seen before. "I love you, Levi."

Tears stung my eyes. "Love you too, Lil," I choked out.

Lily fiddled with her purse rather than holding

my hand while walking toward the church's side entrance, so I shoved mine in my pockets to keep them from shaking.

Mrs. Vale greeted us just inside, a bag over her arm as though she was heading out for the day. "Good afternoon, kids. You can go right on into Zeke's office."

We started that way, and Mrs. Vale slipped outside, the door snicking shut behind her.

Mr. Astbury's office door further down the hallway stood open, the lights out.

"Was your dad home?" I asked while Lily scooted around me, softly touching my forearm.

"He had a dentist appointment at three-thirty today," she replied, her tone breathless. A soft giggle escaped her, and she shifted back and forth in her white Adidas before knocking on Zeke's door.

"Are *you* nervous?" I whispered.

"A little." She took my hand.

I'd expected Zeke to call out for us to come on in, but he pulled the door inward.

The scent of leather and subtle cologne wafted off him, and my instincts expanded my lungs as I drew him in as deep as I could.

His gaze flitted over Lil's smiling face as she greeted him. She sauntered past, brushing against his arm, but his focus landed on our clasped hands.

I dropped my hold on her, slower in approaching, certain I hadn't imagined the tic in his jaw.

"Levi."

My groin tightened at the heat in his eyes I caught a peek of before he shut it down.

"Come on in."

I didn't brush against him like Lil did, but energy crackled between us as though we'd touched skin on skin. Backside perched on the couch beside Lil, I fought the need to watch him cross his office and take the chair in front of us. My periphery tracked his every move though, my ears straining for the shifting of material from his pants, the squeak of his left dress shoe.

He cleared his throat while sitting back. "So, how are the two of you doing?"

Lil filled him in on the news of the week—my failed interview, but she sounded upbeat about the possibility with Sabrina's father.

I'd expected her to launch right into her proposition for Zeke to join us in bed.

"And how are the wedding plans going?" Zeke asked the second Lil paused for breath.

I looked to her to answer since she, her mother, and Sabrina were taking care of all the details. Even my mom hadn't been invited to help out, but Lily knew she couldn't be bothered with much outside the church.

Lips pursed, I half-listened as Lil went on and on about wedding stuff...caterers, the cake, the gown she'd picked up earlier in the week, how everything was coming together.

Except for us.

Hell, I wanted to sink into the couch, but I reminded myself that by following through with the engagement, I was making one of her dreams come true. A fairy tale wedding with her best friend.

Zeke kindly listened, but his gaze flicked toward me enough I wondered if he only tolerated her presence.

If I'd had things my way, it would have been another solo session, and I'd have been bent over his desk. That truth should have prickled me with guilt, but it only heightened my arousal.

I fought the urge to adjust myself but couldn't help the flick of my tongue over my lower lip.

He caught the subtle move and honed in on it, his stare on my mouth not doing anything to help my erection go down.

Lil's voice died away, and I glanced at her.

She smiled as though joyful as the day is long—and laced her fingers through mine seemingly to show solidarity. "So." She turned her head back toward Zeke. "We were wondering if you would like to come over for dinner again one night this weekend—or both nights." Her nonchalant shrug came across as practiced, but it was her once more breathless tone that gave her away.

And if Zeke noticed the pulse jumping in her

neck like I did, he had to know exactly what she wanted.

There it was, the opportunity to sin tossed out in the open. A young woman inviting her marriage counselor to join her and her fiancé in their bed for a night of debauchery.

My dick leaked, and I held my breath, my palm growing sweaty against Lil's.

Say yes, please say yes.

Zeke peered at her, his eyes unreadable, hands lightly clasped on his lap. His crossed leg hid any evidence of what I or her suggestion caused to his body.

Even if I didn't get a chance to brush my fingertips over a single inch of his skin, even if our mouths didn't come anywhere close to one another's...I needed him there with us.

Sharing heated gazes while we pleasured Lil.

Imagining he touched my skin rather than hers.

"A party of three?" Zeke asked, finally giving me his attention.

I tugged my hand from Lil's, swallowed hard, and nodded at the same time Lil vocalized an affirmative.

"With me being the dessert, of course." Lil didn't pull any punches.

"Is that what you want, Levi?" Zeke asked me, our gazes still holding.

I jerked my head up and down in a single nod.

"You have no issues with me putting my hands

on your fiancée?" he continued as though I hadn't answered. "Touching and tasting her?"

I envisioned him doing those things to me. "None," I rasped out, expecting covetousness would twist my guts up tight—but I couldn't say no.

"I want you both to fuck me."

I blinked as did Zeke, and we turned toward Lil as though of the same mind.

Chin tilted up and pink flushing her cheeks, she watched him rather than me. "I've dreamed about having two lovers at the same time, and I'm afraid that if I don't get to have that fantasy before we settle down, I'll always be left wondering, you know? Not that I would ever cheat on Levi, but I don't even want to give the devil a hold in my mind. If I get this idea out of my system, I'll be able to settle down with my best friend so we can live happily ever after."

I glanced at Zeke who studied her, his face still bland, revealing nothing.

"I know it's not right that I'm asking you to sin," Lil rushed on when he didn't answer.

"It's not right," he agreed.

"But it will only ever be between the three of us, like we said before. Levi and I don't gossip, we wouldn't tell a soul." Lil's voice shook a little, her hands tightening their clasp together on her lap. "After this weekend, we can go our separate ways, no one the wiser."

"Okay."

Lil and I stared at Zeke.

"Wh-what?" I asked, sure I hadn't heard right.

Zeke met my gaze, allowing a little of his yearning for me to light his eyes. "One night."

Lil squealed, jumping off the couch. She took two steps, leaned down, and planted her lips on Zeke's.

Not long enough for tongue, definitely not as dick-swelling as the kiss he and I had shared—and he looked at me when she backed off.

He licked at the gloss she'd left behind, and I bit back a groan, desperate to give in to the need to shift my aching balls around a bit in my jeans.

"So, Friday night," Lil said, grabbing her purse off the floor where she'd put it. "Six?"

"Sounds good," Zeke agreed, not getting up to see us out.

Giggling, Lil pranced to the door, and I stood as she passed me by.

Zeke's gaze slid down my body, lingering on my groin. "Until then," he stated quietly and lifted his focus to my face.

I couldn't find a word to say, so I followed my fiancée from his office, my backside once more on fire after a glance at the clock above his door.

Twenty-five hours, three minutes, and six seconds until I'll see him again.

17

———

ZEKE

I'm going to be a sexual catalyst. To break up a couple who's been together since sixth grade.

That thought should've made me fall to my knees to beg for forgiveness, but I felt nothing other than excitement. I told myself no one would be hurt in the process like my friend Braden had been by his father's affair. I simply agreed to a night of debauchery to point out the error in the path they'd chosen.

Isn't that what a good counselor would do?

Skewed thoughts...but my stubbornness had chosen, and I wouldn't be swayed a different way.

I brushed my teeth and glanced over my face in the mirror, my eyes clear of any trace of being under the influence.

So where did the numbness toward sin come from?

"Fuck if I know," I muttered at my reflection after spitting and rinsing. "I'm going to outright sin, go against everything I've stood for, all in the hopes of revealing their mistake in getting engaged so they can find happiness in life."

I tossed my toothpaste into the top drawer and slammed it shut, studying my reflection once more.

"Excuses."

Huffing a snort, I turned my back on the man in the mirror, willingly leaving the new creation in Christ behind.

That desire for just one taste of Levi prompted me more than the reasons I'd stated out loud. And while my old sin nature would have loved to take him from Lily for my own, I would adhere to my path—and avoid the thoughts of Levi with a man who wasn't me once I accomplished my task.

Although butterflies hovered in my stomach, my hands didn't shake while holding my car's steering wheel. No sixth sense raised the hairs on my neck—hadn't since Wednesday.

The stalker supposedly still lived in Pittsburgh, and without proof she stalked me, there was nothing the police could do.

Maybe she fucked with me because I'd ruined her life.

No way she knew what I'd done in the privacy of Levi's apartment and my office, just pure fucking coincident with timing.

Pulling to the curb beside the place they'd rented, I pushed aside thoughts of my past.

I'm going to live in the present. Live—if only for tonight.

We would sin. Lily's fantasy would be fulfilled, and unlike her thoughts on sowing oats and ridding that shit from her system, she would only crave more. Lily wouldn't ever get over her wildness, the mischievous nature she tried to squash. And Levi's heart would pay the consequences.

"Better now than five years down the road," I muttered and climbed from my car.

Catalyst—because I cared about them both and didn't want them to be miserable any longer than necessary. I could just tell them the truth of what I expected, but people needed to learn from their own mistakes.

Right?

What I planned on would do the job better than words ever could, and besides, I wouldn't uncover Levi's secrets to the woman who ought to know him better than I did.

Levi answered the door, jacking my heartrate right the fuck up with the clash of our gazes. "Hey." His nervous smile lifted my own lips.

Rather than shy away or keep my distance, I brushed against him while stepping into the apartment because why the fuck not? I wanted every second of contact I could get to think about once he went on to find his forever man. Levi's rushed inhale swelled my chest—and my dick even though the idea with another man furrowed my brow. "Hey, back."

A quick glance around didn't reveal Lily. "Where's the woman of the hour?"

"Bathroom." Levi motioned me to follow him toward the kitchen, which I gladly did.

"Fuck, you've got a great ass," I whispered, crowding in close, almost touching what I craved.

A shiver slid over him, and he pulled up short of the kitchen, bumping me into his back. My dick pressed against his ass.

"Fuck," he whispered, and I leaned down to exhale over his ear.

"What was that?" I asked, grinding against him, the thrill of getting caught in my lust for Levi elevating the need already rushing through me.

The toilet flushed, and he moved forward, escaping me.

Adjusting my dick, I stalked after him like a lion on the prowl, every flex of his ass cheeks in those damn jeans weakening my knees.

I wanted him—but would content myself with stolen touches and heated looks while we gave Lily what she fantasized about. One night.

I had to make the most of it.

Levi bent to take something out of the oven, and

I sat down at the table rather than crowding him again since footsteps sounded behind me.

"You're here."

I turned to find Lily beaming at me, her dark eyes twinkling, the pulse already pounding in her neck. Flushed cheeks and glossed lips...damn beautiful.

She wore a low-cut shirt to tempt me with her cleavage and a skirt that barely covered her thighs. Had she bent over like Levi did, her ass would've hung out. My already hard dick throbbed.

"I'm here," I stated what she had, letting her know I wasn't going anywhere until we finished our "dessert."

"I made baked ziti," she said, prancing around the kitchen to fill our glasses with ice water.

Levi set the casserole dish on the table, not looking at me, his face just as flushed as hers.

They finally settled into their chairs, their gazes catching for a few seconds, soft smiles revealing their love for one another.

Envy lanced through my chest—but dissolved when they focused on me. Lily's eyes filled with lust. Excitement.

Levi guarded his better, but I didn't miss the heat before unease took over.

Silence settled over us, tension rising enough that they both cleared their throats and shifted on their chairs at the same time. Fucking cute as hell.

"So." I bit back a grin.

Lily laughed a nervous giggle and started to serve us.

"How's the job hunt going?" I asked, turning to Levi while she scooped ziti onto his plate.

A frown flitted over his face but smoothed out almost immediately. "Lil was supposed to ask Sabrina's dad last night about a position he has opening in his accounting department."

Her lips thinned as she let out a heavy sigh. "I said I was sorry, Levi."

I glanced between them.

"We got talking about wedding stuff," Lily said before I could ask what happened, "and I completely forgot."

Levi faced me, allowing me to see the hurt in his eyes.

She had to know how important finding a job was to him. As the future man of their household, I imagined the stress hung heavy on his shoulders.

"I said I was sorry, Levi," Lily repeated, giving herself a small portion of ziti. "Anyway." She smiled brightly in my direction, but Levi didn't perk up nearly as quickly as she did. "I'm picking her up tomorrow to go to the caterer's. I'll speak with him then."

Levi nodded and forked up a bite of ziti, not lifting his head.

Lily and I made small talk, but the reminder of

their little spat had dimmed the mood. Add in the sexual tension, and dinner became uncomfortable enough that none of us finished the portions Lily had piled on our plates. She ushered us into the living room afterward, same as before, insisting on cleaning up herself.

I followed on Levi's heels, giving in to the need to touch the back of his bare arm with my fingertips. Electrical currents zapped up toward my shoulder, arced through my chest, and went straight to my groin.

Pink crept up his neck, and he rubbed his hands down his thighs when he settled on the couch.

"What do you want out of tonight?" I asked, jerking his focus toward my face.

"To make Lil happy."

I raised an eyebrow, taking my time looking down over his navy T-shirt and the bulge in his jeans, raising the thickness of lust in the air. "Nothing for yourself?"

Dishes clinked—water ran—and Levi crawled over the couch to plaster his mouth to mine.

Fuck, yes, I love when his insecurities vanish in lust.

I yanked him onto my lap like Lily had been the week before, tugging him close until his hard dick crushed against mine. He tasted like garlic and tomatoes, and thank fuck I loved both.

Devour didn't begin to describe what I did to his delicious mouth, but we kept quiet except for gasps and heavy breaths. My hands on his ass, kneading the flexing muscles as he thrust against me.

It was Nashville all over again, two men desperate for a taste of what they shouldn't want. Greedy and hungry, I sucked on his tongue, his groan tightening my balls against my body.

"You're going to come if we keep this up," I murmured over his lips, squeezing a handful of his ass to the point of bruising.

He whimpered and sagged forward, tipping his forehead to mine. "I-I can't help myself around you."

I ground against him, cursing the clothing between us. "Same. All my self-control goes out the fucking window whenever I lay eyes on you."

The water shut off out in the kitchen, and Levi pulled away with a sigh, leaving me cold.

Aching.

He settled into the corner of the couch, holding my gaze with a hooded one of his own. No shielding rose, and we both sat vulnerable. Open and willing.

Waiting with bated breaths and pounding hearts.

"Are you okay with me fucking her?" I asked quietly.

His brow furrowed. "Not really."

"Because you can't stand the idea of my dick in her body?" I pushed for clarity.

He held my gaze, the green of his eyes eaten by

black pupils. "Because I don't want her having what I need more than my next breath."

Fuck. Me.

Those frowns, the sure jealousy that night she'd propositioned me the first time...

I moved a bit to ease the ache in my groin. Levi had been upset alright—but of Lily getting my attention.

"Would she mind if I touched you too?" I had to ask.

He glanced at the doorway leading into the hallway. "She has no idea what I fantasize about—I'd like to keep it that way."

"Okay," I agreed rather than spewing curses or begging him to just tell her the truth—because that would without doubt end our one night together before it even began.

Selfish asshole.

Lily showed up in my periphery but stopped in the doorway rather than joining us. "Do you want to go upstairs?" she asked, her small voice revealing her nervousness.

Straight to the point at least, thank fuck. I hadn't visited for small talk bullshit. I needed release, and since it wasn't going to be between her thighs or in Levi's body, I'd have to settle for her mouth.

I stood, and she grasped my hand, leading me through the hallway.

A glance over my shoulder showed Levi hot on

my heels, his focus on my ass. I wondered if he fantasized about topping or being on the receiving end. I wanted both. Ached for it in my balls and my untried hole.

Not that I would experience either. I would be content to get what I could in the hours to come.

The queen-sized bed wouldn't fit three comfortably, I thought while eyeing it, but I didn't plan on sticking around for cuddling afterward.

"So, um." Lily's laugh came out shaky, and she dropped my hand when we stood in the middle of the bedroom. "I had all these plans, but now I don't know what to do." She let out another soft laugh, glancing at Levi who stepped up beside me.

"Kiss him like you did last week," Levi told her, his voice strangled.

I wondered how much it cost him to tell her that.

Her lips parted, and she took a step closer, her dark eyes on my face. Such a beautiful woman—all curves and gorgeous features. I could give her what she wanted.

For Levi.

And find release in knowing he wished my mouth was on him instead.

I took Lily's lips more gently than I would have his, allowing her to taste my tongue, to do as she pleased until she sighed and melted against me. Reaching to my left, I bumped my hand against

Levi's arm and tugged him closer...slid my hand down his forearm...put his hand on her waist.

He figured out what I wanted, turning to step in against her back.

Our gazes met while I kissed her—and I grabbed his ass, pulling him in tight, leaving no air between the three of us.

A shudder rippled through Lily's short frame, and I swallowed her moan.

Levi moved her long hair off her shoulder and kissed her neck, his hands trailing up her sides to her breasts.

"Oh God," she whimpered, tearing her mouth from mine, her head tipping back onto his chest. "I'm so wet. So damn worked up." Her throat moved while she swallowed, grinding over my dick.

I stepped back and pulled my shirt off overhead, causing a pause for both of them. Dark and green eyes trailed over my chest, down my abs.

"Lose the clothes," I said, my voice ragged as fuck.

A flurry of movements, shaking hands, left us all naked. It took every fucking ounce of self-control I had to stop myself from devouring Levi with my eyes, but I held my gaze firmly on beautiful breasts in order to keep our secret.

I grabbed Lily's silken hair and kissed her mouth, my dick rubbing against her soft belly. "I want to watch Levi fuck you, Lily," I told her between nipping teeth on her lower lip, "and you're going to suck my dick until I come down your throat."

She whimpered, but Levi's groan oozed precum from my slit.

"On the bed," I rasped. "Hands and knees."

Lily scrambled onto the mattress, and I grabbed the base of my dick while shooting a glance at Levi since her back was turned. He'd have no problem giving her what she wanted. Hard and leaking, his length jutted straight out from his body, enticing a shit ton of drool to flood my mouth.

A vision to remember...

My throat tightened, but I pushed thoughts of a future without him from my mind.

"Good?" I croaked out, and he nodded, turning toward the bed, his backside flexing—fucking tempting the hell out of me to touch and taste *him*.

Fuck, that ass.

I tugged on my balls harder than necessary, but it kept me from blowing too damn soon.

"Fuck me, Levi," Lily said, wiggling her backside while watching him crawl onto the bed behind her.

He sank into her without a word, and I forced the gnawing jealousy away.

I would be content with what I could have.

Lily sagged onto her chest with a deep moan. "God, Levi...you're so hard."

I jerked myself slow and easy, same as he pushed inside Lily's pussy, every flex of his ass mere feet from me, making me wish I could sink into his tight hole while he fucked her.

"Zeke," he croaked out, and I clenched my teeth against the tingles in my spine.

"Yeah," I murmured, rounding the bed and getting in front of Lily.

She peered up at me, her dark eyes already hazed, lips parted while she panted.

"Open up that sweet mouth, Lily."

Her jaw dropped—and I slid my dick along her tongue, lifting my gaze to meet Levi's over her back.

Found...

I held Lily's head while allowing myself shallow thrusts, not enough to gag her, wishing I cradled Levi's face in my hands instead.

He watched my parted lips while fucking her, and I wondered where his mind went.

Did he imagine himself down on his knees for me? Or was it my mouth he fantasized over?

I'd gladly take either, and I held nothing back from my gaze when he finally lifted his focus to my eyes.

Ensnared, I fell down a dark hole of depravity in my mind, full of lust for his smooth, hairless chest, his hard body against mine. I wanted the heat of his ass wrapped around my girth, his hole clenching while he shot his release all over the bed.

I thrust harder, gagging Lily, but I couldn't stop—

and Levi picked up the pace, keeping in time with me.

Can't do this…can't give her what I want him to have.

Tearing my attention off his face hurt, but I backed away from Lily, my balls ready to fucking blow. I lifted her torso upright, pressing her against Levi's chest.

He settled on his haunches, pulling her onto his lap, her thighs spread wide.

Sprawling out on my front brought a curse from Lily when she realized what I planned to do.

Levi's hips continued to move, their upright position making for shallow thrusts—and I dove in for a taste of them both, knowing I would leave with the biggest case of blue balls known to man.

18

LEVI

Lil was a sopping mess around my dick, the wet sounds of my thrusts louder than her whimpers when Zeke licked over her clit. She grabbed my hands on her waist, twining our fingers together.

"Oh God...holy hell." She gulped and shuddered, her back arched to keep me deep inside her. "So good...so damn good."

I sucked on her neck, clasping her tight while watching Zeke's dark head between where he grasped her thighs.

Having him with us made me harder than I'd ever been, like a damn steel rod, and I jabbed into Lil's warm body over and over, the telltale tingling in my balls almost unbearable.

But she needed release first. The whole night was for her.

Zeke's hands moved in closer, shoving her legs

wider—and his thumbs brushed over my dick where I sank into her body again.

I gritted my teeth to keep from uttering a sound, and he continued to stroke me while suckling her clit.

"I'm gonna come..." Lil whimpered, shivering in my arms, her head tipping back onto my shoulder.

For the first time, I didn't hope she found release quickly. I wanted Zeke's touch on my length—

"Fuck!" I gasped as his tongue slid lower, lapping at my dick before swirling up around her clit again.

"Don't stop," Lil begged, her hands tightening around mine, her mouth panting against my ear.

Don't stop...don't stop...

I chanted in my head, groaning at every flick of Zeke's tongue tasting me, watching his ass flex as he humped the bed.

He latched onto her clit, lifted his eyes to mine— and slid a hand beneath Lil to stroke my balls.

"Ung," a grunt gripped from me, and I thrust deep.

Lil shrieked her release and clamped down on my pulsing dick, but it was Zeke's hand on my sack that had me spurting cum from my length. My damn ears rang, every inch of my skin hot.

A droplet of sweat slid down my spine as I finally finished, clutching Lil's lax frame in my arms, her head still tipped back on my shoulder.

Zeke kissed his way up her torso, his scruff

scraping along my jaw while he softly pressed his lips to Lil's. He pulled away, the blue of his eyes overrun by black pupils—focused on me.

A shudder rippled through me as we stared at one another. I panted for breath while he grimaced and reached down.

His dick remained stiff, flushed, and leaking.

I licked my lower lip involuntarily, and he groaned, shaking his head.

Lil sighed, and I lifted her off me, laying her onto the bed.

I wanted to take care of Zeke. Every cell in my body screamed to reach for him, suck him into my mouth, and give him release.

But he crawled off the bed, heading for the bathroom.

Lil peered up at me, a contented smile on her face when I looked down at her. "Best. Night. Ever."

Happiness bubbled up inside me, and I let out a soft chuckle. "I'm glad."

Zeke returned with two wet face cloths, handed them to me, and began pulling on his clothes.

I took care of Lil first, and she snuggled into my pillow, her eyelids fluttering shut. She sank into the bed with a heavy sigh but opened her eyes to find Zeke who bent to tug on his sneakers.

"Thank you," she whispered.

"My pleasure," he said, even though he hadn't finished...

I hopped off the bed and grabbed a pair of sweats when I realized Zeke had no intentions of sticking around. "I'm going to walk him out," I said, and she smiled again, her eyes closed.

"Take your time," she murmured. "I'm just going to rest for a few minutes."

I knew my Lil—she would pass out in twelve seconds and sleep until I woke her and told her to head home before her parents called looking for her.

Zeke strode from the bedroom, and I scurried to keep close, my pulse picking back up. He grasped the door handle.

"Wait," I whispered.

His head tipped down, but he listened.

It was my turn to crowd close, to press against his back. Zeke held still and didn't pull away when I slid my hands around his waist and closed a hand over his hard length.

He hissed, swiveled his head, and let out a whimpered groan while taking my lips.

My dick swelled like I hadn't just emptied my balls at the hungry way he ate at my mouth. A twist brought our fronts together, and I pressed him against the door, my fingers shaking while trying to free him.

One yank of his hands took my sweats down my thighs, and without breaking our kiss, he helped me with his jeans. A swift shimmy, a firm grip on my hip, and he pulled our bodies together again.

Bare flesh. Hot and hard. Soaked by his precum.

Holy hell, better than a wet pussy…

I clung to him as he held us both in his grasp, working our lengths in a slickened mess—his precum all over my dick.

"I couldn't," he gasped, his mouth finding my ear. "Couldn't give her what I wanted you to have."

"Fuck, Zeke." I swallowed hard, hanging onto his head for dear life as his hand moved faster—so damn good. "I want it. Give it to me."

A low rumble escaped his chest as he took my mouth again.

My balls tightened, every lash of his tongue along mine in time with his hand taking me closer. I yearned to watch us come together, but I needed the connection between our lips, the shared, heavy breaths.

He let go first, wet heat shooting all over my chest, and I followed, my knees going weak as we swallowed each other's groans. A few last spurts, and his hand simply held us as our foreheads met, our panted breaths mingling.

A shuddered exhale and he pulled back, his eyes dark in the bit of light filtering from behind me.

We'd been quiet, but had Lil heard us?

He glanced beyond my shoulder but didn't jerk away like he'd have done if she stood there. Even if he had—if she had caught us in the act—my high of release from Zeke's touch wouldn't have allowed guilt to filter in.

Releasing his grasp on our spent dicks sent coolness over my wet skin.

Zeke lifted a fingertip and painted my lower lip with our cum—and he leaned in to lick it away.

I moaned again, clutching at his shirt to stay upright.

This right here. How can I live without his taste on my tongue, the subtle scent of his cologne in my nose?

My eyes stung when he slowly pulled back as though reluctant to let me go.

I dropped to my knees without thought and took his flaccid dick into my mouth, needing to taste his flesh like Lily had. Salt and bitterness coated my tongue, and I groaned, greedily sucking and licking every trace of us from his skin while he gently held my head.

Once finished, I allowed myself a few extra strokes over his slit, hoping for one last hint of him to coat my tongue.

"Levi," he croaked as though I'd gifted him with eternal life.

I rocked back onto my heels and tucked him away, buttoning and zippering him back up. Shaky legs barely got me to my feet.

We stood, two feet apart, the silence heavy between us. Sexual tension radiated in the inches separating our bodies even though we'd finally found release together.

Zeke cupped my chin and stroked his thumb over my lower lip while I lost myself in the depths of his eyes. Open and sated, more beautiful than anything I'd ever seen.

My heart couldn't be more full—

"I'm sorry." Zeke's words ripped the warm fuzzies from my brain, and I stood frozen, staring as he turned and let himself out, quietly shutting the door behind him.

Sorry.

For the threesome? For jerking us off? For allowing me to clean our cum from his skin with my tongue?

What the fuck is he sorry for?

The sting returned to my eyes. Lil hadn't been lying when she'd said best night ever. I couldn't fathom how he might think we'd made a mistake.

I returned to the bedroom, guilt finally snaking in to spoil my high.

My fiancée lay passed out exactly like I'd expected, lips parted, breathing heavily. So damn beautiful, most men would kill to have their diamond on her ring finger.

Usually whenever we messed around and she slept, I would snuggle against her soft body and breathe her vanilla scent into my lungs, telling myself I would eventually find contentment in our marriage.

Zero desire to do the same prompted me forward.

Chest tight, I put distance between us and headed for the bathroom. I washed Zeke's scent from my skin as my tears swirled down the shower's drain with our cum, wishing that I could feel the way he did about what we'd done.

Once I had myself under control, I woke Lil from her short nap. She smiled like a kitten who'd sucked down a bowl of warm milk—and was just as sleepy.

"We have to do that again," she said, stretching lazily.

I didn't reply but pulled on a pair of shorts and a T-shirt.

"Did you have fun?" she asked, and I bent to grab her clothes off the floor.

"Yes."

"You were hard as a rock—again behind me. I'm starting to think you're an ass guy, boo."

I made a noise of agreement but didn't look at her while putting her clothes beside her. It should have been a shitload of shame, guilt, keeping my head low, but disappointment over Zeke leaving weighed my shoulders the most.

"Think he'll go for round two?"

My emotions wouldn't survive it. "Don't know," I

muttered. "I'll get your shoes and meet you at the door."

"You seem anxious to get rid of me." Lil let out a soft, teasing laugh.

She readied to leave, and I walked her out the front door and down the walkway to her car, lost to the loudness in my head.

"Are you okay to drive home?" I asked on autopilot like I did every night.

Lil leaned up and kissed me, her hand going around the back of my head. I couldn't force myself to bend and enjoy her soft lips when all I could think about were Zeke's and the greediness of his tongue.

"Are you okay?" she asked quietly, searching my eyes, her hold still clasped on my nape.

Teeth clenching, I nodded, glancing away.

"Hey."

I steeled myself and met her gaze.

"No guilt allowed, boo. We were three consenting adults enjoying ourselves. And no one needs to know about it, okay? No one but us." She kissed me again. "I still love you and always will, no matter what."

"Same," I managed.

She released me and slid onto her front seat.

"Don't forget to talk to Sabrina's dad," I said the second I remembered, holding her door open.

"I won't. Promise."

I nodded again and shut her in.

Shoulders hunched, I watched her drive off, not turning away until her car passed from sight.

My bed lay rumpled when I returned, and I honed in on the damp area where Zeke had been humping the mattress while licking my dick and sucking Lil's clit.

A glutton for punishment, I laid down face first in the still damp cotton and filled my lungs with his scent.

Divine. Perfect.

I cried myself to sleep.

Call me when you're done.

I'd shot off the text I stared at eight hours and twelve minutes earlier. How long did it take for Lil and Sabrina to sit down with a damn caterer? The meeting had been at nine in the morning.

Where are you? I finally texted again, my nerves as shot as my emotions.

My cell rang three seconds later.

"Boo! I'm so sorry! Sabrina and I ran into some girls from high school while we were at the mall, and time got away from us."

"I thought you were meeting with the caterer?" I sank back into the couch.

"We were done there at ten-thirty and decided to look for my *something blue*."

"Did you ask her dad about the job?"

A silent pause answered that question.

"What the hell, Lil!" I sat up, my forehead denting with a frown. "You know how important this is to me! If I don't get a job soon, I'm going to have to move back in with my parents."

"He and Sabrina's mom are out of town today, but I'll definitely talk to him tomorrow after church. I promise."

Yeah, she'd promised a few times before and forgotten.

I gritted my teeth, my constricting lungs making it hard to breathe. "I have to go. My mom's calling me."

"Oh...okay. Will you be at church tomorrow?"

"Yeah."

Two lies. There'd been no call—hadn't been since I'd returned home—and I couldn't stomach the thought of sitting beside Lily while the pastor thumped his Bible and I fantasized about a man's hands on my body.

I tossed my cell onto the couch the second we hung up.

Lil knew my damn triggers...how the hell could she just forget? Again? Since I couldn't trust her to get the job done, I searched Sabrina's dad online until I found his number.

One simple phone call, a short conversation, and I hung up even more pissed. He'd filled the position the day before and had he known I was interested, he would've hired me.

He told me he would keep an ear open, but I barely heard his good luck wishes.

For the first time in my life, I cursed Lily Astbury.

19

ZEKE

I didn't feel I deserved God's grace, but I went to church anyway—and I'd never been so uncomfortable in my entire life.

The praise and worship team opened the service like always, and I wanted to leave. My feet flared as if they were on fire, like hell lay below the sanctuary's floor ready to ignite every man and woman who defiled God's word.

But strangely, guilt didn't eat at my guts. I just didn't want to be there, in a church, while others sang praises.

Levi didn't sit beside Lily in their usual spot.

I'd apologized before leaving him the night before because I knew he had a bumpy road ahead of him. I hated to be the one to cause him heartache, but it'd been necessary.

He must realize he couldn't marry Lily.

Maybe they'd had it out after I'd left. Maybe they'd already broken up and the worst was out of the way.

But I didn't want to see him pulling away from the church because of it.

And me? Part of that apology had been for myself—because it hurt like fuck that I couldn't stray from my path and make him mine instead. It was like fate had smashed our lives together in a head-on collision, but my livelihood, our beliefs, demanded we both walk in opposite directions.

Teeth clenched against the thickness growing in my throat, I sat as the assistant pastor, Jed Simpson, stepped up to the podium. Aaron settled beside me as usual, appearing well rested for a change. No bags hung beneath his eyes, and last I'd heard at the gym on Friday, his dad seemed to be in better spirits.

While Pastor Jed rolled through the announcements, my brain wandered to the hour I'd spent in Levi and Lily's bed. Rather than replay what we'd done, I turned my thoughts to the dream I'd had afterward.

Bending Levi over my desk and fucking him raw. Dirty and deep. Rough and bruising.

My dick twitched.

You godless heathen. Pay attention.

Frowning, I turned my focus on the weekly

announcements. A secretary came and spoke in Pastor Welker's ear where he sat on stage behind the pulpit. He nodded and stood, approaching Pastor Jed in front of him.

A brief touch to the arm, a quiet whispering of words, and Pastor Jed gave him the pulpit.

Pastor Welker stepped in front of the mic, his gaze scanning the crowd. "A call came through a few minutes ago. Pastor Ezra's wife passed unexpectedly earlier this morning."

Murmurs broke out—Aaron gasped beside me. He leaned forward, staring at the stage.

"As you all know, the two of them labored for the Lord over in the Ukraine the past fifteen years—"

Aaron hopped up. "I have to go," he whispered, pushing to escape the row. People twisted sideways, some standing to let him pass.

"Aaron!" I called quietly, but he didn't slow. Didn't hesitate. He rushed up the empty aisle, slamming the door open into the foyer.

The woman beside me tapped my forearm, turning me back around. "Pastor Ezra is his father's best friend."

Her words explained what Aaron couldn't take the time to do.

Knowing his father watched the live stream, he'd gotten the news in real time.

Not good.

I glanced at the back of the auditorium again, tempted to go after Aaron, but I expected with how quickly he'd fled the auditorium, he would be gone. I pulled my cell from my suit coat and shot off a text.

Call me if you need help.

He didn't text back, but I didn't expect him to until he got home and could assess the damage the news had brought to his father.

Pastor Welker prayed for comfort and healing, all the usual words men of God offered up when one of their flock hurt, but I added my own words for the best friend left behind since I didn't know Pastor Ezra and hadn't ever met him.

A somber mood settled over the church, and thankfully, Pastor Welker kept his sermon short. He had the ushers take up a second collection, a love offering to send to Pastor Ezra over in the Ukraine.

And still, Aaron didn't text me back.

No loud praise music swelled at the service's end. Instead, the pianist played quietly while everyone shuffled out.

I texted Aaron again the second I stepped beneath the sun. **Is your dad okay? Do you need any help?**

I started around the right side of the church toward where I always parked, and my cell dinged before I rounded the corner.

Aaron: **He's a mess but hanging in there.**

Me: **Want me to come over?**

Aaron: **No. It's probably best if we're alone.**

Me: **I'm sorry for his loss.**

Aaron took some time before replying, so I crossed the parking lot.

No Levi stood near my car, and while I should've been relieved, my chest ached.

Aaron: **I'm not.**

I stared at my cell, reading again and processing the typed words. He'd never mentioned his dad's best friend or any altercation that would prompt him to text such a reply.

"Zeke!"

Lily strode toward me with a sassy sway to her hips, and I stood by my car waiting for her, even though I wanted to get the hell out of there.

"Hey, you." She beamed up at me. "You took off Friday night like your ass was on fire."

"You got what you wanted, so there was no point in sticking around."

"Not *exactly* what I'd hoped for." She glanced down over my body, her gaze lingering too long on my groin.

Yeah, she'd hoped for double penetration between her thighs, but my dick in her mouth would have to suffice. I wasn't about to fuck any other hole. One, my dick being in her pussy wasn't what Levi or I wanted, and two, I'd never had anal and didn't plan to until I found someone willing to settle down with me.

Levi.

I pushed against the image flashing in my head that brought my dick to life when I should've been thinking about a faceless woman who would fit into God's will for my future.

You can't have him, or you'll lose everything.

"I won't fuck you, Lily," I whispered through the tightness in my throat, glancing around to make sure no one was within hearing range. "Where's your husband-to-be?"

Her brow furrowed. "I don't know. He said he would be here, and he isn't answering my texts."

So, I hadn't managed to be that damn catalyst... all I'd done was create an even more urgent longing for what I couldn't have.

"What happened after I left Friday night?" I rasped, giving her my full attention.

"He woke me up and walked me out like always." She shifted in her heels, clutching her purse tighter at her side. "But I let him down Saturday. Again. He's probably still really upset with me."

"What happened?" I pushed as my body tensed over the fact she'd hurt Levi again.

"I was supposed to talk to Sabrina's dad about that job and forgot."

"You forgot." My lips pressed into a thin line

while I ground my teeth, and I fought the desire to shake my head.

"Sometimes I get caught up in my own little world and everything else falls away, you know?"

I did know, and I also knew Levi's triggers, thanks to her sharing all about his childhood in our first counseling session. It was my responsibility to guide her in doing what was right for him, but I couldn't find it in myself to be the bigger man. My intentions had been to break them up—for both their sakes.

My cell dinged, and I glanced down.

Aaron: **Any chance you could grab some KFC and drop it off?**

Me: **On my way.**

Drop off wasn't an invitation to stay, but I grabbed hold of the excuse to flee Lily.

"I have to go." I shoved my cell in my suit pocket and fished out my keys, angry enough at her I couldn't look her in the eyes.

"So are we done?"

Yes—in all ways.

"If you feel you need further counseling," I said, "I suggest speaking with someone else. I'm sorry, Lily, but I think it's best if we don't see each other outside church."

"Well that sucks." She let out a huff.

I could have said a hundred different things about trusting God, choosing His path toward righteousness, or offering to pray for them, but I kept my mouth shut and climbed into the car. I hoped to leave the mess of our threesome in the past as easily as she disappeared from my rearview.

If only memories and thoughts of Levi could fade from my mind with such finality. I feared my future would be haunted for years to come.

20

LEVI

Lily called me right after church, and I lay in my bed, gay porn playing in the background while I stared at her name on my cell. My hand clutched my aching dick.

Already on edge and still pissed from the day before, I froze the video on my laptop and answered.

"Hey," I grumbled.

"I thought you said you would be here." She didn't really sound that upset with me for not showing.

"Yeah, I overslept."

Lie.

"You'll never guess what happened."

I didn't bother asking—she would launch into the tale of the day's excitement without encouragement.

"Pastor Ezra's wife passed."

I recognized the name, that he was a missionary overseas somewhere, but didn't know much else. "That's a shame," I replied on autopilot, my dick flagging, pissiness officially taking over the need to paint my abs with cum.

"We took up a special offering. I wonder if he'll finally come back to the States?"

She went on chatting about the man's possibilities as if I cared, as if she hadn't devastated me the day before.

"Did you talk to Sabrina's dad like you promised?" I asked, cutting her off midsentence about setting up a fundraiser.

"Oh, shit."

"Yeah," I snipped the word. My insides quivered, my nostrils flaring. "I called him yesterday. The position was filled on Friday."

"Boo, I'm so sorry."

"Sorry isn't cutting it this time, Lil. He told me he would've hired me if he'd known I was looking for a position." I spat the words out, my anger all too evident in a tone I'd never once used with her.

"I guess it wasn't meant to be," she offered quietly. "God will provide, Levi. He always does—it just might not be exactly what we think might be best."

More canned shit from having been raised in the church that didn't encourage anything outside God's will, God's word, or placing our trust in Him to see us through.

"I have to go," I rasped out, my stomach clenching and the stinging in my eyes too much to handle at the moment.

"I'm really sorry," Lil said again, her tone full of remorse.

"Yeah."

"We'll find something."

Don't promise...don't promise...

"I promise," she said anyway.

I clenched my eyes shut.

"I have a lot of stuff to take care of this week preparing for school starting in the fall," she continued, "but can I come over Wednesday night after church?"

A few days off from our relationship sounded fine by me. Maybe by then I would have some answers on what the hell I should do.

"Fine," I muttered. "I'll see you then."

She offered a sweet goodbye, her voice still sounding sorry, but I wasn't moved by her contrite spirit.

Dick no longer interested in release, I turned off my laptop and decided to work out by doing push-ups and squats until I fell the fuck over. My anger, my confusion remained though, and it carried through into the week.

There were still no job openings to be found—

unless I wanted to flip burgers. The idea made me cringe, but desperate times and all that shit.

I applied for a cashier position at the drugstore. The grocery store was looking for baggers, so I filled out an application there. Anything would be better than moving back home with my parents where I at least knew I could live for free.

Depression sank her claws into me, and all I wanted was someone's warm arms to hold me, to tell me everything would be okay.

I even called my mom about my fruitless job search, thinking she might give me words of comfort for a change.

"Well if you'd sought out God's plan for your life rather than try to fulfill your fleshly desires, you'd *be* at work right now," Mom said, her tone matter of fact. Short. As though my voice, the fact I breathed, bothered her.

A muscle ticked in my jaw. What the hell had made me think she'd say something different?

"At this point, Levi, your only option is to trust God," she went on when I didn't comment.

A canned response I'd grown sick of hearing.

"Thanks, Mom." *For absolutely nothing.*

Well, I was tired of trusting in a being I couldn't see, hear, or feel, but I sure as hell couldn't say that to her without causing World War Three.

Staying faithful to His word hadn't gifted me jack shit, and a seed of bitterness began to fester inside me. It fed off my lingering anger with Lil and the fiasco of my identity, my desire for a man I barely knew.

"I gotta go, Mom."

She didn't offer me best wishes, didn't extend an invitation to me and my fiancée to go over for dinner —so I didn't either.

Wednesday night, I sat on the couch, knee bouncing in the silence while waiting for Lil to show up like she said she'd do.

Something had to give. I just didn't know what.

Lil had always been able to put my broken pieces back together, but for the first time, I felt as though she'd helped in the breaking. I floundered, needing guidance the Bible didn't lay out in black and white.

If I'd had Zeke's cell number, I would've called him and poured my heart out. But his 'sorry' on Friday night left me thinking he wouldn't have anything to do with me or Lil ever again.

Talk about sucking ass, and not in the better way I'd seen on my favorite gay porn site the day before.

I glanced at my watch, teeth clenched to keep my stinging eyes from welling.

Church had let out forty minutes earlier.

"The hell, Lil."

Fucking promises. I shot off a text asking her where she was.

Rather than calling like usual when she disappointed me, she texted back.

Lil: **I stayed after to help your parents with some fundraiser details for Pastor Ezra.**

Church first.

My heart ached while I read her words again. No apology—not that one would've made her forgetting to call any better.

Me: **I'm going to bed. Talk later.**

Lil: **Sabrina and her boyfriend asked us out on a double date Friday. Want to go?**

I considered telling her off, but Lil had been my only support for most of my life. Letting her go, taking separate paths in life, didn't feel right even though our relationship moved toward that direction.

Me: **Sure.**

And with one word, I stayed trapped in what I'd created, stuck in the bed I'd made.

———

I had five bucks left of the hundred Lil had given me the week before, and I used some of it to stop at the corner store to buy a box of Milk Duds early Thursday evening. Maybe having a peace offering would get me where I wanted to be.

My knees quaked—but my need proved greater than the possibility of additional hurt. I didn't think I could be more disappointed and upset with my life.

What was one more blow to the emotions?

Just do it.

I strode up the stairs in my old flipflops and didn't allow myself hesitation before knocking on the condo door.

Zeke answered fifteen seconds later, gray shorts hung low on his hips, and he went barefoot. A faded blue T-shirt brought out the lighter shades in his eyes, and water clung to his eyelashes, making them spiky and sexy as hell. Water dampened his mussed hair.

"Levi."

"Hey."

He didn't step back, didn't invite me in.

"Sorry for dropping by like this," I rushed to say, thrusting the box of candy at his chest. "I-I just needed someone to talk to, and you're the only one who knows about all the shit in my life outside of Lil."

A corner of his lips rose as he took the candy from my outstretched hand. "My favorite."

My smile wobbled. "Mine too." I shoved my hands in my pockets so he couldn't see how they shook. I kept my focus on his eyes as he studied me, but every inch of my body buzzed to move, look away. Hide my face.

Damn insecurities.

Zeke let out a slow exhale. "Come on in."

I shuffled past him, filling my lungs with his clean scent—so, not cologne like I'd thought, but a woodsy bodywash that took me back to Nashville every time I got near enough to sniff.

Dick-achingly delicious.

"Have a seat." He motioned toward a couch. "Want anything to drink?"

For the first time in my life, I'd have loved something more than water or soda. Whiskey sounded about right, considering how my insides clenched tight, but I doubted Zeke partook.

"I'm good," I said, sitting in my usual perch-like position.

Zeke took the chair across from me like we settled in for a counseling session, peeling the top of the box open. He popped a Milk Dud in his mouth and offered me the box.

I shook my head, too worked up for sugar. "No thanks."

"So, what's going on?"

Filling my lungs to bursting didn't offer any relief from the angst ripping up my insides, but I dove in, regardless of my stammering, shaking voice. I told Zeke about the weekend—Lily forgetting time and again and learning about the position being filled. I topped that shit with the stuff from my mom and how the last thing I needed to hear was to trust God, that He had all the answers.

Blah, blah, blah bullshit...

"I'm so fucking lost," I croaked out, my hands clenched tight on my lap as I stared at the gray area rug between us. "Depressed. Angry. Second guessing everything...and the only person I have to go to for answers is half the problem. I've never had anyone but Lil, and I love her dearly, but..."

"But?" Zeke prompted when I fell quiet.

I finally looked him full in the face after rambling for a good twenty minutes. No pity shone in his features, but concern warmed the eyes I wanted to get lost in.

"But I'm starting to feel like she isn't my person anymore." My voice caught, and I swallowed hard. "I'm stressing big time over finding work, our relationship, the future."

Zeke didn't spew biblical bull at me. He didn't offer to pray for God's leading. "When you think about your future, what do you wish for?"

It had always been Lil. Always. But only darkness lay in my path. "I-I don't know anymore. I want what everyone does—love. Affection. Someone to lean on, someone to hold when they need me."

"I understand what you went through as a kid." Zeke popped another candy in his mouth and studied the box while chewing. Every twitch of his scruff along his moving jaw reminded me of how it had felt along my cheek when he'd kissed me.

My dick woke back up, and I tore my focus off him to study my white knuckles, hands still gripped on my lap.

"My parents loved me unconditionally," Zeke

finally said, "but once they met God and the church in Boston, I took a backseat in a lot of ways. Forsaking the assembling of God's children became like a sin, and we spent more time at church than we did together as a family."

I relaxed and listened. Soaked in every word Zeke spoke about his childhood, how he'd gone off to a Christian college for counseling because of his old pastor who'd broken his best friend's heart. How he'd hidden and squashed the part of him that always tempted his flesh.

The sexual energy that had flared to life the second our eyes had met all those months ago morphed into more...a connection of shared heartache.

I hardly knew the man I sat across from, but I experienced emotions swelling I'd only felt for Lil—and they added to my confusion.

It seemed there were no answers.

21

ZEKE

I'd fucked up by giving into Lily's request. Failed the two of them, Levi especially, in agreeing to be a catalyst to rip them apart.

He sat on my couch, shoulders slouched, face pale, almost...shrouded in visible depression.

Which I'd caused with my unsuccessful attempt to send them both down the path toward happiness.

I thought that revealing some of my past would show him I could be a friend, someone who understood, but studying his gorgeous face while trailing off with more of my backstory than I'd shared before made me aware I could never just be his friend.

The second the knock had sounded while I dried off after the shower, I knew who stood outside my door. Keeping my dick in check while rushing to dress and sprint across my condo hadn't come easy. Proved even worse when our eyes met.

I wanted Levi with an obsession that bordered on evil. Beyond a sinful nature—the attraction between us was instinctual, as though my subconscious even recognized the fact he belonged to me.

But.

Levi lifted his head, and my breathing grew shallow, the lance of pain across my chest more real than the rug beneath my feet. "Is there any hope?" he whispered.

A few canned phrases came to mind, Bible verses he'd probably heard quoted a million times, but I couldn't bring myself to say them—because I wasn't sure myself.

"I don't know, Levi." I let out a heavy exhale, questioning everything I'd been taught, everything I'd learned about being a Christian. "The struggle is real. The push and pull of the old man versus the new. Choosing to live a godly life is a tough decision we have to make every single day."

"And what if there is no God, Zeke? What if there's no heaven, no reward for denying ourselves during the one life we have? What if it's darkness, zero consciousness, after death? You knew nothing before birth, so what if it's the same after you breathe your last?"

"I suppose life wouldn't have meaning beyond the years we have here on earth if that were the case," I answered truthfully.

"Is it the fear of hell that keeps you from living?"

His green eyes peered deep inside me as though sifting through the thoughts and shit I dealt with almost every day.

"No," I answered truthfully, my reasons for steadfastness as real in my mind as his body mere feet away from me.

"Then what is it?"

My lips lifted in a wry grin even though I considered disliking part of my personality for the first time ever. "Stubbornness."

Levi didn't smile but held my gaze as my convictions and desires warred inside my head—the Bible's truth and eternity versus longing in the present.

My mind agreed with the first because of how I'd been raised, but my body fought hard for the second.

"Do you believe in God?" Levi asked, quieting my inner struggle, but I wasn't quick to answer since I wasn't sure exactly where my beliefs rested.

Did I only accept the truth of God because of where and when I'd been born? Did I only pray and trust God because my parents did?

"If you had a son, Zeke, would you allow someone or something to physically alter his make-up?" Levi asked when I didn't answer.

"What do you mean?"

"His DNA, the chemicals in his brain—would

you allow something to mess him up in a way that would cause misery for his entire existence?"

His question hit me like a punch to the gut, bringing Braden to mind. I'd experienced his brain and heart's reaction to what his father had done to him—and I refused to be such a man. It was why I had set my path toward counseling and chose a godly existence all those years ago.

"Would you force him to live a lie in order to be on good terms with you?" Levi continued with his powerful questions. "Tell me that isn't fucked up, Zeke. Explain how that isn't cruel."

Fuck, he sounded like Malachi.

"My human mind can't fathom it, but I have to believe that someday I'll stand before the throne of God and be given understanding—"

Levi pushed to his feet and took the three steps to close the distance between us. He stood looming over me, shaking hands fisted at his sides, his eyes full of green fire that rushed blood straight to my dick.

"What I feel for you, what I want you to do to my body—" Levi swallowed hard "—no heavenly father would allow his child to experience that yearning, knowing it would cause pain. Don't give me canned phrases. Tell me I'm wrong, Zeke. Share your truth with me. *Show* me."

Fucking hell.

My truth—in that tense moment, I wanted him more than I wanted breath.

Self-control?

Gone.

I grasped his waistband and yanked him close, tugging his shorts and briefs down past his thighs. His hard length slapped up against his abs, and I didn't waste any time before closing my mouth over him.

"Fuck." He grabbed hold of my head, a shudder rippling down over his body as I swallowed him as deep as I could.

Saltiness oozed over the back of my tongue, and I pulled away, lapping, probing his slit for more.

So damn delicious.

I cradled his balls in my hand, and he kicked off his shorts to widen his legs.

"Holy hell, Zeke...fucking hell."

I couldn't stop, every whimper and groan I pulled from his mouth spurring me onward. My sinful nature took control.

And I willingly submitted to sin, allowing us one last moment together.

Levi's sack tightened, and I rubbed the smooth skin behind.

"Yes," he whispered. "Please."

My dick leaked to touch where my fingertips wandered—over soft, puckered skin.

I popped off his dick and watched his flushed face while gently rubbing over his asshole.

Lips parted, he stared down at me, black eating at the green of his eyes.

"I want you to come undone in my mouth," I said, my voice haggard with lust over the clenching ring of muscle I pressed against. *Want inside you so fucking bad.*

Levi whimpered when I removed my hand from his body, but he gasped when I licked the forbidden taste of him off my fingers.

A deep groan rumbled from my chest at his musky flavor. Goddamn delicious, ten times better than his pre-cum. I lusted to bury my face between his cheeks and eat the fuck out of his ass.

I shoved forward, taking him to the ground like an animal, hell bent on having my feast. Both of us let out a grunt at the impact, but our hands continued to grasp at one another as though unfazed by the tumble.

"Hold yourself open for me," I half-growled the words, so far gone in my need I couldn't focus on anything but taking what I had to have.

Levi spread his legs, grabbed the back of his thighs—and I dove in. Lapping. Sucking. Rimming his tight hole until he whimpered. My mouth flooded with saliva, and I pressed with my tongue.

"Let me in." The words rumbled through me, and I pushed my tongue against him again.

"Yes," he hissed.

Levi relaxed the slightest bit—and I penetrated his body, shoving in as far as I could to taste the most secret, hidden part of him while he let out a curse. I'd never known hunger before. The yearning to take everything I knew he would give barreled over me like a steam engine.

I licked up his perineum, my fingertip once more finding his hole.

Our gazes met, and I sucked down his dick while sinking my finger into his body.

"Fuuuuuuck," he groaned, his head tipping back, dick leaking on my tongue.

I rutted against the rug beneath me, moving in time with my finger fucking his ass. He hissed when I added a second, and I returned to his hole with my mouth, using more saliva to ease the stretching.

"So good," he gasped. "So fucking good, Zeke. Don't stop."

No fucking way in hell his untried hole could take a dick without lots of prep. And without lube or condoms...no fucking.

"I want your cum in my mouth," I told him and lathed my tongue over his balls, lusting for so much more than a mere taste of him. "Shoot it down my throat."

"Oh fuck."

I shoved my face over his length, gagging myself,

but I couldn't stop. A twist of my hand, a few deep reaches, and I found the magic spot inside his body.

Levi bowed off the floor, a strangled cry ripping from his lips.

And he came.

Like a bottled up can of soda shaken too long, he erupted, shooting hot semen into my mouth, half of which I swallowed. I stroked his prostate, milking every drop from his writhing body, my mouth still full of his cum.

The second he went lax, I shoved up onto my knees, yanked down my shorts, and spat his release onto my waiting hand.

Hot. Wet.

I wrapped my fist around my length and fucked my hand.

"Zeke," Levi whispered, and I fell into a one-armed plank over him, my fist slamming against his ass with every tug on my dick.

"Gonna come all over your hole," I told him, my voice fucking wrecked, every muscle in my body tensed and ready to explode.

He grabbed my head and took my mouth.

My balls seized, and I pressed my throbbing dick head against the softest puckered skin, shooting my release. I lusted to shove into him. To finish emptying inside his body, to claim his goddamn soul, but I held onto some self-control.

Because I couldn't bear the thought of damaging his body.

And it hurt—fuck, how it ached to not take advantage of our final time together. Every spurt of cum pulled a grunt from my lungs, and I muttered curses against Levi's perfect mouth, knowing I would want him forever.

Long after the final shudder dribbled cum from my slit, our mouths stayed fused as I soaked in every second I could. Our moans mingling, breaths eventually quieting.

I needed another shower, but I'd never felt so spent, so...right.

Tearing my mouth from Levi's, I buried my face in his neck, waiting for my heartbeat to calm the fuck down and fighting off the desire to mark the fuck out of his skin with sucked bruises and bites.

"I should bring you Milk Duds more often." His ragged voice filled with laughter, but I rubbed my cum-soaked fingers over his asshole, quieting him right the fuck up because I wasn't ready for our moment to end.

22

LEVI

My body buzzed beneath the weight of Zeke's body, the scent of his bodywash, clean sweat, and cum flooding my nose. My senses overran with all things him—and I couldn't want for more.

He rimmed my asshole with his cum, and all trace of teasing erased from my mind. I'd thought to lighten the mood, but I guessed Zeke wasn't ready for guilt to creep in.

And I was fine with that.

Relentless, he tormented me, his breath hot on my neck, and my body responded like a well-played instrument, dick thickening and pulse fluttering.

Living.

My eyes stung at the swell of emotion rising in my chest, and the second he breached my body with his finger, I pulled his head away from my neck. Held his face in my hands, held his gaze with mine while he defiled my body in the most beautiful way possible.

Both of us remained open, laid bare. Nothing but passion and panted breaths between us as he made himself one with my body.

He added a second finger, fucking in and out of me with slow, steady motions...deeper to rub my prostate, backing out, leaving me hanging on the edge of sanity.

My ass stung, but the pain only made the pleasure better. I lifted my hips, needing him where he wouldn't be able to escape.

The distance between our faces closed, as did our eyes. We shared exhales, lips caressing as he continued to rub deep inside me, every brush over my prostate leaking fluid from my dick trapped between our bodies. Every pause and press catching my breath.

"G-Gonna come," I gasped as he kept his fingers right fucking *there*...coaxing, enticing my body to give him another.

"I want it, Levi." Zeke licked over my lower lip, and I came, his mouth taking mine and swallowing my cries as I shuddered beneath him, completely wrecked.

My asshole ached, my dick throbbed, and my body shifted to escape his persistent touch while my heart and mind yearned for more.

"Shh," he murmured against my lips, easing his

fingers from my sore hole. "Shh." Zeke kissed me softly, settling his full weight atop me once more.

And I melted into the carpet, exhausted yet fulfilled to the point my brain couldn't function. Didn't want it to. Death could have claimed me, and I wouldn't have cared one bit.

"Shit." Zeke let out a huffed exhale and pulled away, glancing over the mess we'd made. His eyes closed off, brow furrowing.

I went from blissed out to tensed, clarity of thought smashing into me. "Don't say you're sorry," I spewed, pushing up onto my elbows as he collapsed back against the base of his chair, his face revealing the sentiment times a million and five.

"I am."

"Don't."

"Levi." Lips pressed tight, he studied my face while I stared and waited for him to rip my heart to shreds. "We can't do this."

My throat stung. "We can. We just did."

He pulled his shirt off overhead, but I was too spent to drool over the muscle rippling down his chest and lower torso. "And it won't happen again." Zeke moved to clean me with his shirt, but I snatched the soft cotton from his hand and wiped my own ass, my insides boiling, roiling with emotion.

Too much.

I shoved my legs through the shorts I'd half-worn while we'd fucked around, my weak legs barely holding me when I stood over him.

His flaccid length still glistened with our combined cum, his own shorts mid-thigh. For once, I stood firm, gaze unwavering as his slid away from my face in what could only be shame.

Zeke would allow his guilty conscience to win, to take away the beautiful moment we'd experienced together.

"Zeke," I croaked out his name.

"What's there to say?" He refused to look at me, refused to give me the attention I needed like air. "I did what I thought would be for the best, and now it has to stop."

The hairs on my neck raised. "What are you talking about?"

"I slept with you and Lily so you'd come to realize that she'll never make you happy, that marrying her would be a mistake."

"What the hell?"

"Fucked up counseling, I know," he muttered, shifting to yank up his shorts. "I chose wrong, Levi, and I have no excuse."

He chose wrong.

After all we'd talked about, the connection I'd felt between our souls, he still found me...wrong.

Not enough.

I stumbled while shoving my feet back into my flipflops.

"Please don't come back." Zeke's whisper barely reached through the ringing of my ears as I grabbed hold of his door handle.

As if I would survive another rejection.

I slammed the door on my way out, the finality of the bang breaking the dam holding back my heartache.

Somehow I managed to drive back to my empty apartment, the quiet, dark interior welcoming me with open arms. My misery sank me into my mattress, and I soaked my pillow with tears that usually would've been shed on Lil's shoulder.

I had no one to share my grief, the pain shredding my insides. The temptation to call Lil rose, but I squashed it down, expecting she was probably too busy with the fundraiser thing for Pastor Ezra, some other church event, or Sabrina shit.

Eventually, I stopped crying and decided to sit in the hot tub until my skin pruned and the water cooled. Escape would've been good, but I didn't have drugs or alcohol, or cash for either. Nothing on the TV I'd pilfered from my parents interested me, and the book I'd picked up couldn't hold my attention.

Melatonin for the win, I remembered after staring at my bedroom's dark ceiling for close to an hour. Tears well emptied and my body aching—one part deliciously so—I downed two of the strawberry flavored pills.

And thankfully passed the fuck out.

23

———

ZEKE

I took a personal day on Friday, asking Mrs. Vale to reschedule my handful of appointments for the following week. Good thing too, since my cell started dinging while I showered away the sweat from a seven-mile run that hadn't done shit to empty my mind.

Her.

"Goddamnit."

She'd gone silent after spewing all the shit that had gotten me riled enough to check on her ass, and I'd hoped she'd finally disappeared for the last time.

Psychobitch: **Lying cunt.**

Psychobitch: **You're a piece of shit.**

Psychobitch: **A goddamn hypocrite.**

Psychobitch: **Fucking failure.**

Psychobitch: **You're going to rot in hell.**

Psychobitch: **What I wouldn't give to get my**

hands on you. But not for pleasure this time. Oh no. You're going to pay for what you did.

For what I did?

My hands shook as I started typing a reply—and my fingertip answered a call before my brain processed the number.

"What!" I barked, ready to light the fuck into her, to threaten her within an inch of her useless life—

"Zeke? Are you alright?"

"Mr. Astbury." I shuddered and closed my eyes. *Fuck.* "Yeah. Sorry. I just...dumped hot coffee on my hand when I answered."

"I can call back."

"No. It's okay. Not a problem."

My cell dinged with another text I ignored.

"I wanted to invite you for dinner," he said. "I know it's last minute, but Lily and Levi are out on a date with friends from the church tonight, and her mother and I were hoping to talk to you."

Shit. Fucking hell...

They were on a date, so not broken up. And Mr. Astbury sounded too jolly to be pissed off which he definitely would be if he'd learned about the shit that had gone down between his daughter, her fiancé, and me.

"Sure. Yeah, dinner sounds lovely." I grimaced as another notification dinged.

"Wonderful. I'll have Sandy set another place at the table. Is six alright?"

I glanced at the clock. Two hours. "Six is perfect. I'll see you then."

I hung up—and shut down my cell without bothering to check the other messages. Time to hand my cell over to the police and get a new one.

It took me five minutes to get ready, and I spent the next hour and a half at the police station, sitting down with the officer I'd spoken to after the psycho's first barrage. They downloaded all of her shit off my cell for evidence and just told me to block the number and let them know if she tried from another.

She would. No fucking doubt.

He had the texts, the outright threat. Enough to pursue the issue even if she didn't.

I left only feeling slightly better.

Sandy Astbury answered the door at six, and I noted again how much Lily looked like her mother. A bit shorter and with graying hair, Mrs. Astbury was still very much a beautiful woman. "Sorry for the short notice, but Lily just told us this afternoon that she wouldn't be home for dinner. Please, come in."

The foyer smelled like baked ziti, and if Lily's mom had taught her to cook, I was in for a treat.

But the scent also brought back memories of our night together. Images in my brain I'd rather forget, my first taste of Levi's flesh I'd craved ever since.

Mouth watering even though my chest ached, I

followed her into the living room where Mr. Astbury rose from his chair in front of the TV.

"Are you a golf man?" he asked, reaching out his hand to shake mine.

"I'm more a football fan, to be honest," I replied, thankful to have small talk to take my focus off the regrets and unfulfilled longings inside my heart.

"Eagles?" he asked, settling back in his chair.

"Patriots." I grinned. "Boston born and raised."

"Well, thank God for the ability to love unconditionally." He winked, and we shared a laugh.

I glanced around the room, scanning the dozen or so pictures on the mantle and bookshelf. The Astburys had three daughters, the two oldest having already married and blessed them with a half-dozen grandchildren. All six lined up from tallest to shortest in an eight-by-ten framed image to my right.

A few meandering footsteps took me in front of the picture, and I smiled over the six kids—every single one had Sandy's dark eyes. "Quite the crew," I said, noting the only boy, the youngest, had the type of smirk that promised a three-year-old terror.

"You should hear them when they're all in the same room." Mr. Astbury made a tsking noise. "Lord have mercy."

Both of us laughed again, and I ambled along the wall, taking in the other pictures. A few of their daughters and their families, Lily's graduation picture. One of her and Levi at Christmas where she had a sparkling diamond on her left hand.

She beamed as though he'd just handed her the moon, but it was his shy smile that caught my eye.

Timid and insecure. He needed to be built up, shown what an amazing man he was. A loyal friend. Yes, he had one hell of a wounded past that had shaped him, but the potential he had hidden inside...I wanted to watch him bloom. Own who he was. Find happiness with a man who could give him every inch of his soul without regret or shame—

Fuck, no.

I couldn't handle seeing him with someone other than me, but he wasn't *for* me. And the way I'd handled the fall out after our...*moment* together couldn't have been worse.

Fucking asshole.

My throat clenched up tight along with my fists at my sides, and I tore my focus off his face for the next picture.

Mr. Astbury stood with his arm around a blonde woman's shoulder.

My heartrate jacked the fuck up, ripping all thoughts of Levi from my mind, and I leaned in closer, sure my eyes weren't seeing right.

"That's my sister, Denise."

Denise Foster. Psychotic stalker bitch from hell.

My stomach churned, the blood draining from

my face so fucking fast I wanted to put my head between my knees.

Fucking hell. Fuck!

I cleared my throat, praying like hell for a steady voice. "Does she live around here?"

"Pittsburgh, last I'd heard," Mr. Astbury replied, not offering any further information.

He had no fucking clue I was the one responsible for her stint in the psych ward. Or did he even know how I'd helped get her locked up the year before?

"Do you keep in touch with her?" I managed to force out the words.

"Not lately." Mr. Astbury shifted on his chair behind me. "She...isn't well. Hasn't been for years."

"Oh?" I took the bait and turned, needing whatever shit I could rustle up.

"Drugs. Alcohol." Mr. Astbury shook his head. "She left the church years ago, giving us no reason to keep in touch. We'd heard she married a decent enough man. They have a daughter named Haley who lives in California and calls once in a while. Haley is Lily's favorite cousin—and nothing but trouble, just like her mother at her age."

"Are they still married?"

He frowned, giving his attention to the TV as one of the announcers said something about a birdie. "No. Haley told me they divorced, but I'm not surprised, considering the lifestyle she lives."

"I'm sorry to hear that."

Fucking lie from hell.

"They'd gone for marriage counseling, and the supposed Christian man meeting with them talked my sister into his bed. He broke her heart and her mind. Last I'd spoken to Haley, Denise was still there. But that was six months ago."

Mr. Astbury had no fucking clue that supposed Christian man stood right in front of him. Otherwise, I never would have been asked to offer premarital counseling to his daughter. No way in hell I would have been invited into his home, either.

Sandy arrived in the doorway. "Dinner's ready."

I followed Mr. Astbury from the room, scrubbing a hand down over my face and eyeing the door where my feet itched to take me.

I needed to get the fuck out of there, not attempt to enjoy a goddamn family dinner.

"So what did you want to talk about?" I asked, once seated with a pile of steaming ziti mounded on my plate. Anything to get the conversation going so dinner would end and I could leave.

"We wanted to discuss Lily and Levi."

I nodded, chewing a mouthful of food I couldn't even taste thanks to the jumping pulse beneath my skin and the churning guts keeping my focus.

"We have...concerns."

I gave Lily's dad my attention.

"She's been acting strange. Restless."

"In what way?" I asked, forking another bite even though I couldn't stomach another one.

Mr. Astbury pursed his lips and shook his head, glancing at his wife. "Her spirit just seems...dim. We've asked if she's struggling with anything, and she assures us it's just pre-wedding nerves."

I forced a smile. "I suppose every bride-to-be has their moments."

"Has she shared anything with you?"

I met Mr. Astbury's gaze head on. "I'm sorry, but whatever is said inside my office isn't something I can discuss with you."

"But we're her parents."

Sandy patted his hand, but I didn't take my focus off his face.

Our stare down lasted for a few seconds while I considered the gall of the man. A fellow counselor asking me to break the confidence—of his daughter no less.

"If I deemed something serious enough to warrant sharing with you, I would," I said, barely keeping my anger from my voice.

"Surely you can understand our concern. They're both quite young—"

"Yes, but they're both adults. They will stand or fall before God alone, and quite frankly, their relationship isn't yours to meddle in." I wiped my mouth and stood. "Sandy, thank you for dinner, but I'm afraid I have to go."

"Zeke, wait." Mr. Astbury followed me to their entryway, but I didn't do as he asked.

I opened the door.

"I'm sorry for upsetting you."

A quick nod was all I offered before striding down their sidewalk.

"We'll talk next week."

Don't get your hopes up.

I hopped in my car and drove off.

"Fuck my goddamn life," I muttered, punching my steering wheel. "Goddamnitalltofuckinghell!"

What were the goddamn chances? Seriously… fucked the hell right up.

"Why, God?" I barked a laugh while stopping at a red light. "You have one fucked up sense of humor."

A car drove through the intersection—Lily's. Levi sat in the passenger seat closest to me, staring out the window. Lips downturned, that shroud once more seeming to weigh him down.

Lily smiled and chatted away with the people in the back.

As though feeling my gaze, Levi lifted his eyes and ensnared me as usual until the car passed from sight.

Someone laid on the horn behind me.

"Fuck off!" I hollered, glaring in my rearview. I waited at the green light because why the fuck not— and drove off the two seconds after it turned yellow.

The horn followed me, and I gave them the bird.

24

LEVI

I never should've agreed to this.

Lil, Sabrina, and her boyfriend Jarod all enjoyed the after-dinner conversation while driving toward the club we often snuck out to, but I wished to be a hundred miles away. Anywhere other than where they laughed and enjoyed life.

Because mine sucked.

Lil hadn't touched me once since picking me up. Not once. Usually, she had wandering hands beneath the dinner table when we went out on dates, and even having friends with us didn't deter her. No soft brushes of shoulders, no gentle bumps with her knee to let me know she was there for me.

It was like a wall had risen between us, and even though a part of me recognized us both pulling away, it hurt like hell.

She was no longer my rock, my other half.

And I couldn't bear to be in the car another minute—

Zeke.

Pulling his car to a stop at a red light.

My chest ached, eyes welled as we stared at each other for the brief five seconds it took Lil to drive through the intersection. He passed from sight, once more ripped from my life.

"Can you take me home?" Lil didn't hear my whisper, and I leaned forward, turning down the radio. "I don't feel well enough to go dancing. Can you please take me home?" I repeated.

Her focus flitted over my face quickly before turning back to the road. "Are you going to puke?"

"No." *Maybe.* "But that pizza isn't doing my stomach any favors."

"You only ate three bites."

So she had noticed. Even knowing her motherly instinct to watch out for me remained, I didn't feel any comfort from that fact like I used to.

"Can you please just drop me off at home?" I croaked out, tilting my forehead against the warm window heated from the summer evening. At least air conditioning blasted from the dashboard vent, cooling my face.

Lil didn't poke or prod, didn't reach for my hand. She simply took the next turn that would lead us back to the apartment.

I climbed out of the car ten minutes later

without a goodnight kiss—not that I wanted one. The wall between us felt fifty-three miles thick, unscalable physically and emotionally—thanks to my cheating and her disappointing me.

"I'll check in on you later," Lil said out the window as I shuffled up the walkway.

I waved Lil's statement off, knowing she would lose track of time like she always did when on the dance floor. The three of them drove away, and I once more collapsed on the bed I hadn't straightened that morning when I'd finally crawled off the mattress at eleven.

No dishes waited in the sink since I hadn't been able to stomach the thought of food. The three bites of pizza sat like a rock in my stomach, so I hadn't lied about it being upset.

I'd never experienced such darkness before. Like a thick, putrid ooze of the blackest tar, it seemed to coat my insides, cover my heart, and infect my mind.

Not a good spot to be.

I pulled out my cell and swiped the screen on, refusing to second guess myself while dialing up Mrs. Vale who was good friends with my mom.

Zeke had caused half the shit, so he ought to help me deal with it because I sure as fuck didn't know how to on my own.

The number I got from Mrs. Vale went straight to voicemail.

"Hey," I croaked out and cleared my voice. "Um...

sorry to bother you, but I just really need to talk to someone. I'm...not good. I feel like I'm drowning. Can't keep my head above water." My voice broke. "Anyway. You made it clear you don't want me in your life at all, so I'm going to just turn off my cell."

Not bothering with a goodbye, I hung up and powered off the phone like I said I would.

Silence settled heavily over my head, and I decided to try meditating. I let out a heavy exhale, counting and losing myself to the thrumming heartbeats in my head. At two-sixteen, I lay in bed like a hypnotized blob of shit. Maybe I'd taken too much melatonin the night before.

I stopped counting, but the quietness in my head lingered, my body like a sand bag.

Would death's arrival feel the same? Blessed numbness? A slowing tick of the heart until it just simply...stopped?

I wish mine would stop.

Blinking brought the dark ceiling into focus.

"Still alive," I whispered to myself, not upset in the least. I was too chickenshit to take my own life.

Lil would be heartbroken, and I couldn't bear the thought of her standing over my grave dressed in somber colors and holding a single, blood-red rose.

She would be beautiful in grief. Pale and stunning...but I refused to hurt her like that.

I would hurt her in another way though. I would break her heart by setting her free—ending our engagement. I had no other option. Living a lie would never fulfill me, and she would always feel the lack too.

Tomorrow. I'll call her tomorrow.

My throat tightened, my sweet numbness fading away on a wave of fresh agony.

Why did loving and letting go hurt so damn much?

Tears slid down my cheeks, hot on my skin, and I allowed them to drip.

Fucking *hell*, emotions hurt.

Someone pounded on the front door, and groaning, I rolled off the bed.

"Guess that talk won't wait," I muttered, ready to face the woman who'd actually followed through on her promise to check up on me.

25

ZEKE

The memory of the pain in Levi's eyes mocked my conscience until I got home, and I powered on my cell, knowing I had to make things right. Apologize for what I'd said Thursday night when he'd left me.

I had asked him to not come back as though I hated him, couldn't stand the sight of him. But it'd been a near silent plea for him to set my emotions, my aching heart, free so I could live the life I'd chosen without wondering of the 'what ifs'. He must have heard my mutter and misunderstood with how he'd slammed my front door.

And to see his face in the passenger window, those beautiful eyes broken...his soul bleeding...

"Asshole."

Shaking my head, I paused my thumb over the

screen rather than clicking on my contacts to find his number I'd taken from their file at work.

He'd tried calling me minutes earlier and had left a voice mail.

I played back the message, his low voice stumbling in my ear—and ripping my heart to shreds, shattering my nerves.

"Fucking hell." I clenched the cell and put through a call. "Don't do it—fucking hell, please, Levi. Don't do anything stupid—"

Straight to voicemail.

"No!" I tried again, a cold sweat breaking out on my brow.

Voicemail.

"Shit!" I grabbed my keys and sprinted back outside, my heart racing faster than my feet, faster than my tires eating up the miles, the minutes it took to reach his apartment.

Thoughts and fear clouded my mind, creating a hell of my own making, one I wanted to escape but couldn't. I gulped down breaths to keep keening noises from filling my car as images of what I might find flashed through my mind with lightning speed.

If he contemplated suicide, if he...

"Fuck!"

I can't lose him...can't...

I drove up onto the curb at the first available parking spot at his apartment complex and hopped out, tripping up the stairs in my haste to get to him.

Slamming my fist on the door, I spewed curses—not prayers—desperate for it to pull inward. Such fucking *need* to hear footsteps inside coursed through me even though my thudding heart wouldn't allow me to make out much above them.

"Please, Levi, please." My voice choked, and I pounded again, resting my forehead on the wooden door to keep dizziness from toppling me over. "Please," I whispered, my guts twisted beyond repair, my temples throbbing.

Every inch of my body burned with the desire to scream, to thrash around and show how badly I'd bankrupt my entire life.

The door swung in.

Levi.

Red-rimmed eyes...so broken.

Alive.

A release of tension rolled over me, and I rushed forward, pulling him into my arms, barely holding back a sob.

He melted into me, clung to my back with greedy hands as though it was my strength alone keeping him upright while my knees threatened to buckle beneath us.

"So sorry...so fucking sorry," I murmured, soaking in the thump of his heart beating against mine, the warmth of his neck on my lips. The solid form of muscle and bone—tangible—pressing along my front.

Alive, I reminded myself again, a rush of thankfulness clogging my throat.

Wetness coated where our cheeks met, and I pulled back, grasping his face, wiping the tears away with my thumbs. Sooty lashes clumped with wetness around his pale eyes, creating such an ache deep inside my chest I could barely breathe.

"Okay?" I managed to croak.

Levi shook his head, his fingers still grasping at my back.

"What do you need?" I couldn't get the words out fast enough. "Anything—tell me, Levi, how I can help you."

"Kiss," he whispered.

Fucking hell, I couldn't say no.

I claimed his mouth as a cry of my own echoed between us. There was no lust of the flesh between our mouths, no hunger for sin—only compassion and connection, a communion of souls.

Fucking *life*, and the tears rolled as we clung to one another, tongues twining, breaths shared. How could I deny him? The connection between us had been a collision course since we first laid eyes on one another. God, the church, my job be damned...I just...couldn't say no to us in that moment of thankfulness he still breathed, his exhales filling my lungs and reaching clear into my soul.

Yearning to make him mine in our present

defeated the supposed truth I'd claimed since childhood.

As though Levi noticed the war's outcome inside my head, he pressed closer, his lips tasting, devouring, rather than taking solace in my affection.

He moaned into my mouth, the thickening of his dick against my thigh all the encouragement my body required.

I grabbed his ass like I'd done in Nashville, grinding against him until I throbbed. Leaked. Lips bruised, teeth clashed in our desire to be closer.

"Need you," he whispered, and I shoved my tongue into his mouth with a deep groan, knowing there would be no turning back.

I stepped away, but only long enough to rip my shirt off. He did the same, and we came back together, mouths fused, hands mapping out bared skin and restless muscles. We managed to stumble into the living room where the rest of our clothing hit the floor.

Couch.

I shoved him over the back, face down, and he lifted his gorgeous ass in offering.

"Fuck." I grabbed my dick and squeezed, my knees hitting the floor and my face finding his crease.

His musky scent filled my lungs, and I moaned, shoving my tongue right into his hole.

A sexy as fuck hiss escaped him, and I speared

into him over and over, my hands bruising his cheeks, keeping him spread wide for my mouth.

"Zeke, please...I want you. Please."

"Don't have condoms or lube," I muttered and shoved my tongue back into him, curses ringing in my head.

"Don't care."

"You would if I tried to fuck you right now." I exchanged my tongue for my finger, letting him get a reminder of what penetration with only saliva felt like.

He lifted onto his toes when I didn't take it easy on his hole.

Fucking couldn't. Levi wrecked my goddamn self-control.

"L-Lotion," he whimpered, pointing to the left.

Lotion and tissues sat on the side table.

Thank fuck.

Exhilaration rushed through me, quickening my breaths and making me feel as giddy as a kid standing neck deep in a vat of Milk Duds. "What do you get up to in this living room when you're bored and all alone?" I asked, swiping the bottle into my shaking hand.

"Masturbating to gay porn," he stated, no hesitation, no hint of shame.

"Fuck, I love brutal honesty coming from your lips." I squirted lotion onto my hand and added it to the copious amount of pre-cum coating my dick.

"I always think of you when I watch it," Levi said, shifting against the couch like he couldn't stand the wait. "It's your name I cry out when I come with my fingers buried in my ass."

"Fuck." His hole clenched in front of my eyes, and I took one last lick from his taint up to his lower back before giving him a lotioned finger.

"Oh God." He squirmed, and I grabbed hold of his dick trapped between his hips and the back of the couch. "Don't come until I'm balls deep inside your body, Levi."

"Then hurry the fuck up because I need you— I've been waiting forever to feel you inside me."

"We can't hurry this." I eased in a second finger, scissoring like I'd seen done on the porn I'd jerked off to during college.

"Ung," he moaned as I stroked over his prostate.

I leaned over his back, thrusting my dick against my hand fucking his ass, going light-headed over the truth I would be balls deep inside him, making him mine in a matter of seconds. "Fuck yes." I groaned at the thought of his tight hole clenching around my girth.

He hissed again as my knuckles slammed over his backside. "More. Another."

"Greedy."

"For you," he gasped. "Always."

I eased in a third, my breath already ragged as fuck, my dick dripping on the floor between our feet.

"Ready for me?" I asked along the shell of his ear, every cell in my body on the verge of busting a goddamn nut.

"Mmm," he whimpered an affirmative, and I moved back, pulling my fingers from his silken heat.

"I've never done this before," I told him through clenched teeth, my focus on where my leaking slit pressed against his puckered skin—like the softest kiss.

Levi twisted, giving me his eyes. "I trust you."

"Christ." I gritted my teeth, held his gaze, and pressed forward.

He blinked, lips parted on a gasp. "Fucking *hell*... don't stop, don't fucking stop."

"Bear down," I remembered to say—and lost myself to a deep as fuck groan as the head of my dick slipped past the tight ring of muscle protecting his forbidden hole.

"Oh God...God*damn*!" His head dipped down between his shoulders, a full body shudder rippling him beneath me.

"Shh." I stroked his thighs with trembling hands, blinking at the constriction around the tip of my dick. "Shh...I have you." My legs trembled, and holding back from shoving balls deep set me on edge. "Tell me you're okay, Levi...please, fucking hell, tell me you're okay."

"Ok-kay." He let out a heavy exhale—and pushed back onto my dick.

"Oh *fuck*." I held still, watching my dick slowly sink into his body one inch at a time, sheer fucking torture of the best kind.

He paused, his breaths labored. "Need," he choked out, his hands grasping at the cushion below him.

I gathered him up in my arms, his back to my chest, and a grunt ripped past his lips. "Let me in," I whispered against his ear and flexed my ass, sliding in a little bit deeper.

"Oh fuck," he cried out, arching his back, his hands grasping mine atop his chest hard enough I hesitated from taking him fully. "Holy fucking hell!"

"Too much?" I bit his earlobe, my balls drawn up tight.

"No—yes. Shit, I don't know."

"Tell me to stop and I will," I forced myself to say.

"Fuck me, Zeke. Fucking own me. Wreck me and put me back together again."

"Jesus." I thrust—fucking balls deep into the only heaven I wanted for eternity.

26

LEVI

The burn ran from my ass clear up and down my spine, curled my toes, and caught my breath. Stuffed full...exquisite pain—I'd never felt so alive.

I fought for oxygen, forbade the welling tears from falling, and floundered in such a sea of need I couldn't think straight.

The pull and push between our bodies, the dragging of his hard length in and out of my ass, along my prostate...too much. Not enough. My brain turned to nothing more than static, my nerve endings alive with zapping energy.

Precum dripped from my dick with every thrust of Zeke's hips, the smack of his balls against my ass like beautiful music to my ears. And his groans, his grunts while fucking into me like an animal...

Worth the pain.

So delicious, so right.

I clung to his hands on my chest as he clasped my back tight to him, the flex of muscle behind me absolute perfection. He slid our hands down my torso, and I released one to wrap around behind his neck, keeping him close.

His hot pants of breath bathed my neck, my ear, sending shivers over me, pebbling every inch of my skin.

Zeke wrapped his free hand around my length and tugged, his mouth closing over where my neck met my shoulder—and he sucked in tandem with jerking me off.

"Ung." I groaned and gulped, tipping my head down and forcing my eyelids open to see him milk my aching length.

"You're so fucking hard for me," he murmured against the back of my neck, thrusting deep and squeezing my dick.

I couldn't find my voice, just sucked in wind, my mouth dry as a damn desert while watching his hand work me over in time with his dick in my ass.

"So fucking perfect. This hole." He backed out and slammed in, our clasped hands on my hip holding me in place. "Are you going to come for me, Levi?"

"Yes," I whispered, gasping at the tingles in my balls, the constant friction across my prostate. "So hard...so much."

"Give it to me. Fill my hand."

"Zeke. Oh fuuuuuck." Cum shot from me, and my head tipped back again while I rode the wave of his erratic thrusts. My ears rang, every spurt through my length pulling a grunt from my chest—and still he fucked my ass.

Hard. Rough. Biting my shoulder enough to leave a bruise.

Better than any porn, better than anything I could've fantasized about.

He grabbed my chin and turned my face, our mouths coming together.

Heat erupted in my ass, and I swallowed down his groan, another dribble leaking from my flagging dick at the deep rumble, the feel of his release inside me.

Nothing—absolutely fucking nothing—had ever sounded so satisfying.

Zeke stayed hard, his dick lodged deep while our kisses turned languid. I rested against his chest, one hand on the back of his head, the other lacing through his cum-covered hand at my groin.

"Okay?" he whispered, pulling away from my mouth.

"Mmm." I smiled, wondering if the floating feeling in my head was similar to being high. "Never better."

"I heard your voicemail and thought you were

going to..." his voice faded as he buried his scruff against my neck.

"I wouldn't," I told him, knowing where his mind had gone. "I'm too much of a chickenshit to off myself. I'll always find a way to go on."

Especially now that I'll have you beside me.

"Come here." Zeke pulled out of my ass, and I hissed at the sudden emptiness, the wet heat dripping down my thigh. He tugged my hand, leading me a few steps around the couch to the rug, enough to know my ass wouldn't be happy with me come morning.

We went to the floor as though of the same mind, and Zeke crawled between my legs—his dick still like steel. "Not done with you yet," he murmured, lifting my feet and pressing my knees toward my chest.

A shot of lust rolled over me, twitching through my spent dick. How he stayed erect...

I pulled the backs of my knees higher, not caring if the ache ahead of me would cause regret in the hours to come.

"So sexy." Zeke ran his fingers through the cum that had slid from my ass to my thighs. He coated his dick with it and sank back into my stretched hole with one slow glide.

My toes curled, a breathy groan ripping from my lungs. I bit the inside of my lip at the uncomfortable as fuck sting from being stuffed full of his dick after being ridden hard as hell.

"So good, Levi, Christ, you feel so good. Hot and silky." He planked over me, slowly lowering his head.

My focus followed his parted lips, and I rose to meet him, giving him my mouth.

My heart.

My soul.

No holding back, I poured every emotion welling inside me into the kiss as he began to slowly rock in and out of my body. Zeke made love to me, as rhythmic as lapping waves soothing a sandy shore. Comforting. Hypnotizing.

I want him forever.

Zeke covered every part of me like a soothing balm, wiping away the blackness from my mind, the choking tar that smothered life. He washed me clean. Created a new man.

One that loved him—

The front door creaked, tearing my eyes open, my focus toward the right.

My fiancée paused on our apartment's threshold, eyes darting over our sprawled bodies.

"Lil." I croaked her name, the blood draining from my face.

She blinked.

I blinked.

Zeke backed out of me with a whispered curse at the same time I scrambled to get from beneath him.

"Lil—" I started, but she spun on her heel and closed the door. "Shit. Not like this...not like this..."

"I'm sorry, Levi."

I ignored Zeke's stupid as fuck words while yanking up my shorts. The last thing I needed out of his mouth was a goddamn *sorry,* same as the other time his guilty conscience had reared its ugly head.

Jerking the door open, I hollered out Lil's name again—and hurried after her into the night.

27

ZEKE

Levi ran after Lily within a heartbeat of my being deep inside his body.

He'd chosen her—without a backward glance.

My apology for the shit he was about to face hot on his heels went ignored too, and I stared at the open apartment door, my heart weeping as the blood drained from my face.

Even though I'd turned him away over and over, the first time he did the same to me, I couldn't handle my inability to breathe, to blink.

All I'd finally given in to, allowed myself to hope for...gone in the blink of an eye.

The devil's laughter came to life in my head, swelling until I cringed, folding in on myself. Reality slapped me across the face, and guilt poured over me like a cold as fuck tidal wave.

Christ, what have I done?

Curses spewed from my lips, and my guts churned while I pulled on clothing beneath a weight of which I'd never felt before. I'd been wrapped up in heaven, and hell came knocking—and my goddamn dick stayed hard as fuck. Wanting more. Needing to finish.

Lusts of the flesh were never satisfied, I'd been taught. One sin led to another, piling higher until even the mighty fell.

And fallen I had.

Shame slid through my mind like a serpent, sending shivers down my spine.

I need to get the hell out of here.

Levi and Lily's voices reached me through the front door, but I couldn't make out what they said.

"Shit."

I moved into the kitchen before realizing self-preservation itched my feet to leave through the back door. Flee like a craven piece of shit because I couldn't face his verbal rejection too atop how he'd left me without a word.

Jaw clenched against the ache stabbing at my chest like a goddamn jagged knife, I slipped into the night.

Be sure your sins will find you out.

Lily would uncover my transgressions to her father, and a shit storm would arise worse than any nor'easter, just like the one at my church in Boston years ago.

No children would be crushed, but a fucking disaster all the same, worse than any fire and brimstone hell could singe me with. I already felt burned to ash by Levi's turning away from me so damn easily after the intimacy we'd just shared.

I snuck around the back of the apartment building like a goddamn thief in the night, peeking around the corner.

Lily and Levi stood in front of her car in the extra parking area, a few dozen feet away from my car where I'd left it half on the curb. They were deep in conversation, gazes locked, standing close, ignoring the woman walking on the sidewalk who passed them and the cars driving by.

Nausea rolled in my stomach, and pain lanced through my chest, but I shoved my hands in my shorts' pockets, tucked my own head, and hurried toward my car.

Feeling like the chickenshit I hadn't realized I was deep in the marrow of my bones.

Sweat slid down my spine—from exertion, the hot summer night, the nerves jacking my heartrate and causing every muscle in my body to tremble.

But I made it to my car without drawing attention.

Same as when Levi went after Lily, I drove off without a backward glance, every swallow to keep tears away like jagged glass ripping down my throat.

I had finally given in to what we both wanted,

turned my back on all I'd stood for...and he showed me where I aligned in level of importance in his life.

Nothing but a way to fulfill the lusts of his flesh, a sowing of wild oats. Answers to his questions—but he'd chosen safety.

Eyes stinging, I pulled my cell from my pocket and hit speed dial for the one man listed. Once on speaker, I clicked the cell to the magnetic holder on my dash.

"Ezekiel," Malachi greeted me after two rings, jolly as hell.

"Hey, Zeke!" Isaac called out, letting me know Malachi had answered on speaker.

"I fucked him, Malachi," I spewed, uncaring if his lover heard. "Submitted to my sinful nature and took what didn't belong to me."

"It's heaven, isn't it?" Isaac responded before Malachi did.

"The fuck!" I hit my steering wheel. "This isn't funny! Lily walked in on us while I was balls deep in his ass."

"Did she stick around to watch?" Isaac pushed, and Malachi quietly hushed him as I cursed through clenched teeth.

"Sorry," my friend grumbled, his voice clearer— no longer on speaker, thank fuck.

"She took off—and Levi went after her." My voice broke, revealing the shattered heart fighting to beat.

"Shit," Malachi muttered. "What happened?"

"I don't know." I swallowed hard, scratching at my pec where a smear of dried spunk tightened my skin—or maybe I tried to ease the bone-deep ache beneath that wanted to spread over the rest of my body. "I managed to toss out an apology, but he didn't even spare me a glance. Just yanked on shorts and sprinted out the door like I was nothing more than desiccated, irritating cum."

"And your heart is broken and bleeding." Malachi didn't ask a question.

I refused to focus on the hurt in my chest when I had bigger shit to deal with. "I'm no better than him. I'm a fucking fornicator who broke up an engage-ment—but it turns out, he wanted her after all. One goddamn wrong choice after the other, and now my livelihood is fucking doomed too. The *fuck* am I supposed to do?" I ran out of steam, gasping for breath.

"Isaac is the best decision I've ever made," Malachi said as though every word I'd vomited revolved around him.

"The fuck does that have to do with my situa-tion?" I snipped, taking a turn fast enough the wheels of my car squealed.

"You called me knowing what I lived through, the angst that filled my life for months. And you've heard me say I would do it all over, dozens of times, if it meant one lifetime with my love."

"Fuck." I punched my steering wheel again.

"You're looking for confirmation of what you feel, Zeke, not spiritual guidance which you *know* you'd never get from me. You've already made your decision."

"My heart has," I admitted, grimacing at the pain beneath my breastbone, the tightness in my throat.

"And the rest?"

I'd thought I could do what Malachi had done—I'd made the goddamn decision in my head, gave Levi everything—and I paid the price for my sins by having my heart shit on. Well, a partial payment. Fuck knew what awaited me in the near future.

"I can't, Malachi," I rasped out what I'd realized had to be my truth. "I can't give up the path I've striven to stride down since Braden's dad did what he did. Every decision I've made for my future, every choice before meeting Levi had been to prove a point. And I fucked it up."

"What about *God's* calling on your life, Zeke?"

I opened my mouth to toss out the same answer I always did, but the words I'd just stated about what I pushed for in my daily living sat heavy in my brain.

"Consider that path *you* placed before yourself," Malachi continued as though reading my mind. "Search your heart, your conscience. Hell," he snorted a sarcastic laugh. "Get on your knees and beg God to shed some light on your situation. Either the Holy Spirit you claim to believe in will give you answers and fill you with peace to continue on, or you'll be left floundering. And if that's the case, which I'd bet our first million in sales on, step up and make the hard decisions for yourself. We were always prompted to just trust God when shit got real —but sometimes, all the faith in the world won't help."

I pulled into my condo's parking spot and shut the engine down, allowing silence to settle over me. Malachi had spewed out some shit for me to consider, especially his thoughts on why I'd called him when I should've sought out a spiritual leader who would give me Biblical truth.

Faith—not reality.

"Still there?"

"Yeah," I rasped out, tipping my head back and closing my eyes.

"Cling to what you know—the tangible. Everything else in life is nothing but a breeze you can't capture with your fingertips."

I longed to do what he suggested, the same as he'd chosen. I yearned for the love he'd found, the obvious joy he'd portrayed while on stage with Isaac.

Malachi had found his place, his peace.

I need to find mine.

And the fact it wouldn't be with Levi constricted my lungs, making it hard to breathe. "I gotta go," I rasped out and pulled my key from the ignition.

"I'm always here for you."

Grabbing my cell, I climbed from the car on weak legs. "Thanks, brother."

"Keep me in the loop."

I powered off my phone after a goodbye and let myself into my condo. A light shone above the stove, illuminating enough I didn't bother flicking on more.

Walking through the kitchen with heavy feet, I tossed my keys and phone onto the small island, my focus on a shower first.

Prayer—repentance and begging God's mercy —second.

Quietness of mind didn't come until sleep took me under hours later, and I found no answers, no guidance in my dreams.

28

LEVI

Torn in two.

The saying held real meaning for me as I hurried after Lil regardless of my desire to stay with Zeke, my bare feet slapping the sidewalk and causing an ache through my backside with every step.

"Lil!" I whisper hollered, not wanting to call any more attention to us than I already did wearing nothing but shorts as she rushed to escape what she'd seen. I caught her before she climbed into the car. "Lil, please. Please let me talk to you."

"Are you going to offer an apology?" She tossed her purse and keys onto the driver seat and spun, her dark eyes luminous in the night.

It was what I should have said—first thing. That I was sorry for cheating. But I wasn't, and rather than get weighed down by shame, only an ache settled in my chest over the knowledge I'd hurt her. It was time for honesty, the type I'd given Zeke when he'd asked about the lotion and tissues.

I straightened, swallowing hard and mentally pulling up my big boy panties. "I met him in Nashville last fall." My voice held surprisingly steady.

Her eyebrows furrowed. "What are you talking about?"

"Isaac and Malachi's tour kicked off not long after classes started, and I went. Zeke was there in the crowd. I-I didn't know who he was, but we made eye contact in the mass of people crowding the stage. He came to me—and I kissed him. I-I didn't even get his name, just felt guilty as hell and fled the second we got jostled apart." My voice faded, and I wrapped my arms around myself even though I sweated. "I had no intention...I didn't mean to hurt you."

"He's been the issue this whole time, hasn't he?" Lil's voice didn't spew anger or hatred. Her dry eyes held my gaze when I'd expected tears.

"Yes," I whispered.

"You're attracted to men."

My gaze dropped to the warm sidewalk beneath my feet, my shoulders falling. *Honesty is the best policy.* If only I'd listened to her before. "Yes, since as far back as I can remember."

Lil wrapped her hand around the back of my neck, and I gasped, lifting my focus to her face, blinking at the acceptance on her face. "I love you,

Levi. Always have—always will no matter what, but I'm not what you need in life."

"It's *desire*," I hastened to correct her, "not need. It's wrong to want him like I do."

"Do you love him?"

My eyes stung, and I couldn't find my voice.

She caressed my cheek with her thumb, peering up at me with sadness tugging at the corners of her eyes. "I didn't just come here to check on you. I left the club because two guys had boxed me in, grinding all over me—and I loved it." Her voice escaped as merely a whisper, as though the admission pained her—for me.

The image flashing in my head of two strangers being all up on her body should have pissed me off, but instead, I found my lips curling upward at what she must have experienced sandwiched between the two men. "Was it hot?"

"Was it?" Lil snorted a shaky laugh, and I knew she'd been concerned about my reaction. "What you, Zeke, and I did can't be wrong. It felt too damn good, and I want more of it. Two lovers. I realize my flesh is greedy, but I'm tired of living a lie. It took two random guys beneath flashing lights and thrumming bass to make me realize what I hope for in life, not just my dreams."

Same as it'd done for me but with one man.

"I needed to tell you that tonight," Lil continued, sadness once more flooding her face, "but also that the three of us won't ever work. I've never been anything but a third wheel with you and Zeke."

"What? No!"

"Please." She patted my cheek before dropping her arm limply to her side. "I might be immature, but I have eyes—discernment to a degree. The sexual tension between the two of you is off the charts. Sexy as hell even though I'm not in the equation. I want a puzzle of three matching in our dreams, our desires.

"I know Zeke touched you that night in our bed —and it only made me hotter. I've also seen the way he looks at you when neither of you realize I'm watching. He wants you just as much as you want him." Lil let out a shuddered exhale and tugged off her engagement ring. She eyed it lying on her palm for a few seconds while I held my breath...

Twelve agonizing seconds ticked away in my head while I waited at the precipice of a splitting rollercoaster where our lives would rush onward in opposite directions.

She finally held out her hand toward me, eyes welled with tears. "So here's your freedom to find happiness, boo. Go back in there to the man who makes you come alive in ways I never could."

Tears rose in my eyes too—but I closed her fingers back around that damn ring, clasping our hands tight, feeling as though the bars to my prison had been sprung open. "It's yours, Lil. Keep it, sell it...I don't care, but how will you explain this to your parents?"

She shrugged, her smile wobbling. "Only that we agreed to end our engagement amicably. I won't tell them why," she whispered. "I think we both have always known our friendship ended up as more because you're desperate for love and acceptance and my parents thought you were good influence on me."

Her honest summary didn't offend me. "I fucked up with that suggestion of a threesome though, huh?" I said, my face heating as I finally let go of her hands, my arms dropping to my sides.

"Nope." She popped the P as though trying to lighten the moment on purpose. "Yet another good decision on your part that brought about the truth we refused to acknowledge on a conscious level." Lil reached for one of my hands, our fingers threading together on instinct as always. "But me finding myself and you coming out is ours to do separately —just know that I will support you in any way I can. I'll only ever be a phone call away."

"Promise?" I couldn't help but ask, biting back a grin even though her face wavered from my unshed tears.

"I think we both know I've got some maturing to do in that area," she said with a wink, causing a droplet to spill down her cheek.

I threw my arms around Lil and hugged her

tight, wetness sliding down my face. Heartache, happiness, and relief all jumbled up in a pile of emotions I didn't know how to handle. "I love you, Lil."

"I love you too, boo, but you smell like sweat and sex."

I jumped back, a rush of blood burning my face. "Sorry."

She laughed lightly, grabbed my wet cheeks, and kissed me soundly on the lips.

Purely platonic, soft and sweet.

"Nothing, huh?" she asked, stepping back with a smile and swiping the tears from her cheeks.

"Um...not really, no. Sorry?" I shrugged, and she reached up to dry my tears too.

"Don't be. Seriously, Levi, don't regret this. It had to happen, but you just caught me off guard. I'm sorry for running out like that. I'm kinda wishing I could go back in time and just sit down on the couch to watch the show."

Heat flushed my face again, and I shifted on my feet, wishing the ground would swallow me.

"Don't be embarrassed." She squeezed my hand and released it. "That memory I have of the two of you will fuel fantasies for a long time."

"Oh God."

She laughed while I shook my head. "Seriously hot. Like I'm thinking about heading back to the club hot."

Our chuckles and smiles died as we stared at one another, the finality in the moment settling over us.

"What are you going to do, Lil?" I asked quietly, needing to know she would be okay, that she would find a way to traverse the muck we'd allowed between us by not being honest with one another.

She inhaled a lungful while glancing over the front of our apartment complex. "Well, now that I'm free, I think I'll take off for a while. Go find myself. Maybe visit my cousin in California."

"The heathen?"

"The one and only," she said with a wink, her easy smile reappearing.

"Are you going to go seeking those two lovers to keep you satisfied?"

Her dark eyes twinkled in the street light. "I'll try."

She pulled out of the parking spot a minute later, and I waved, watching her drive off.

I let out a sigh, my chest heavy—and yet lighter than it had been in too many days to count. My apartment door still hung open, and I hurried inside, my pulse picking back up.

Freedom—to live, to love the one man I wanted. No longer chained, no longer caught up in a prison of my own making...

Zeke wasn't in the living room.

The lotion and tissues still lay on the floor.

"Zeke?" I called, hurrying toward the tiny

hallway as chills rippled over me. The bathroom door stood open, the light off. He wasn't waiting for me in the kitchen either. "Zeke!" I called again, my voice breaking, but I knew, could sense he'd gone.

Somehow, he'd snuck off under his cloak of guilt. He had bowed down to shame rather than facing what we'd done, not giving a shit things might've worked out for the best.

Or maybe he hadn't wanted anything more than to satisfy the lust that flared between us.

His departure without a goodbye, without a note, spoke loud and clear. He didn't want me.

I sank to the floor and wrapped trembling arms around my upturned knees, the tightness in my chest making it difficult to breathe.

I'm not enough.

29

ZEKE

I sat in my condo Saturday morning in a mental fog, waiting, trying like fuck to keep my thoughts off Levi going after Lily and the painful longing wracking through my body.

Once the news broke, Mr. Astbury and Pastor Welker would be the two elders of the church to visit me. Being the spiritual ones, they would approach the transgressor like the Bible commanded in Galatians. But I didn't expect they would come with mercy to restore me in a spirit of gentleness like God's word commanded.

Even if my actions hadn't ruined Lily's dream wedding which I wondered over with how Levi lit after her, Mr. Astbury would demand my resignation which I wouldn't be able to get out of.

Not that I hoped for a different outcome. I couldn't figure out what the fuck I wanted.

Couldn't make sense of time or my tumbling emotions.

Noon came and went without a morsel of food passing my lips to my heavy stomach, and still no somber knock sounded. I went out for a long run until my legs went rubbery and my lungs burned. After a dinner I barely picked at, I turned on my cell, steeling myself for hateful texts.

Hoping for a missed call from Levi.

Only one text—from Malachi: **Find heaven again?**

I scowled over Levi not reaching out to me and took it out on Malachi in my reply. **Fuck off.**

Malachi: **No thanks. I've got my man. Did you get yours?**

Me: **I'm waiting for the roof to cave in.**

Malachi: **No peace to be found?**

I snorted. **Can't even pray for it.**

Malachi: **Sounds familiar ;)**

My fingers itched to type out another *fuck off*, but I shot off a promise to let him know the outcome of the sure shitshow waiting for me.

No calls came through from Pastor Welker or Lily's father Saturday night, no spiritual leaders showing up to condemn me to hell.

And no word from Levi.

I slept like shit, wishing for him—dreaming about being in his arms—and studied my scruffy jaw and bagged eyes in the mirror Sunday morning when the truth he'd chosen her for good solidified in my guts. "Face the loud, ugly music?"

Lips pressed tight, I straightened, looking myself in the eyes because I didn't deserve anything less for making wrong choices like Braden's father.

"Don't continue to be like Pastor Hardy," I said even as my heart ached for Levi. "Don't run away and hide. Own your shit. Be a better man than him."

I showered, stopped at Clyde's Cafe for a black eye coffee, and drove to church. Service hadn't started yet, so I sat in my car, the morning outside my air-conditioned car already sweltering, and finished my coffee even though my stomach churned.

Straightening my too-hot suit coat, I lifted my chin and strode inside on trembling legs.

The praise and worship team sang on stage, lifting their voices to God.

My skin prickled—with lingering heat, with the urge to turn around and walk out over a sense of being a fraud, over not belonging.

Over fear of seeing Levi—with Lily, without, broken or reunited with her through forgiveness on her part.

Aaron sat in his seat, the one beside him empty. "What's up?" he asked as I shuffled past him to take my usual spot out of sheer stubbornness.

I shook my head, not ready to tell him anything —I had to see how things went down first. Hands clasped on the back of the chair in front of me, I inhaled a deep breath and allowed my gaze to drift to the front of the church, my heart yearning for a glimpse of the one every part of my bleeding soul wanted.

Lily stood beside her mom. She didn't sing or raise her hands like those in worship around her—and Levi wasn't on her other side.

A sense of relief I hadn't expected settled my hitched shoulders, but I wondered over his absence, over his mental and emotional health. He'd run after her as though she meant the world to him which I knew she did. If she refused forgiveness and our choices screwed up their friendship, how did he fare? I imagined his possible grief and cursed myself for leaving my cell in my car.

But he'd have reached out to me if he'd wanted —needed me, I reminded myself, once more causing pain to strike my chest.

The service dragged on for an eternity, and I didn't hear a word Pastor Welker said from the pulpit. Rather than fighting to focus on what I'd been taught for most of my life as truth, I lived in mine from Friday night, searching my heart just like Malachi had told me to do even though it hurt like hell.

I wanted Levi. That would never change with how the connection between us only got stronger every time I saw him. Touched and tasted him.

But I'd been so set in my stubborn ways, the need to follow through the life's path I'd laid for myself. I couldn't let down anyone, couldn't crush souls like my old pastor had done to me and Braden.

Confusion played tug of war in my head once more, causing my flesh to want one thing and the supposed new man in Christ another.

I made my usual plans with Aaron for Monday morning as we waited our turn to escape the auditorium. His dad's physical health had declined, but his depression had lifted a bit because his best friend would be back in the states in a few weeks.

Aaron's face closed off when talking about Pastor Ezra, and I didn't pry. God knew I had shit of my own that didn't need spoken out loud.

We stepped out in the bright sunshine, and Aaron clasped my shoulder before skulking off.

"Zeke!" Mr. Astbury called out my name.

I held steady, slowly filling my lungs before turning back toward the church.

Here it comes.

Mr. Astbury stuck out his hand with a smile as usual.

I nodded a greeting, glancing beyond him and Sandy toward Lily who stood with some friends by the church's front doors a few feet away. She met my gaze and waved with a ringless hand, her lips smiling, a twinkle in her eyes.

The fuck?

"I wanted to thank you for spending time with the kids." Mr. Astbury's statement jerked my attention back on him. "I'm not sure if they told you, but Lily and Levi decided to end their engagement. While Lily didn't go into details, she said it was an amicable break up and that they're both content in their decision and excited to move forward in their lives."

I cleared my throat, not sure what to say. At least his explanation sounded as though Levi handled the breakup well.

So why hadn't he called?

"They've been together forever," Sandy said, her eyes welling with tears. "I just don't understand."

Her husband hugged her close. "We have to trust God for their future," he said and kissed her forehead. "He'll lead them in the direction they need to go."

I realized I no longer believed such canned words.

I wondered over Lily, but her actions—or *lack* of actions toward me after what she'd walked in on Friday night didn't match up.

My expectations of being outed, of being tied to a stake and smothered with fire and brimstone hadn't come to fruition.

"Levi is okay?" I had to clarify, my focus still on Lily and her smiling face.

"Lily said he's relieved. Ready to move on and

find the life he's meant to live."

Relieved.

Ready to move on—obviously without me.

And not a hint of scandal, no fallout for the ages.

I made my escape quickly, bafflement rising atop my broken heart. Was God offering me yet another chance to prove myself? Had he allowed mercy when I didn't deserve anything but job loss and shame?

I sat at my small kitchen table, my untouched lunch in front of me, wondering why I wasn't filled with the joy of the Lord. Loneliness hung over me, an emptiness so deep, my chest felt hollowed, stripped of everything good.

Somehow God had redeemed my mistakes with Levi and Lily—or perhaps God had used me to set them both on a different path just like I'd planned, but I wasn't happy like Mr. Astbury claimed the two of them were.

And what about Levi? He'd told me he'd changed his mind on his engagement, but he'd gone after her as though fire licked at his heels.

Lily relayed to her parents he was ready to find his future—and his silence since she'd walked in on us stated I wouldn't be a part of it.

I scrubbed a hand down over my face, still confused as fuck over what we'd had, what I'd thought he wanted.

Guess I'd read him wrong...

Accept the grace you've been given. Move forward in the light.

A heavy exhale deflated me in my chair. I'd been offered a second chance I didn't deserve. God's mercy.

Nodding at my thoughts my heart didn't want to agree with, I decided to cling to stubbornness as I should have done all along. I picked up my sandwich I'd made an hour earlier. I'd sat so long wondering over my thoughts, the various truths in my head, that the bread had begun to stale.

"To moving forward," I croaked and lifted my sandwich as though toasting the Holy Spirit. "I won't fail this time."

I forced myself to take a bite, grimacing at the hardened bits of crust and the dust-like texture on my tongue.

A snort of bitter laughter escaped my nose at the bread's parallel to my life.

Fitting.

But it would sustain my body same as I hoped God would my soul.

My cell rang, the name flashing on the screen bringing a sense of happiness I hadn't felt in what seemed forever.

"Braden," I greeted, sitting back in my chair and pushing my sandwich away.

"Zeke, my man! How are you?"

Just hearing the lightness in his tone, the joy he'd

found again eased my insides. "Been better, but how about you?"

"Excellent. Excellent," he breathed out with a soft chuckle. "I just got hired on to our old church in Boston."

"No shit!"

"Yes. God is giving me an opportunity to redeem my family name, Zeke. I can't believe this gift he's offering me after all my father did to the church. Healing is taking place, brother, and I am beyond ready to step through this door into a new ministry."

His unexpected call at that moment wasn't the Holy Spirit speaking to me, but a sign from God all the same, I had no doubt.

We chatted a few minutes, the peace and joy he'd found following God's path making me wish for forgiveness, to just once get caught up in the emotionalism of Christianity.

"But tell me about you," he said.

"What about me?"

"You've been on my heart lately, and I've been wanting to catch up with you. How are things in Philly?

I longed to dump on him like I'd done with Malachi—but couldn't bring myself to soil his happiness or remind him of his past. One man's self-ishness had upended his life for a time, and I wouldn't be the one to bring him down.

"Better than Pittsburgh," I said, lying through my

teeth.

"I would love to have you come back to Boston," Braden said, his excitement almost infectious. "We could serve the Lord together on this path we'd set in stone all those years ago. Stand strong in our faith and be good role models for other kids to look up to."

His reminder spoke to my soul—or maybe the quiet Holy Spirit inside me. Having failed, I longed for what Braden spoke of. Forgiveness to ease my shame. Mercy to override the hurt festering inside my soul.

Grace to cover my sins that had already been found out—even if they didn't end up ruining me like I'd expected. My bisexuality would remain a secret, and I could continue on in the stubbornness that had taken a backseat to lust.

Same as the last time we'd spoken over the phone, Braden initiated prayer, and I closed my eyes while he asked God for guidance in both our lives, pleading Him to open doors to bring me back home to New England so we could minister together.

When he said *Amen* and hung up soon afterward, things quieted in my soul. I settled in my heart where I knew I needed to place my trust even though doing so meant leaving Levi in my past where he belonged. Braden had set my focus back on where it should have been all along.

Living in the new man, accepting God's grace.

LEVI

I'd lost Lily.

Lost Zeke.

And the burden of having no job and an apartment to pay for on my own made me desperate. I didn't want to move back in with my parents, but what choice did I have?

I couldn't rouse any desire to watch porn and jerk off like I'd been doing the previous couple of Sunday mornings, and I shot off a text to Lily as soon as service ended. We needed to talk details so I could get my shit in order.

She called a half hour later while I sat on the couch and stared at the carpet where Zeke had made love to me.

"Hey, boo."

"Hi," I croaked a greeting.

"Are you okay?" She'd always known my mood by my voice over the phone.

I tore my gaze off the floor, pushing against the image of him atop me from my memory. "I will be." *I hope.*

"Zeke didn't look good at church this morning. Things didn't go well after I left Friday night?"

"He snuck out while I was talking to you." I swallowed hard against the tightness creeping up my throat.

"Did you go after him?"

"He left, Lil," I whispered. "He didn't stick around to fight for me or face the truth of what went down. He took off without a goodbye, without a note. I wasn't enough for more than a release that had been brewing since that night in Nashville."

"I'm so sorry," she whispered, tears lacing her tone. She knew my insecurities, the triggers that sent me down a dark path. "Did you try calling him?"

"If he wanted to talk, he'd have stuck around."

"Maybe he's just running scared. Think about his mission in life he set for himself. Imagine where his head is right now. I'm sure guilt is clinging to him like a too-small pair of briefs, Levi. Uncomfortable doesn't begin to describe how he appeared this morning at church."

"He's probably swamped by remorse, feeling like a massive failure—but he's opened our eyes, and while it hasn't been completely pleasant, I think we're on the right paths now."

"Then go tell him," Lil stated, her sweetness, her desire to see me happy coming through her voice. "I know you hate making yourself vulnerable, but think of the glass as half-full—you could end up where your heart longs to be."

"Or I could end up even more battered and bruised," I spoke of the truth I expected from past experience with him.

"Is he worth the chance, Levi?"

More time with him, getting to know him, perhaps having more than friendship and lust seemed a fantasy. Unattainable. "He could be." I admitted to the deep yearning inside me that couldn't stop replaying the beautiful moments we'd had before being interrupted.

"Then call," Lil insisted. "Talk to him. See where he is in his head, convince him of what you feel, of what I *saw* grow and erupt between the two of you—and I'm not just talking about dicks and cum."

I laughed with her but sobered as my quickening pulse fluttered my belly full of butterflies. "And if he says no?" I whispered, rubbing my hand over my thigh.

"Then you have your final answer, and you'll have direction."

Her words sounded good in theory, but my heart

didn't agree. Without her, without Zeke, where would I go? What would I do?

One step at a time. I blew out an unsteady exhale. First, I needed to talk to him, and with how he'd left after Lil had walked in on us, I knew he wouldn't want that.

I showered, puked up my coffee, and hopped in my car. After a stop at the convenience store at the corner, I set my sights on getting answers.

My stomach churned when I stared at his door. I clutched the gift in my hand—not roses, but something I hoped would break the barrier between us to at least allow conversation. Hand shaking like mad, I knocked, the raps of my knuckles against wood sounding more like nails being pounded into a coffin.

A chain slid, lock disengaged.

And my racing heart stalled out, same as it had when our gazes met at the concert and the world fell away. Dark blue eyes ensnared me, lighting my skin on fire.

"Levi," he whispered my name and swallowed hard, the bob of his Adam's apple flooding my mouth with saliva.

I thrust the box of Milk Duds at him.

He eyed the candy in my trembling fingers as though chocolate had become a serpent, ready to strike.

"I'm not here for a blowjob," I rushed over my

words, my face heating. "Well, I wouldn't say no to receiving. Or giving. Shit." I closed my eyes and filled my lungs. "I just want to talk. Can we do that?" I met his gaze.

He'd closed his face down to an unreadable mask same as he'd looked at me in his office.

My heart cracked, but he took the gift I'd brought him without touching my hand, widened the door, and moved back, allowing me entry.

I wanted to relish in the hope his actions brought, but I'd never been one to expect things to go my way. Stepping past him, I breathed in the scent of his bodywash, swallowing another rush of drool, wondering if it would be the last time I stood close enough to fill my lungs with him.

He didn't offer me a drink like last time, simply motioned toward the couch. Not exactly promising.

"Lil and I broke up," I said the second he sat, rubbing my hands over my shorts.

"I heard."

"You talked to her?"

"Her parents. They don't know what really happened."

I studied his bland face while he focused on opening the candy box. "We agreed to keep things between the three of us. It's no one's business."

"This morning she seemed to be over her anger of catching us fucking."

"She was never upset to begin with."

Zeke's head jerked up, one of his eyebrows raised. "She walked in on us when I had my dick buried in her fiancé's ass. How is she not mad as hell over our transgressions?"

The memory twitched life through my groin. "She'd come over with the intentions of ending our engagement for reasons of her own. Finding us was more a shock to her than anything, but trust me, she's not mad. I told her about Nashville."

He nodded slowly, going back to his candy. He opened and held out the box, but I shook my head, knowing my roiling stomach wouldn't handle the sweetness. I stared as he popped one in his mouth and studied the back of the box. Obviously, he wasn't worked up over the whole affair like I was.

"I apologized, but she said things have worked out as they should. She's free to explore her desires outside what we've been force fed our whole lives, and I'm free to be the man I was born to be, to have what I yearn for."

My pulse thundered, shaking my voice, and when Zeke didn't press for me to finish my suggestion or meet my gaze, the crack in my heart widened.

"I want you, Zeke," I spewed the truth and held my breath, vulnerability like a chasm I hovered over—hoping, praying, Zeke would span a bridge to save me.

He let out a slow exhale, his shoulders slumping. "My path was set in stone years ago," he reminded me quietly, finally lifting his head, but his face showed no sentiment. No pain over having to let me go, no hesitation in ending whatever had started in Nashville.

My emotions tumbled down, the ground rushing to meet them.

"I'm sorry, Levi."

No thoughts filtered through the hurt flooding my mind, my heart. But I'd heard his words loud and clear.

I stood and walked on numb legs, desperate to escape the connection tethering my body, my soul to his. Like a live wire, a tangible energy linked us together.

How could he deny the truth of it? Its power? Hadn't he seen the truth in my eyes, tasted it on my tongue while we'd consummated what had begun months earlier?

Zeke didn't follow me, didn't utter another word —and I let myself out of his condo, shutting the door behind me.

I drove away, tears soaking my cheeks and sobs ripping from my chest. Being out on my own had only created more distance between me and my parents, but I had no choice.

Like a wooden marionette, I returned to the apartment and packed up all my things into the same boxes I'd brought from college and had stuffed in the closet.

All of my possessions once more in my car, I headed to the house that hadn't ever felt like a home.

At least by the time I let myself in, my tears had dried like the husk attempting to beat inside my chest.

"Levi?" Dad sat reading the Sunday paper—who fucking did that anymore? Mom lounged on the couch beside him, a book in hand.

"Hey," I croaked out.

Mom eyed the duffle bag I clutched in front of me. "You're back."

"If you'll allow it," I said to them both.

They exchanged a long look which I couldn't decipher.

"Mrs. Astbury told me before service this morning that you and Lily broke up," Mom said.

I nodded, swallowing hard.

"You said she was God's gift to you, your future. What happened?"

Mom and Dad had found out at church and hadn't called to check in on me. Hadn't reached out in the hours since they'd heard.

"After a lot of prayer and discussion, we've realized we're not ready for marriage." I kept my focus on the scuffed hardwood flooring of the living room's entryway where I stood. Lies—all lies. But being truthful would leave me on the streets.

"Well, I for one am disappointed," Dad said, his voice stern enough I cringed. "The Astburys are well loved in the church. Godly people—you'll never find a better match than Lily."

I have, but he doesn't want me.

Unable to voice a sound other than the sob I choked back, I nodded.

"Well," Mom said, standing and approaching me. She laid her hand on my shoulder briefly, and I longed to lean into her and have her arms around me, but she moved off before I could make myself vulnerable. "Stay faithful to God, and He'll direct your steps."

Dad made a noise of agreement under his breath, and I managed one in return.

I went upstairs into my old bedroom to deposit my bag, my heart shattering all over again.

Trust God. Just what I wanted to do.

Seventeen minutes later, all my belongings once more in my childhood bedroom, I shut the door behind me and let the tears fall. First thing I did once they dried again was boot up my computer and begin job searching—but far from Philadelphia. I set my heart on taking the first offer I found, trusting *myself* to create a new life.

One without the church, without the easily led sheep supposed to love their child and see to their emotional welfare.

Without Zeke.

But I knew the memories of our short time together would haunt me for years to come.

31

ZEKE

Somehow, I made it through work on Monday without a hint of my sins arising. Tuesday passed in the same vein. Wednesday and Thursday, even better. I breathed easier even though heartache over missing Levi and having to set aside what I wanted with him for God lingered in my heart and head. At least I didn't shift in my office chair, my pulse leaping, every time someone knocked on my door.

I began to think that physically, the entire affair lay behind me—us—but I did fear the arrival of the weekend and Sunday service.

Aaron met me at the gym every morning before work, and I continued to keep the truth of why I couldn't smile from him. Not that he needed to shoulder another burden. His father required constant care, and he wore himself out because they couldn't afford a full-time nurse or to put him in a home.

I offered him money, something my family had plenty of, but he declined.

And I'd thought myself stubborn.

But my stubbornness to stay away from the one I yearned for had intensified with every passing day that God allowed my sins to remain covered. Still, I dealt with a level of guilt for hurting Levi as I'd done, and my thoughts lingered on him more often than not.

At least he hadn't seemed torn apart when I'd turned him away. He'd stood without a word and left. Accepting my word as final.

Thank fuck, because if he had begged, reached for me, I wouldn't have been able to say no.

My entire body ached, and my heart lay heavy in my chest. I hadn't even been able to lift half my max while bench pressing on Thursday.

Friday morning, I arrived at the church at the same time as Mr. Astbury, and we met up in the parking lot to walk into the office together, my feet dragging.

"Lily has decided to take some time away," he told me as we fell in line beside each other.

"Oh?" I didn't attempt to sound too anxious for news, but I'd been wondering how she fared.

"Her cousin lives in California, and she's going to

visit for a few months." His voice didn't sound too pleased.

Her cousin, I remembered from having dined at the Astbury's a few weeks earlier. Denise's daughter Haley. Unsure what to say, I kept my mouth shut.

"While Sandy and I aren't thrilled with her choice, we believe it's best to let her stretch her wings a bit since Levi's parents told us he would be relocating in less than two weeks too."

He must have gotten a job.

Both happiness for him and agony swirled like a toxic brew inside me at the finality of knowing he moved on like he'd said he always did on the night I'd thought he'd taken his life.

For the best.

I cleared my throat. "Where is he—"

"Zeke Sipe!"

Oh holy fucking hell... I went lightheaded, all thoughts of Levi ripped from my head, and turned slowly at her shrill tone.

"Denise!" Mr. Astbury called, his voice raised with surprise. "What are you doing here?"

His sister kept her gaze on me while stomping across the parking lot. Blonde hair hung scraggly around her pale, thin face, the sweat pants and shirt hanging off her frame making her appear skeletal.

She stalked toward me like she brought death in her wake.

The type of death that didn't involve a grave but

the demolition of the path I'd decided to once more faithfully follow.

"You lying, hypocritical cunt!" she screamed at me, and I automatically stepped back.

"Denise, what is going on?" Mr. Astbury glanced at me. At her closing the distance between us.

And I said nothing, simply held up my hands in an attempt to keep her quiet.

Twenty feet—and she screamed obscenities at me.

Ten feet—and I could see the track marks on her pale arms, the bloodshot redness of her eyes.

"You ruined my life!" she spat, less than five feet from my personal space.

And you're about to ruin mine.

"Denise, you're unwell," I tried, while fishing for my cell. "If you come any closer, I'm going to have to call the cops."

"Oh good Lord." Mr. Astbury stepped back, his eyes wide. "You," he whispered toward me. "It was *you!*"

Fuck!

"You ruined my life!" she shrieked again, ignoring everything but my face.

I dialed 911 with shaking fingers, knowing they would send a cruiser without my saying a word into the cell.

"You need to stay calm," I told the psychobitch

from hell, trying to keep my tone level, "or you're going to wind back up in the psych ward."

She leaped at me, jagged fingernails first—and Mr. Astbury grabbed her in his arms. Denise flailed and howled like a wild animal, hair and spit flying. Still, her brother handled her.

I barked a few words to the operator, giving her our location, and stayed on the line until Denise calmed. Mr. Astbury continued to hold her upright while murmuring to her, his gaze finally turning my way.

He stared with a calculating look in his eyes, his brain working so damn hard I could feel the gears shifting aligning the truth of my sins, my secrets into line inside his mind.

I held up my hands. "Mr. Astbury, I can explain."

"What? How you ruined my sister's marriage? How you tore apart Lily and Levi?"

"What are you talking about?" I asked with feigned disbelief, my pulse thrumming in my neck.

"The Lord gives wisdom to his faithful children. Discernment," he half-spat the words as sirens raised in the distance. "You tried to steal Lily from Levi, didn't you?"

"No," Denise whispered before I could answer the same, shaking her head, her voice ragged. "It was the other way around this time. He fucked *Levi*."

I blinked as the blood rushed from my face. She would ruin me—spill the *whole* truth of me—

"What?" Mr. Astbury jerked his focus toward his sister. "What are you talking about?"

"Friday night," she said with a sneer. "I watched them through the window."

Oh fuck...fucking hell!

She hissed at me while carefully peeling her stunned brother's hands from her arms. Mr. Astbury stood in shock, staring at me.

Denise took a step my way, her manic eyes, the twist of her lips raising the hairs on my nape. "And now you're going to get what you deserve."

Damnation.

The wages of sin...death.

She leaped at me again, her hands reaching for my throat—and I instinctively swung a right hook, catching her on the chin. A soft grunt left her as she crumpled to the ground.

My chest heaved for oxygen as I trembled over her, hands fisted, wanting to take my dress shoe's sole to her face time and again.

"What have you done?" Mr. Astbury barely gasped out the words. "Levi...my *daughter*." He glanced at Denise who whimpered, curling in on herself.

So, not dead. Pity.

"You'll never counsel another soul," Mr. Astbury hissed, his shoulders hunching, eyes glinting with the same kind of unhinged anger I'd seen on his sister's face countless times.

Flashing blue lights burst in my periphery, and I stepped back a few feet, keeping my silence.

"I. Will. Ruin. You." Mr. Astbury's promise didn't mean jack shit to me.

"I've already ruined myself," I whispered what I knew to be true as two police cars pulled up alongside us, allowing me some breathing room.

The shit show had begun.

———

Five hours later, I let myself into my condo, shedding my suit coat and loosely knotted tie before making it over the threshold.

I pulled my lone bottle of whiskey from beneath the kitchen's sink cabinet where it had been sitting since I'd moved to the Philadelphia area. Only three shots had been poured from the amber bottle—all on the night I'd bought the damn thing.

The night I'd returned from Nashville and found Denise in my bed.

But I didn't stop at three shots while replaying the morning through my head. Three *more* shots, and I finally didn't give too many fucks about the summer I'd experienced while seeking out "God's will" for my future.

Two more, and I cursed myself, wondering why the fuck I couldn't just pass out and forget about reality for a while. The crap shoot of my life.

After finishing at the police station, I'd returned to the church to gather my things, stopping in to see Pastor Welker to give him my resignation.

Mr. Astbury had gotten to him first, and the man who preached tolerance, grace, and mercy wouldn't even allow me to explain what had happened in Pittsburgh with Denise—the truth. Mr. Astbury believed his deranged sister's story about my manipulating and making advances on her regardless of the police records I'd offered to share with him, so why would he listen to anything I said about Lily and Levi's break up?

At least the assistant pastor, Jed, had kept silent, his lips tight even though his eyes didn't reveal judgement like Welker's.

Not having the energy to care about what people thought though, I'd left the church property, allowing them to believe what they would. There wasn't a goddamn thing I could do to right the situation or heal the hearts I'd broken, mine included. I'd fucked up. Majorly—and my sins had found me out to the point shame made me want to bury my head in the sand. Escape my reality.

Now what?

I studied my tenth shot of whiskey in the bottom of a clear juice glass. Or was it only the eighth? Shrugging, my numb lips tipped upward. Levi would undoubtedly have kept track. To the ounce. I blinked at the sudden sting of tears while rubbing a hand over my shirt. I'd thought I'd drank enough to numb the pain.

I'm a selfish asshole. No different than Pastor Hardy.

Leaning to the side a little too fast, I swiped my cell off the end table—and it clattered to the floor.

"Shit," I muttered and tried to stand. The room spun, so I downed my whiskey, set the glass on the coffee table, and dropped to my hands and knees, crawling toward my phone. No way in fuck could I walk.

Malachi didn't answer.

"He's probably on stage with his lover," I muttered.

My fucking chest ached.

Aaron, I thought and nodded to myself while pulling up his number.

"What's up, Zeke?" he answered almost immediately, his voice sounding upbeat for a change—or maybe I was drunk.

"I feel like shit." I huffed a laugh and quickly sobered—but not from the whiskey. "I fucked Levi, Denise showed up, and now I'm fucked."

Aaron didn't say jack shit.

"Did you hear me?" I asked, raising my voice like he hadn't. "I said I fucked—"

"I heard you loud and clear, man," he cut me off. "Are you drunk?"

"Maybe." I studied the bottle of whiskey beside the juice glass, closing one eyelid thinking it would help me focus better. There wasn't much left at the bottom of the bottle. "Yep. I'm drunk."

I leaned against my couch and found darkness behind my eyelids, smiling, but I didn't know what the fuck for.

"Are you okay?"

"Nope." I popped the P like Lily would've and laughed at myself. "Something's funny, so make that nope a yep."

"Shit, man...I can't leave my dad right now."

"'S'okay," I slurred, my world spinning like a Tilt-a-Whirl. "Remember that psycho bitch from Pittsburgh? It's Lily's aunt. She showed up at the church this morning and told Mr. Astbury that she saw me and Levi fucking on the floor last week."

Aaron swore. "Tell me she was lying."

"She wasn't," I stated matter of fact as my throat tightened up.

"Zeke...I'll get my neighbor to stay with my dad so I can come over."

"Nah." I waved a hand. "No need. I'm gonna go puke my guts up and pass out so I don't have to think about this shit anymore."

"Are you sure you're okay?"

"I'm gonna be." I opened my eyes, fighting to focus on the far wall, knowing I lied. "Gonna head home to Boston since I don't have a job and I've been marked as evil by your pastor."

"Shit."

"Yeah, but that's what I get for giving in to my sinful nature. My mighty fall from grace." Just like Pastor Hardy, another selfish asshole whose dick got him into trouble. For the first time in my life, I understood what he had faced—and I didn't hate him quite as much.

But now Braden will hate me too.

I swallowed hard, wishing like fuck the whiskey would just make me pass out and forget for a little while.

"What's going on with Levi?" Aaron asked.

Fuck.

The relentless, crushing weight returned to steal my breath. I couldn't answer right away—the truth hurt too much. "I fucked up his relationship with Lily." My voice broke. "Ruined what was probably a good thing because I thought I knew better. I'm a selfish asshole. Arrogant. A hypocrite. I'm bisexual, Aaron."

"I don't give a shit."

"You're gay," I told him with my matter-of-fact tone, latching onto anything but how much I missed Levi, how Mr. Astbury had told me he was happy and moving. "And I don't give a shit about *that.*"

He let out a heavy exhale, loud enough I could make it out over the phone. "Call me when you wake up in the morning, okay? I want to know you're alright. I'll help you pack if you're serious about heading north."

"Dead *fucking* serious."

I needed a vacation.

A break.

Fuck, who was I kidding? I wanted to run away like a scared little kid so I wouldn't have to deal with the steaming pile of shit that was my life.

But first, I needed off this spinning carnival ride.

I had to puke.

32

———

LEVI

L il called me on Friday late morning, telling me what had happened at the church, and I sat on my bed afterward, wringing my hands while waiting for my parents to get back from work at dinner time.

With how the gossip mill ran in the congregation, I knew they'd be made aware of my affair with Zeke long before walking in the door. And forget disappointment—they would see me as an abomination, an evil creature on my way to an eternity in hell.

I puked up my coffee and the toast I'd eaten, my nerves shattered, fear cramping my guts.

I heard the front door open before I managed to calm myself.

"Levi Townson!" Dad hollered from downstairs.

Two hours and seven minutes early.

"Shit," I muttered, my heart thrumming hard enough I could barely breathe.

The door slammed, and I got up, knowing I couldn't hide away forever. I made it to the top of the stairs and hesitated, my legs trembling beneath me.

Both parents stood below in the entryway, faces red. Dad actually quivered with anger, his eyes hard and just as cutting as flint.

"Tell me it's a lie," he said through clenched teeth.

There had been a witness—unhinged or not, Lil's aunt had seen Zeke and I together, and the Astburys would believe her.

"I can't," I whispered.

"How could you?" Mom hissed as Dad shook his head.

"Perversion...in my house! My own son!" he barked.

We hadn't fucked in his house, and he didn't treat me like a son, but I wasn't going to argue. I hung my head and tried to block out the words slung at me that hurt as much as a stoning would.

Vile sinner.

Lost soul.

Beyond disappointment.

I hadn't expected anything less, but every sentence spewed hit me like a crushing blow until I cowered beneath my shame.

"Two weeks," Dad muttered. "And you are no longer welcome in this house."

A cloud of pitch black hung over me, thick enough I couldn't conjure a single ounce of appreciation for having time to find a place of my own.

With what money?

"Your mother and I are going over to the apartment to help the Astburys remove all the furniture and Lil's personal belongings. You will stay here and beg God's forgiveness for your wretched ways."

I nodded again, even though I would do no such thing.

"You're lucky the landlord is a friend of Pastor Welker's, or you never would've gotten out of the lease." Mom's haughty tone brought on a cringe deserving of a gold medal. "Go to your room. There'll be no dinner for you this evening, nor are you welcome to join us for meals in the two weeks we're graciously allowing you to stay."

Knowing better than to talk back, I did as told on legs shaky as Jell-O, quietly snicking the door shut behind me and leaning against it.

I'm fucked.

I slid down to the floor and buried my face in my hands. No tears rolled for a change, but anger— bitterness—festered inside my heart. I clung to the burning that brought life to my chest so I wouldn't give in to the feelings of my soul being shredded into a million and one ribbons of trash.

Raining curses down on my parents, on Zeke, on God didn't make me feel any better, but it helped pass the time.

Kept me sane.

The next morning, I snuck down early to get a cup of coffee even though my stomach wasn't too keen on the idea.

Mom had beaten me to the pot. "You're going to church this morning," she snipped without looking at me. "You're going to repent and beg forgiveness."

Refusing could get me kicked out of their house, but no way in hell would I stand in front of anyone —even just the stage—and plead for a God I no longer believed in to cleanse me from my instinctual desires for love and affection from the same sex. I couldn't change my body's wants any more than I could the pigment of my skin.

I lifted my chin even though she didn't give me the time of day. "I won't do it."

She clunked Dad's coffee mug onto the counter. "I'll pray for your soul," she stated, her shoulders rigid as she stood with her back to me.

A quick escape up the stairs kept me from Dad's wrath, but he never approached the subject. An hour later, the door closed behind them, and I watched their clunker drive away, taking them to church.

I'd never experienced such a sigh of relief.

I still have a roof over my head.

And being alone meant I could grab some food. My stomach cramped over its emptiness, but I piled a plate high with peanut butter and jelly sandwiches on cheap white bread, snagged two apples, and a handful of baby carrots.

Enough sustenance to see me through the day— if I could keep it down. I headed up the stairs, but a knock on the front door drew me up short.

Zeke.

Swallowing hard, I set my food back on the kitchen counter and rushed to throw open the front door even while telling myself I didn't want to talk to him. See his face. Hear how sorry he was.

But it wasn't Zeke on the stoop.

"Aaron," I said, my disappointment all too evident in my voice and the sudden sag that pulled my body earthward.

"Just me. Sorry." He smiled kindly, even though no joy reached his blue eyes, and his shoulders slouched same as mine. "Got a few minutes?"

"I've got an entire lifetime to spare," I muttered, stepping back to let him in.

Mom's papers and flyers scattered atop the kitchen table, so I pushed them to the side and motioned to the chair. "Coffee?"

"I'm good, thanks."

I sat, hands on my thighs.

Aaron's steady gaze shifted my ass on the chair after three seconds. Was he going to rain down judgement on me too? Suggest I repent and get right with God?

"I just came from Zeke's."

"How is he?" I burst out, my throat going tight.

"Miserable as hell. He shared with me what happened."

"Everything?" I asked, cringing.

"Everything."

"I suppose you're here to tell me what a heathen I am, how disappointed you are in me."

His brow furrowed. "Why the hell would I do that?"

"Why wouldn't you?" I shot back, sounding like a miserable bastard.

He leaned onto the table, crossing his beefy arms. "Because it's not my place to judge, and quite frankly, I think people should be allowed to love whoever they're drawn to."

I stared, sure we hadn't been raised in the same church even though I'd known him and seen him there since I could remember.

"You heard about Lily's aunt?" he asked.

"Yeah...Lil called me yesterday." And all the shit Zeke had explained about his past had made even more sense, had become real to me in a way it hadn't before. I'd been desperate to reach out to him, knowing how he must have suffered emotionally— still suffered from what Aaron had said.

But he'd chosen God. I wasn't enough.

"He's going back to his parents in Boston."

My heartbeat stumbled. "What?" I rasped.

"He didn't admit it to me, but he has feelings for you. His heart is broken, and he's fucking lost."

I twisted my fingers together on my lap. "He doesn't want me."

"His fear probably tells him that. He desperately needs someone to cling to—and that person is not me. Take a chance on him, Levi."

"I already did," I whispered, my eyes welling. "And he told me his path is *set in stone*. He won't deviate, Aaron. He's proven that countless times. He'll find another church, another place to live a life of ministry."

"Try again." Aaron's stare didn't waver, his tone hard.

"Isn't that harassment like Lil's aunt? Not hearing no as a no?"

"Not when the one you want needs you."

Thickness clogged my throat. "I don't know how to make him see that." A tear slid down my cheek.

"Show him he's not a failure, that everything that's gone down over this summer has been the best thing for your life. Yeah, it hurt, but it brought the two of you together."

Only to rip us apart again.

I swiped at the wetness on my face with the back of my hand. "I don't have the balls to let myself be vulnerable again."

"You're still here in the land of the living, aren't you?" Aaron asked, his face softening a bit as though he knew how the darkness sometimes overcame my senses. "Choosing to continue breathing takes more balls than most men have between their legs."

I blew out an exhale, shuffling around some of Mom's papers while gaining control over myself.

Aaron stretched to pick up a flyer, his gaze sliding down over the full sheet Mom had created a few days earlier.

"Fundraiser for Pastor Ezra," I muttered.

"Yeah," he whispered, his forehead denting—but not from anger.

"You know him?"

"He's my dad's best friend." Aaron cleared his throat and set the flyer back on the table.

"I heard he's coming back to the States later this week," I said.

"I'll be picking him up at the airport. He's going to stay with me and my dad for a month or two."

"You must be looking forward to the company—having some help."

Aaron wouldn't meet my gaze while nodding. "Do me a favor, Levi."

"What?"

"Live," he said and rapped his knuckles on the table while standing. "Life's too short."

I followed him toward the door, not sure what to say since I didn't want to pry over the story that prompted his advice. He walked toward his car, hands shoved in his pockets, shoulders rounded.

Yearning to see Zeke again made my feet itch to go to him, but self-preservation, my aching heart, kept me rooted in my bedroom. I puked up more than I managed to keep down of the food I forced myself to eat.

For twenty-three hours and five minutes, I considered Aaron's words about Zeke needing me. More than anything, I want to be there for him. While Lil had claimed to need me, I knew she would be fine on her own. She was the closest I'd ever come to feeling appreciated.

No job offerings, no interaction whatsoever with my parents, and Lil calling me asking me to take her to the airport later that week revealed to me just how thoroughly my life sucked.

How could Zeke turning me away again possibly make things any worse?

I stood in front of his condo door less than a week after he'd bent me over the back of my couch and claimed my body along with my heart. But I couldn't knock, could barely breathe.

Every cell in me burned for him, every muscle quivered at the idea of having the chance to look into his eyes again and get lost.

Found.

I knocked and held my breath for thirty-six

seconds before sucking oxygen into my starved lungs.

I knocked again.

Still no answer.

"Are you looking for Zeke?"

I turned to find the neighbor across the hallway peeking out her chain-linked doorway.

"Yes," I said, trying for a smile.

"He left for Boston this morning."

My upturned lips fell, and I choked back a whimper. Too late. Too fucking late—because of my fear.

"Thanks," I managed to croak out before fleeing.

I sat in my car and stared at his building. Would he answer if I called? Respond if I texted?

Lower lip between my teeth, I pulled my cell from my pocket and found his number.

But what to text?

I miss you.

I need you.

I feel lost without you.

The memory of you haunts my dreams. I remember every touch, every kiss. My lungs are desperate for your exhales, and my heart...

Tears rolled down my cheeks—and I hit send to put a call through instead of texting the various thoughts and memories flying through my messed-up head.

"The number you have dialed is no longer in service," a feminine robotic voice informed me.

I held the back of my hand to my mouth to keep my sobs contained.

They escaped anyway.

33

ZEKE

y parents welcomed me home with open arms, not that I expected anything less. I'd called and informed them I was coming home and that I would explain shit once I got there.

Mom sat me down at the kitchen table with a cup of strong, black coffee after we got all of my stuff unloaded from the U-Haul I'd rented. Boxes and bags of clothes stacked in my old bedroom, but they could wait.

It wasn't like I had any plans for the near future.

"So tell us why God brought you back to us," Mom said, and I glanced at Dad across from me. He didn't appear concerned, but he'd smoked enough pot in his lifetime I was pretty sure the high fog remained even while sober.

"I went to Malachi's concert in Nashville last fall,

and I met a man." I sipped my coffee—Dad didn't blink. "I kissed him."

Neither parent made a sound, so I dove into the story, not bothering to leave a goddamn thing out. They already knew about Denise, and Mom muttered a few curses when I explained her arrival at the church Friday morning.

Once I ran out of steam, I slouched in my chair, eyeing my half-empty coffee.

"How the hell did that bitch escape the psych ward in Pittsburgh?" Mom asked, her tone hard.

I caught her gaze, my lips twitching. "I just told you I had an affair with an engaged *man* and that's what you're worried about?"

"I don't have a fuck to give over who you love, baby boy. You know that."

Love. I blew out a breath at the truth of her assessment of my feelings for Levi and glanced at Dad even as my heart cracked all over again.

"Dicks aren't my cup of tea, but you do you, son."

"It's unnatural," I pushed what I'd always believed, what I'd been taught by every spiritual leader I'd placed myself beneath in order to avoid the ache in my chest. "Sexual perversion goes against God's word."

"One of the many parts of the Bible I can do without." Mom got up to retrieve the coffee carafe, and Dad murmured an agreement with her statement while she refilled our cups.

She sat back down and grasped my hand resting on the table, squeezing it tight. Warmth lived in the dark blue eyes I'd inherited. "We love you no matter what. Always have, always will."

"I'm no better than Pastor Hardy," I whispered, a reflooding of shame making me want to melt into the floor.

"Is that what all this *woe is me* shit is really about?" Mom asked, her brow furrowed while studying me.

"You know how I had him on a pedestal until he crushed Braden," I said.

"Braden has moved on," Mom told me. "He's happily married with a family of his own and just got hired at our church as an assistant pastor."

Yeah, I'd learned that bit, and I hated he might find out I'd done the same damn thing as his father. Yet another relationship doomed. "I looked up to Pastor Hardy more than any man on earth."

Dad cleared his throat.

"Besides you," I said, shaking my head. "But seriously. In my eyes, he was God's man. Ordained by God, blessed by the Holy Spirit. A man above reproach."

"Yeah," Dad said. "A *man*. Human—nothing more, nothing less. Hardy just had a piece of paper that said he'd studied scripture and got to share pretty words from the pulpit."

Mom nodded, and I looked back and forth

between them a few times. "You mean to tell me," I said slowly, "you didn't see him the same way I did?"

Both shook their head.

"So, you just took me to Sunday school every weekend, allowed the teachers and eventually Pastor Hardy to fill my head with…"

"Shit," Dad stated with the matter-of-fact voice I often heard on my own lips.

"Shit," I repeated and stared at him, leaning onto the table, arms crossed. "Care to tell me what the fuck is going on here?"

Mom and Dad shared a look, but not a lick of shame or regret lined their faces when they turned toward me.

"We did a lot of drugs back in our younger years," Mom said, but that wasn't news to me. "And even after having you, we struggled to stay clean." She glanced down at her coffee cup, the first evidence of guilt I'd ever seen weigh on her. "We weren't the best parents when you were little, Zeke, and the church accepted us with open arms. Helped us. Supported us when we strove to stay sober for you."

Fuck, my head couldn't handle the shit they threw at me atop the pain riddling my emotions.

"Do either of you even believe in God?" I croaked out.

Dad shrugged, but Mom nodded. "I like to think there's a higher being," she said, "but man wrote that book pastors preach from every week. The words may have been inspired by God, but if man is inherently a sinner, then who's to say it's the infallible word of God on those pages?"

I'd had that same argument in my head dozens of times but chose to believe—because it was what I'd been taught in Sunday school and in the church's grade school.

You don't question the pulpit.

You don't question God's man.

"When Pastor Hardy had his so-called fall from grace," Mom continued, "your dad and I brushed it off as we would with anyone's sins being found out. We all make wrong decisions, and we all do stupid shit."

"I went into counseling because of him," I sputtered past the thickness in my throat, realizing as I said it that I'd never told my parents why I'd gone off to a Christian college. "I dedicated my *life* to proving that man could counsel other souls and make right choices amidst temptation. That a man could remain faithful and not ruin others' lives."

"Oh, my baby boy." Mom's eyes welled as mine did.

"And I've failed just like Hardy." My voice caught. "I f-fucked up a relationship—"

"And they're better off for it," Dad interrupted, his voice gruff.

I inhaled a shaky breath, fighting for calm.

Mom squeezed my hand.

"So now it's time to create something different for yourself," Dad said after a few seconds of silence while I thought over where Lily headed, how I'd heard Levi had found a job and would be starting a new life too. They *were* better off for it—even if I wasn't. "You're done with counseling, I'm guessing?"

I shook my head, studying my mug in front of me. "You know my stubbornness," I whispered, my throat feeling raw—like I'd cried a million tears.

Mom rubbed her palm down over my hair. "You need to take some time off. Relax and rest."

"Smoke some pot?" I asked, a grin tugging on my lips even though zero feelings of happiness enticed the action. I just needed some light in my darkness, something to boost my spirits.

"That can be arranged," Dad said, and Mom shushed him.

"None of that," she chided.

"Stay as long as you want, son," Dad said. "You'll always be welcome in our home."

I tried doing as Dad said, focusing on the "now" and grew restless after two days—but I couldn't put a call through to Braden. Too much emotion clogged my thoughts. Attempting to find a new normal after I'd put the past behind me—Levi, God, the church—I went back to the gym I'd gone to before heading out of state for college. The building hadn't changed much from its industrial style with exposed steel beams to its wooden benches in the locker rooms. At least the place had been freshly painted, new dumbbells replacing the old pieces of shit, and filters took away the stench of sweat and mildew that used to cling to the air molecules.

I dove into my workout, jaw clenched, stubborn in trying to figure out how I wanted to live my life. My muscles remembered hard work, and for the first time in days, I felt...somewhat good.

A twink came in fifteen or so minutes after I did, and I nodded when he passed behind me. I watched in the mirror as he checked my ass out, and while he was cute as hell in his hot pink crop top and tight shorts, he did nothing for my dick.

Memories of Levi slammed into my brain, and I fought to focus.

I finished my set of dumbbell curls with gritted teeth and watched the twink attempt squats with an empty barbell. I couldn't stay away—besides, I needed a distraction.

"Zeke," I said, holding out my hand once he finished a set of five.

"Chase." He smiled while shaking my hand, his dark eyes flicking down over my front. "So are you just here for the eye candy, or..."

I actually chuckled, having wondered the exact

same about him. "The weights. It's a discipline thing for me."

And I'm trying to remember who I was before Levi.

"Oh." His lips quirked like he tried to bite back a smirk. "I enjoy a little discipline every now and then."

"Not interested," I had to tell him.

"Well, damn." He huffed.

"But I'd like to give you some pointers on your squats—if *you're* here for more than eye candy."

His smile returned, all trace of flirting leaving his eyes. "I'd appreciate any help I can get."

I explained proper form to keep him from blowing out his back or knees, not that he'd do it with an empty bar, but still. We added some weight, and he grinned once his legs turned to mush.

"I'm going to have tree trunks," he said, flexing in the mirror and causing us both to snort with a bit of laughter.

"It's not impossible," I told him while we put the weights back on their racks. "My friend Aaron used to be a scrawny shit—"

"Are you calling this scrawny shit?" Chase said, posing and going all Vanna White over his body.

I barked a laugh that felt damn good. "You know you're cute as hell."

"Ooo!" His dark eyes lit up. "So you *do* think I'm cute!"

"Still not interested."

My heart belonged elsewhere. I swallowed hard as the truth hit me like a jab to the solar plexus. Levi had moved on. Would I ever find the ability to do so? He'd ensnared me, captured my soul—

"Tell me about this Aaron with the scrawny body," Chase said with a sigh.

Pushing aside my hurt didn't come easily, but I managed to focus on the twink who needed encouragement and a helping hand.

"He didn't like the way he looked and decided to do something about it," I said. "He eats crazy amounts of chicken and spends more time in the gym than anyone I know, but he's ripped as fuck. Packed on some muscle mass, and no one fucks with him anymore."

Chase eyed the other guys working out, licking his lips over someone behind me. "So lots of protein, huh?" He winked.

I chuckled again. "You're a brat."

"One who's tired of being kicked around."

Both of our smiles faded. "Want me to break a few bones for you, Chase?" Because the shit with Denise still had me on kick ass mode even though my heart lay like lead in my chest.

He straightened, his chin lifting. "I'd rather you showed me how to *pack on some muscle* so I can defend myself."

I held out my hand, thrilled to have someone to

give my attention to rather than my own issues. "Deal."

We shook on it and made plans to meet the next morning. "Can I ask you a question?" I turned toward him as we stepped outside into the bright sunlight.

"Anything."

"For someone who got bullied all through life, you're wicked confident."

"Years of therapy," Chase replied without hesitation or a hint of embarrassment. "I found my person, and she's helped me recognize my value."

Long after Chase hopped in his car and left, I considered his words, considered the hundreds of other kids in the LGBTQ community who were desperate for love, encouragement, and someone to talk to.

Support like I thrived on giving to those who needed and wanted it.

When I arrived home, something...clicked inside my brain. I loved helping people. Who said I had to be in a Christian or Bible based setting?

34

LEVI

Lil held my hand while I drove her to the airport. We didn't talk much, but when had we ever? She knew my heartache, and I could literally feel her excitement to jet across the country.

While Lil didn't exactly have her parents' blessing, she had mine. For the foreseeable future, she would room with her cousin in California who'd already gotten a job lined up for her.

Lucky girl.

I'd yet to find something, that entire week's searching fruitless. It was like fate blocked me from moving on.

Zeke had left.

Lil was leaving.

And I had eight days before the time at my parents' ran out.

"What am I going to do?" I heard myself ask.

Lil squeezed my fingers. "You could come with me."

I snorted a laugh. "That wouldn't be freedom to start over, Lil."

"You told me yourself that seeing me with another guy—or two lovers—wouldn't bother you. Why not come to California with me and start over? We can share my cousin's spare room, I'm sure she wouldn't mind."

My heart ached at her love for me, but she needed to find her way without someone from the past influencing her choices.

"I always feared setting my path and making a mistake," I said, "but now I'm on my own and it's up to me to walk forward."

"I allowed you to lean on me too much."

I shot her a sad smile but shook my head. "No. You were perfect for me, Lil, and you'll stay my best friend forever. You always saw me for who I was, didn't you?"

"More than I let on."

Zeke had seen me.

And he left me as would Lil in seven minutes and fifteen seconds.

But Zeke fled for different reasons, and I still didn't have closure.

"If you won't come to California, will you go to Boston?"

"He doesn't want me," I muttered, hating the

catch in my voice.

"Bullshit," Lil snorted. "That man is so damn hot for you it isn't even funny. He took off out of shame, and you need to show him that he *is* a good man."

Aaron had pretty much said the same, and I'd yet to come up with an argument.

A lawyer I could never be.

Lil rifled in her purse before shoving the tiny diamond I'd bought for her under my nose.

"I told you I don't want it back," I said, turning my gaze back on the road.

She let out a huff and rummaged around some more—and stuffed a hundred-dollar bill into my hand.

"What's this for?"

"Gas."

"I'm not taking this, Lil," I muttered, holding it back out to her.

"Yes, you are. You're going to pull up your big boy panties, take this cash, and get your ass to Boston," she stated, her tone not allowing argument. "I've got a job waiting for me and money in my savings. I know you're dead broke. Fill up this car's gas tank and escape this city."

"And when he turns me away and I'm left destitute without gas money to return?"

"Don't *let* him turn you away," Lil said with a nonchalant attitude that had me snorting again.

"Life isn't all rainbows and happily ever afters," I

pointed out while angling my car into the departures for her airline.

"We're climbing one side of the rainbow, boo."

I put the car into park and angled to face my ex-girlfriend, my best friend.

She smiled, her dark eyes full of warmth and love. "And once we reach the top, we'll slide down the other side right into our happily ever after's arms —or two sets of arms in my case." She winked, and I couldn't argue.

I wanted Lily Astbury to be sent off on her adventure without a hint of dark shadows dimming her sunshine.

We climbed from my old Honda, and I hefted her two suitcases from the trunk. The vehicle behind me honked, but I ignored him, my gaze caught by Lil's.

She threw her arms around me, squeezing me tight, and I breathed the scent of vanilla deep into my lungs.

"Go, boo. Or you'll live the rest of your life wondering. Regretting."

I nodded when she pulled away, my throat too tight to reply.

She grabbed her suitcases, blew me an air kiss, and walked away to start life anew.

"I hope you find them!" I called out right before the automatic doors closed her in.

"I will!" she hollered back over her shoulder.

Such confidence.

The car honked again, and I shot the driver a glare.

Yeah, yeah.

I climbed into my Honda and drove into traffic.

Nothing waited for me at home but negativity and depression.

The hundred dollar bill I'd decided to accept burned a hole in my pocket. Enough to get me to Massachusetts...but after that?

"No damn clue."

I chewed the inside of my lip.

Nothing kept me in Philly. No job offerings came in to take me elsewhere. It was like the only path I could choose led to Zeke, to the man I wanted.

Pull up your big boy panties.

Lil's voice rang in my mind, and I found myself smiling, my heart lighter than it had been in over two weeks.

A glance at the clock and I quickly calculated an estimated arrival time in New England that would mean a hotel before showing up at Zeke's parents' house.

I'd already used the internet to my advantage and learned where they lived thanks to Zeke still being listed as a resident at their address—and I knew how long it would take me to get there. Five to six hours depending on New York traffic...which I would hit at rush hour if I left that afternoon.

Not good.

I could handle one more night at my parents and leave first thing in the morning.

Pulling into our driveway, I let out an unsteady, slow exhale. Tell the truth and be banned for life, or lie and possibly have a place to return to when Zeke turned me away again?

I remembered Lil's confident stride as she walked into the airport, and I wanted to do the same. I wanted to own who I was—and that meant being vocal about my heart's desire.

But that could wait for morning so I at least had a bed to sleep in.

Quiet as a mouse, I repacked up my meager belongings I'd unboxed, knowing once morning came and I revealed my plan to my parents that my time with them would end.

Sleep wouldn't come as I imagined every scenario that could take place in my future. Definite horrible words would rain down on me come morning, but what about afterward?

Would Zeke even allow me into his parents' home?

Did he care enough to at least hear me out when I explained how meeting him was the single most important moment in my life?

Was the guilt eating at him too much to offer himself forgiveness and accept my truth?

Or had he already dedicated his life back to God,

even more determined and stubborn about his walk
to prove man could be good?

I prayed like hell the final thought wasn't so.

And dreams of that very thing left me haggard,
bags-under-the-eyes tired in the morning.

My cell's alarm rang—but I already sat at the
table, the Honda packed, coffee made, and waiting
for my parents to get up.

Mom found me first, pulling up to a stop from
shuffling through the doorway into the kitchen. She
eyed my scuffed-up duffle bag by the front door.

"You're leaving."

Not a question and no hint of sadness lit her
voice.

I suddenly realized they didn't need to know the
truth—I wouldn't be returning regardless of the
outcome ahead of me.

"Yes." I stood and dumped my half-drank coffee
down the drain.

Mom made a noise in her throat I couldn't decipher, but it sounded like an okay, go on, then.

Or maybe my insecurities poked at my brain.

Either way, I approached her where she poured
two mugs of coffee. She finished and turned to face
me, no offer of her arms, no best wishes.

A hundred things ran through my mind, words
to tear her down, to make her feel my depth of
disappointment in her as a mother. Curses toward

her, her church, and the God she'd put ahead of her only child.

She deserved each and every one—but I couldn't be bothered.

I turned my back on her as she and Dad had done to me emotionally my entire life, grabbed my bag off the floor, and let myself out into the early morning.

Breathing in the warm summer air until my lungs ached, I told myself it was time to create my own path.

As exciting as the thought should have been, dread smothered all other emotions like black tar.

Without a clue of what waited in my future, I gassed up my car and headed north on route 95 with forty-six dollars and twenty-two cents left in my pocket.

35

ZEKE

I got up Sunday morning and went to church with my parents because I needed to see the difference my folks spoke of for myself—and try to get answers about what I believed and where I belonged.

The church's structure hadn't changed, but the congregation, the *feel* of it had. Sure, people dressed up in their best clothes, but true happiness seemed to shine on their faces.

Within minutes of Braden Hardy taking to the pulpit—his first time—I understood why. He preached tolerance and unconditional love even though he'd been hurt terribly by his father. He taught grace and mercy—without a hint of fire and brimstone or demands to repent for the old man's evil ways.

Healing had taken place after his father's leaving,

that much became apparent, but I still didn't feel comfortable sitting in the massive sanctuary. They sang songs of praise I recognized, but my lips stayed shut, not one ounce of desire to lift my voice in worship bubbling inside me.

A deep hurt that had festered for years settled in my mind.

Braden had moved on, and there was no more need for me to prove man could make good decisions.

He had done so—and the congregation he'd come back to had thrived.

There was also no need to uncover my sins to him. He'd found contentment and peace, and I could live with him not knowing the truth about what I'd done.

I followed my parents from the church after a shared back-slap with Braden, knowing I would never return, that the whole organized religion part of my life had come to an end.

There was no light above my head moment when I realized that truth for me. It came as more a whispered exhale, a warm breeze across my face.

I found peace in the decision made in my heart. And for the first time in...what seemed forever, I breathed easy, like a boulder had been lifted off my shoulders.

Free.

From chains I'd shackled onto myself, ones that

had kept me from living, from going after who my heart yearned for.

But he would be starting a new job soon, moving on with his life.

Without me.

Pain lanced through my chest when I realized I couldn't live without him, those bewitching eyes, his luscious lips. I couldn't spend another day without hearing his voice, ticking off numbers for some random reason. My soul had recognized its other half even in Nashville—and I'd kept us apart out of sheer stubbornness, thinking that blind faith would lead me closer to fulfillment than my own heart.

The second we got home, I hurried up the stairs to my bedroom to make a phone call.

Levi's cell went straight to voicemail.

I tried Aaron and found out that Lily had left for California the day before.

Levi hadn't been back to church either.

"I saw him while out running errands for my dad a couple days ago," Aaron said. "He looked like shit."

My brow furrowed. "What?"

"Levi. He's pale. Bags under his eyes. He probably hasn't been eating."

"The fuck?" Had Mr. Astbury lied about how he fared, how he'd planned on moving? Or had Levi's parents done the lying? Neither would surprise me —but my gut hardened all the same.

Someone had lied.

And I'd wasted time away from Levi because of it.

"Has he reached out to you?" Aaron asked.

"No." And with how I'd left things, from what I'd heard, I didn't expect him to. I glanced at the clock, wanting to try Levi again, needing shit straightened out in my head and between us, but I hadn't spoken to Aaron since I'd left Philly. "How's that missionary doing?" I asked quickly.

Aaron didn't answer right away.

"He's coming home soon, right?"

A clearing of his throat and Aaron answered an affirmative. "I'm picking him up at the airport."

"What's going on?" I asked, his tone more telling of his discomfort than any shifting gaze or ass on a chair could say.

"Long story for another time," he said.

His answer sounded so much like mine with Malachi over a year ago that I grinned. "Good story or bad?"

"We'll see," he muttered. "How about you?"

"I just signed a lease on a condo yesterday, and I'm trying to decide on work," I replied. My parents had begged me to stay, but I needed my own space that didn't involve Jesus music on twenty-four seven. When I'd asked Mom why she listened to that shit, she said it helped keep her anxiety down. I wanted to suggest a joint instead, but that would be a slippery slope I'd hate to see her slide down again.

I quickly told Aaron about my thoughts on offering counseling at an LGBTQ community home in Malden, and when I hung up with his words of encouragement ringing in my ears, my mind set on doing so—after getting in touch with Levi and finding out the truth about what the fuck was going on.

And if things went well, I would invite him up to Boston.

To stay.

I tried his number for a second time, cursing when I got automated voicemail again. "Goddamnitalltofuckinghell, answer your phone, Levi. We've got shit to talk about. Plans to make. You better not have blocked me...I know I don't deserve anything different, but do *not* take off and leave me in the dust. Christ. Please..."

Heaving a heavy exhale, I scrubbed a hand over my permanent scruff.

Screw waiting to find out. I've wasted too much time already. I'll go back to Philly, guns blazing and steal away my man. Fuck Simply Grace Church, fuck Pastor Welker and everyone there.

I hopped off my bed, adrenaline pumping. Stubbornness set in stone...

But this time for getting what I wanted, what I gave up for the glory of a supposed God of love.

Fear snaked in to blacken my thoughts, stumbling my steps across my bedroom.

But would Levi allow me the chance to get on my knees and beg his forgiveness for all the times I turned him away? Would he even want to look at me again? Listen to a single word I needed to say?

Five hours...it would take me five hours of restless agony to find out. My heart pounded in my chest to the point of pain, my stomach going rock hard again—

"Zeke!" Mom hollered up the stairs. "You have a visitor!"

Chase.

"Goddamnitalltofuckinghell."

Talk about shitty timing.

Limbs trembling, I headed toward the stairs rather than my closet for a duffel bag. It wouldn't be the first time he'd shown up in tears, needing a platonic hug and an ear when his therapist wasn't available. It had been his direction that had led my thoughts to the Humanity House in Malden.

The twink was becoming a fast friend—at least he'd left off the flirting for good.

I stumbled down the stairs in my gray sweats, not bothering with a shirt since I didn't want to waste any time. I needed to help Chase straighten out whatever had his panties bunched up so I could send him on his merry way and get my ass to Philly —and face my fear head on.

36

LEVI

My stomach twisted like a tornado while I perched on the edge of the couch, hands clenched around a box of Milk Duds to keep my fingers from swiping at the imaginary ants skittering across my skin. My knee bounced nonstop.

"Can I get you something to drink?"

I gulped and shook my head at Zeke's mom, knowing I wouldn't even keep water down—and Zeke stepped around her into the living room, pulling up short at the sight of me.

Dark gray sweatpants hung low enough on his hips that the luscious V of muscle flooded my mouth with drool. I dragged my gaze upward.

No shirt covered golden skin and rippling muscle that seemed to shiver beneath my stare.

His Adam's apple bobbed.

Lips parted.

And those blue eyes went dark, widening as our gazes clashed.

"Ooooookay." Mrs. Sipe drew out the word and patted her son's shoulder where he stood frozen, staring at me. "I'll...um...be in the kitchen finishing up lunch."

She disappeared in my periphery, and I sucked down oxygen for the first time since Zeke made an appearance.

He didn't move. Didn't speak.

I pushed up on unsteady feet, my own throat working. "Hey," I managed past the tightness in my chest.

We stared at each other, everything I'd thought to say, all words wiped from my mind. A deep yearning to touch him, to suck his scent into my lungs swept over me, weakening my knees, but I locked them up tight.

At least unease kept my dick from swelling to life regardless of the sexual tension that thickened between us.

Zeke tore his focus off my mouth to glance down over me.

Faded T-shirt, old jean shorts, and scuffed Vans I'd found in a second-hand shop in Nashville— pretty much my usual.

"You're here," he whispered the words as though still unsure I stood in his parent's living room. "W-why?" His eyes held a slew of emotion I couldn't read, but I took comfort in the fact he hadn't closed off or appeared angry like I'd expected.

Rather than drop to my knees and beg for yet another chance, I decided on safer waters. "Lil left for California," I said, my words stilted, breath hitched.

"Aaron just told me," he rasped out and studied my face long enough I shifted. He swallowed hard. "H-how bad was it after I left, Levi?"

"Bad," I whispered the truth.

His brow furrowed, and tension I hadn't realized rode his shoulders slipped away, slumping his six-foot height closer to my five-ten. "I'm so fucking sorry."

I hated those words with passion enough that my hands fisted and my forehead dented. "Don't—"

"Not for what we did," Zeke hastened to say and moved closer, leeching all the fight out of me. "Never for that." He paused at the other end of the couch, the energy crackling in the five feet between us with life enough I couldn't believe the recessed lights overhead didn't explode.

"Then why are you always saying you're sorry?" I asked, not understanding—and needing to. Desperately.

Regret dominated the emotions in his eyes. "For hurting you. For hurting Lily."

"There might have been some heartache over the past couple of months, Zeke, but I wouldn't change one minute, one second of our moments together. You opened our minds to truths she and I had ignored, the things we'd set aside in thinking we needed to do what was right in God's eyes. Well, we've both decided we don't give a flying fuck about anything other than what's real, what is in here." I pressed my shaking fist to my chest. "It's time for us to learn who we are outside the church and our parents' influence. We're choosing our own paths now, creating futures we can be happy with rather than just obeying and trusting God."

Zeke stretched his fingers out at his sides like he wanted to pull me into his arms but held back because I did.

"What about you?" I asked, every cell in my body yearning to lean into him. Touch him. Kiss his mouth and hope like fuck he recognized what we could be if given the chance. "What path are you on now that the door at Simply Grace closed?"

"More like slammed shut," he muttered without a hint of a frown.

"Have you found another church?" I asked, hating the wariness in my tone but unable to hide it.

"No," he whispered, and I exhaled. "And I have no plans to, either."

Hope lit like a flicker in my belly, sending a rush of butterflies through my limbs. "What will you do?"

He took another step closer to me, ramping up my heart rate from fast to flipping out. "Counseling."

I blinked back sudden tears. He hadn't changed his path—

"But with kids who are struggling with their sexual orientation, kids who aren't accepted and loved by their parents because they identify outside the 'norm'." Zeke used air quotes, sarcasm lacing the word.

My throat tightened up. "You're a good man, Zeke Sipe," I whispered.

His gaze dipped to my mouth—dropping my belly to my toes and rushing adrenaline through my heart. "And what are you going to do?" he asked rather than denying the truth I'd stated.

I let out a steady breath and handed him the box of candy that shook hard enough the Milk Duds rattled inside.

Time for the heavy shit. Please don't turn me away.

"Start over...maybe here."

ZEKE

"Here," I repeated, sure I'd misheard, sure I'd imagined him showing up after everything I'd said and done. "As in Massachusetts."

Levi nodded, his bewitching eyes wide and so damn vulnerable I couldn't *not* touch him.

But I hesitated and looked him over again, watching the pulse jump in his neck, the way his chest heaved for breath. Those fingers clenched around an outstretched, dilapidated box of candy rather than grasping at my back like they'd done when I'd been buried inside his body...loving him.

I took the box, rubbing my fingers along his and earning a groin-tightening whimper from his parted lips I wanted to devour. A tremor rippled over him, actually shifted his damn threadbare shirt over his pecs. But he didn't make a move—as well as I wouldn't if I'd been in his shoes.

It was my turn to beg.

Even though Mom was just around the corner in the kitchen, I set the candy down on the coffee table and stepped in closer, electrical charges raising the hairs on my arms as Levi and I stood toe to toe. His head tipped the slightest bit to keep those green eyes latched onto mine, his breath catching.

"I know you don't want to hear that I'm sorry, Levi," I rasped out, needing to touch him so damn bad that every joint in my body ached, "but I never should have left you to deal with the aftermath of my poor choices. I was a selfish asshole and listened to lies rather than reaching out to you myself. For that, I'm truly sorry—for both of us."

Unable to help myself, I slid my hand around the back of his neck and tilted my forehead to his. No fucking way could I look into his eyes if he denied me.

"I don't deserve..." I barely managed to whisper. "But showing up here...fuck, Levi." I swallowed hard, steeling my heart even though he didn't pull away. "Hope has my insides all jumbled up. I'll get on my knees and beg if that's what you want. Tell me what you need," I said the same thing that night I thought he'd taken his life. "Anything—it's yours."

He didn't speak, the lack of hot exhales over my mouth making me wonder if he breathed.

I lifted my forehead off his, opening my eyes to

take in his beautiful face, the dark circles under his eyes I'd caused—the pink cheeks and parted lips.

Still, he didn't speak, black taking over the green of his eyes I adored so damn much I could cry.

"I have a spare bedroom at my condo I'm moving into tomorrow," I croaked when he didn't tell me what I needed to do to close the emotional distance I'd created between us.

"What are you saying?" he asked, his voice small, hesitant.

"I could use a roommate?" I suggested, allowing the hint of a question—but not because I had one in my mind toward Levi Townson. I knew what—who —I wanted. I'd known since that first night I'd laid eyes on him in Nashville, but my stubbornness had denied my heart.

"With b-benefits?" he stuttered.

Fuck, he was adorable, freaked out with nervousness. I couldn't help my smirk as a rush of relief so fucking sweet rolled over me. "I'm not averse to benefits," I said, keeping my voice low, my thumb rubbing the skin beneath his ear.

"I don't have much to my name. No job lined up, no way of helping out with rent," he said as though trying to talk me out of the offer of taking on a roommate.

I wanted a fuck ton more than a guy to share my personal space, but it seemed that needed to be put to rest first in his organized mind.

"I can handle the bills on my own," I assured him, "and finding you a job up here with all my connections won't be a problem."

"I'll pay my fair share," he stated, his chin lifting.

Fuck, did I love him.

"And once you're financially able to, which I know you will be in the next couple of months, I won't say no."

Silence settled between us. So many damn things left unsaid, emotions roiling.

"I'm scared," he whispered, tears welling in his eyes.

"Then let's be scared together," I whispered back, cupping his face with my other hand.

And still, he hesitated from giving me a nod, from closing the distance between us.

"What number are you going to count to before putting me out of my misery?" I asked, half afraid he'd driven all that way just to leave me like I'd left him.

I deserved no less—but Levi wasn't such a man.

"Thirty-seven," he squeaked—and I captured his lips.

Heat rushed through my body, lighting up my insides and settling every bit of fear, unsettled anxiety...Levi laid to rest every question with strokes of his tongue, the small whimpers he breathed into my mouth.

"Zeke!" Mom called. "Lunch is ready!"

Fuck. Fucking hell.

I tore my lips off Levi's but couldn't bear to step away from his body. We both gasped for breath, eyes locked. Wrapping my arm around his lower back, I pulled him in tighter. Our hard dicks pressed against each other—and I kept him right *there*, firm enough I felt his length jerk along mine.

"Hungry?" I asked, my lips curving upward from the happiness ready to burst from my chest.

"For you," he whispered, his smile unsure. Trembling.

I let out a groan and rested my forehead on his again. "Fucking hell, saying no to you is damn impossible."

"You've done it before."

"Ouch." I grimaced and pressed my lips against his forehead. "Never again, Levi.

"Bedroom?" Hope lit in his eyes.

"Shit." I chuckled. "You *would* make me say it again, wouldn't you?"

He shrugged a shoulder while biting back a smirk.

"I'd rather have your mouth than food," I whispered, getting in close enough that his breath ghosted over my lips, "but if we get started, we won't go into the kitchen on our own, and my mom will come looking for us."

"You're telling me no, aren't you?" he asked with a teasing tone although his voice shook.

"Did you drive all the way up here this morning?" I asked rather than answering.

"Yes." Levi ran a hand up my spine, tempting me to drag him up the stairs to where he'd suggested we go.

"Did you eat breakfast?"

"Yes."

"Did you keep it down?"

He shook his head. Big surprise.

I tore myself from his grasping hands but tightly laced my fingers with his. "Lunch first, because you're going to need sustenance for all the plans I have for us."

"Holy hell, Zeke," he groaned, his cheeks flushing.

"Come on." I tugged on his hand. "Meet my dad."

"With that obnoxious tent?" he asked, nodding toward my groin.

I adjusted my dick before pulling him in front of me. "Lead the way," I whispered in his ear.

"As if I'm in a better state," he grumbled.

"At least jean shorts hide it better than sweats."

"Sexy as hell sweats." He halted quickly, and I bumped into his back, my dick right against his ass crack. "Your parents—do they know about me?"

"Yes."

"Everything?" he asked, his voice going high and squeaking like a pubescent kid.

I leaned in and bit his earlobe. "*Everything.* My

parents are a bit…unusual. Fair warning, there's no such thing as TMI in this household."

"And they're okay with…us?"

"They're going to be thrilled to have you here. I've been a miserable grump. Twice, Mom told me to go back to Philly and steal you away like a knight in shining armor. Dad agreed."

"Oh. Okay, then."

We walked into the kitchen and sat down to a family meal, the first of many—I hoped.

38

LEVI

I had trouble swallowing my lunch for three reasons. First, excitement over not being turned away and somewhat having things settled between us. Second, the nerves over what would happen after we escaped upstairs kept me hard and aching...while butterflies fluttered the whole forty-three minutes and twelve seconds we sat at the dinner table.

And the third reason?

Zeke's parents. Their acceptance of me without question, without wary glances...he'd been so lucky being born to them. His dad had called me son when greeting me. And his mom? She'd hugged me tight, welcoming me to the family when Zeke told them I'd agreed to be his roommate.

At least he hadn't shared the benefits part.

I'd glanced at Zeke, and his smirk and shrug

melted my heart. My eyes burned bad enough I barely kept from spilling tears down my smiling cheeks.

Their home was my home, I'd been assured—so I hopped up to help with dishes the second Mrs. Sipe stood.

"No," she said with a wink similar to her son's. "You boys go on. I'm sure you've got a lot of catching up to do. Dad will watch the game down in the den, and I'll clean up the dishes—with my earbuds in so I can listen to my Jesus music. Then I'll head to the basement too so no need to worry about us overhearing anything we shouldn't."

Heat flooded my face when she winked again.

"Mom," Zeke chided with a chuckle but took my hand and pulled me toward the stairs.

"Have fun playing!" his mom called as Zeke grabbed the box of Milk Duds from the coffee table where he'd left them.

"Oh my God," I groaned. "They're not...normal. Is she oblivious? Does she really think we're just going to your room for Xbox or something?"

Zeke kicked in his door, shuffling me into his bedroom where he left me standing to grab up his cell off the bed.

I wiped my hands down my jean shorts as he popped some candy into his mouth and tapped at his phone's screen.

He turned toward me, setting the cell on the dresser. "Dance with me?"

A lone guitar began strumming a song I recognized, one that stole my breath and left me weak in the knees.

Beautifully us, worth the sacrifice. I would choose you all over again, Isaac sang through the tinny speakers.

My throat went all tight, the sight of Zeke hazing in front of me.

My light.

My life.

My love.

Just like that night in Nashville, I made the first move, but there was no tentative press of lips on my end. I dove in with a hunger no food could ever satisfy, one Zeke matched stroke for stroke with his tongue, the sweetness of caramel and chocolate on him making my mouth water for more. My shirt ripped down the center in his rush to get me naked.

"That was my favorite one," I said, gasping for breath.

"I'll buy you ten more."

I kicked off my sneakers and shoved off my shorts. "Are you going to be my sugar daddy?"

Zeke pushed down his sweats, his hard dick slapping up against his belly. "I'll be whatever you need me to be."

I swallowed at the sight of welling precum on the

tip of his flushed length. "My light. My life...my lover," I repeated the words Isaac sang but with a question in my voice.

"Yes...fuck yes," Zeke choked on a whisper, finally giving me the answer I yearned to hear.

We paused, enjoying the sight of each other. Muscle and sinew, rigid dicks, his jutting from neatly trimmed dark hair. A droplet of precum slid down his length, and I moved in, ready to drop to my knees to taste him.

"No." He grabbed my arms and pulled me in close, skin on skin, flush against one another.

"No?" I gulped, my insecurities taking me to the bowels of hell in a flash. "You're fucking telling me no *again*?"

"I want you to fuck me, Levi."

"S-Sorry?" I choked out, sure I'd heard wrong. Only the Zeke of my dreams told me such things.

He dragged his lips over my clean-shaven cheek up to my ear. "I want you to *fuck me*," he repeated, his hot breath sending shivers down my spine.

"As in me on top," I asked, my voice breaking like a hormonal teenager and bringing a flush to my face.

"As in your dick worked deep inside my body. Owning me. Filling me with your cum." Zeke pulled back and held my gaze, the blue of his eyes gone to black as he pressed his groin against mine. "Feels like you're up for it..."

I licked my lower lip and jerked my head in a nod.

"Breathe, Levi. Count to sixty-nine if it'll help calm you down."

I shoved a hand between us to squeeze my dick. "Oh, holy hell, Zeke. I did *not* need that image in my mind too."

"Another fantasy?"

"God, yes."

"Later."

"Oh shit." I gulped and watched Zeke climb onto his bed, knees up, feet planted on the mattress. He crooked a finger, and I realized I'd been frozen, staring at his ass while counting. "Sixty-six," I whispered, and he chuckled, leaning toward the bedstand to pull lube from the drawer.

"Sixty-seven." Precum slid over my knuckles where I still held tight to my throbbing dick.

Zeke snapped open the cap and squeezed the bottle, coating his fingers with lube.

"Sixty-eight," I squeaked again as he widened his legs and slid a finger straight into his ass.

"Shit. You're so hot, Zeke." I swallowed hard, staring while he slowly fucked himself—adding a second finger. I forgot to breathe, forgot to count while watching his slickened fingers reach deep, his harsh breaths in time with mine.

"Levi," he groaned.

"Sixty-nine," I choked out.

"Get over here."

I smashed my shin on the bedframe in my haste to get between his thighs, and the curses spewing from me staved off the need to blow in the next breath.

"Okay?" he asked, fighting off a smirk.

"Shut up," I grumbled, swiping the bottle of lube from his hand. "Hold your knees."

"Bossy," he muttered but smiled while doing as told.

"Damn right," I rushed out breathless, my focus on the puckered pink skin I planned to tongue one day. "I've been dreaming about this for so long...are you sure?" I moved in closer on my knees, his hole clenching as though desperate for me. "I don't know what I'm doing. Not really. You were my only experience, and porn isn't an actual lesson—"

"I want you, Levi. In every possible fucking way. Put your dick in me."

"Fuck." I clenched my jaw and stared down while placing the oozing tip of my length against him. So soft...I rubbed the head around his rim, and my balls seized right back up against my body. "You're so beautiful."

"Hey."

I finally lifted my attention back to his face.

Passion-hazed eyes snagged hold of my focus.

"Give me your mouth," Zeke said, reaching for

the back of my neck. "Swallow my groan when you make me yours."

Holy hell.

I pressed forward, Zeke's grunt hitting my ears before our mouths slammed together. He exhaled hard through his nose—and I breached the ring of muscle, the heat of his body clasping tight to the head of my dick.

A shudder wracked through me, and Zeke clutched at my ass with his heels, pulling me into him while guiding my body atop his.

My head spun at the silken heat in a vise grip around my length. Nothing, no fist, no person would ever compare to being inside Zeke.

Mine.

"Better than every fantasy," I whispered against his mouth as he breathed through the discomfort like I'd done with him. "Silky. Hot and tight." I swallowed, thoughts crashing through my head.

Damn.

So perfect.

"You're never leaving me behind again, Zeke," I spewed the words that rose to the forefront of my mind.

"Never. Sorry—so damn sor—"

I smashed my mouth against his and thrust deeper, shutting him the fuck up. There was no room for that shit while I buried balls deep in his tight ass and staked my claim on the man I wanted for the rest of my life.

I set a slow pace, fucking into him like he'd done with me on my apartment floor on the night we'd got caught. But there was no one to burst the bubble around us, no one to interrupt our gasps and clutching hands. Our deep moans and quickening thumps of the headboard continued, creating a confidence in me I didn't understand—but wasn't about to let go.

My spine took up its telltale tingling, and I propped onto my elbows. "Make yourself come before I fill your ass."

"Fuck, I love when you're sure of yourself. So fucking sexy." Zeke reached between us, grabbing hold of his dick and tugging in time with my thrusts, his knuckles rubbing against my abs. "Harder," he gasped, lips parting to pant when I gave him what he'd asked for.

Steady thumps of the headboard reached my ears, and I didn't care if his parents did hear us going at it. Somehow, I'd managed to get what I wanted, and no way in hell would I stop until I felt his hot, sticky cum smeared over my core.

I swallowed down his soft grunts that escaped with every snap of my hips until I couldn't hold out any longer. "I would choose you all over again," I whispered against his lips, burying deep inside his body.

"Levi—fuck." He came all over our stomachs and my chest, his eyes hazed over with barely a hint of blue remaining.

So damn beautiful and vulnerable. For me.

I gasped out his name as my balls erupted.

He took my mouth in a bruising kiss, swallowing my groans while I emptied inside his body, coating him with my essence.

A sticky mess smeared between us, but I couldn't be bothered to care.

Hairy legs wrapped around the backs of mine, and strong arms crushed me against a hard chest that heaved for breath.

"That was way better than I'd dreamed," I murmured, sinking into his warmth.

"You fantasized about drilling my ass?"

I snorted a laugh, and Zeke squeezed me tighter so I couldn't move off him. "Um...maybe? Did I hurt you?"

"I won't be able to sit comfortably for a few days, but it was worth the wait," he said with a groan that sounded a hell of a lot like pure, unadulterated satisfaction.

I grinned against his neck. "How long have you been thinking about my dick in your ass?"

"Since the first night I saw you."

"Shit. Really?"

A deep sound of agreement rumbled through his chest. "Fuck, yeah."

Zeke finally let me prop up on my elbows but kept me close. The movement jostled us enough that my softening dick slid from his body. He grimaced.

"*Still* worth it?" I asked, knowing exactly the feeling that caused the pinched expression.

"Hell yes."

Silence settled between us, contented smiles on both our faces. The world fell away as I lost myself in his eyes.

"Found," I whispered.

His smile widened as though he read my thoughts—or had similar ones, and everything calmed inside my soul.

I leaned down and softly kissed his lips, my heart delivered from the shroud of darkness that had clung to me for too long.

Free—to live.

To love.

39

ZEKE

I laid on my side, watching Levi sleep. Sooty lashes fanned above the purplish smudges beneath his eyes. Light snores escaped his parted lips that remained swollen and red from kissing for a good hour after he'd fucked me into my bed.

Levi's confidence, his blunt honesty, came out during sex, and not just from his mouth. He'd moved against my body—*in* my body—with pure, unadulterated truth, showing me his thoughts, his feelings toward me without words. The man might be insecure as hell in some areas of his life, but he knew how to fuck.

And my ass ached in the best way possible, but I wanted him again.

Never enough.

I let out a contented sigh rather than kissing him awake. The dark circles beneath his eyes insisted I let him sleep. I couldn't imagine he'd gotten much the previous week while living beneath his parents' roof. It couldn't have been comfortable.

"I'm sorry," I whispered, my throat tight. "I won't tell you again, but I'll *show* you how very much once you're back in the land of the living. I was an asshole who didn't have the guts to communicate, but I'm going to take every minute, every second you'll allow me to make it up to you."

Levi didn't so much as stir, so I pressed my lips to his forehead and slid off the bed.

We'd cleaned up earlier, but my backside protested my quiet movements around my room to find clothing.

Opening my bedroom door brought a rush of sweet-smelling air wafting past my nose.

Mom had baked cookies.

My mouth watered, and I lumbered down the stairs, walking like a goddamn cowboy. Being fucked by my man was going to take some getting used to, but I was up to the task.

I chuckled, pulling Mom's attention off the cookie sheet she took from the oven.

"No hickeys?" she asked after a quick perusal of my neck and bare chest while I tried not to flinch or flush.

I tilted my head side to side, letting her get a good look.

"Humph. Guess not." She motioned toward the

cooling racks with her chin. "Take that boy of yours some cookies. After that marathon, you probably need susten—"

"Mom," I groaned but grabbed a few. "Can we have some level of decency in this house? *Please*?"

She smirked, biting back a bigger grin while tugging the oven mitts of her hands. "Do I embarrass you, baby boy?"

"Yes." I took a large bite of cookie and chewed while holding her gaze. "Yes, you do," I stated around the gooey, warm chocolate.

She swatted me with the spatula. "Don't talk with your mouth full—unless Levi likes to hear you garble words around his—"

"Mom!"

She laughed. "Cold water's in the fridge."

The woman had read my mind.

"Where's Dad?"

"Still hiding out in the den. Is your boyfriend sleeping?"

I retrieved two bottles of ice water while she moved hot cookies to the rack. "How is there a complete lack of judgement? Total acceptance from both of you?"

Mom finished and propped her hip against the sink, smiling with enough warmth to melt an inch of ice off a windshield. "Love is love is love," she said quietly. "I've always believed that, and no God in heaven or higher being in this universe and beyond will change those thoughts. I love you, no matter what, unconditionally."

"Levi never had that," I told her, my smile fading as I imagined what he'd dealt with after I'd left. My heart ached all over again, and I couldn't wait to pull him into my arms and give him all the love, affection, and edification he should have had but didn't.

"Well he does now. And we're going to make sure he knows it's his right—and yours—to love who you want and need."

I choked up and held open my arms. "Thanks, Mom. You don't know how much your words mean to me. And Levi."

Mom eyed my bare chest as though looking for dried spunk. "Is it safe to hug you right now?" she asked, confirming my assumption.

"Maybe?" I offered a sheepish grin.

"You can give me that hug later. After you and my second son shower. Together—you know, to save water." She winked.

"Thanks, Mom." My voice broke, and her eyes welled with tears too.

———

It took us a couple hours to get all my stuff from my parents' basement into the condo, but by dinner time on Monday night, Levi, Mom, Dad, and I had the place pretty well set up.

No one said a word about the fact there was only one bed or that I'd put our desks in the second bedroom.

After gorging ourselves on pizza, Mom and Dad took off, leaving quiet in their wake.

I shut the door behind them, enjoying the sudden silence.

Levi sat at the kitchen table. The dark smudges under his eyes had faded, but he slumped in the chair.

"Tired?"

"Beat. I guess I'll just crash on the couch until I can get myself a bed." He glanced toward the living room and the sectional that was comfortable as fuck —but wasn't going to be his bed.

I leaned against the door, arms crossing and my lips quirking up. "I was hoping those roommate with benefits agreements included you in *my* bed and waking up beside me every morning. Tangled up limbs. Sleepy, soft kisses. Maybe blow job wake up calls?"

Levi tilted his head to the side, studying my face.

"You're important to me," I told him, crossing the kitchen when he didn't reply. "You weaved your way into my heart, and I want you to stay. There, in my bed, and in my life."

"What happens when you grow tired of me,

when I'm no longer enough?" he asked, tipping his head back when I loomed over him.

I dropped to my knees between his and cradled his face in my hands, realizing his insecurities had crept back in. Holding his stare, I rubbed my thumbs along the hint of scruff he hadn't shaved earlier that morning after we'd showered together. "Not gonna happen, Levi."

He glanced away, a slight frown furrowing his brow.

"Hey." I grasped his chin and turned his head, getting his focus back on where it needed to be. His future—if I had a say in the matter. "The second I saw you while my best friend and his lover sang on stage to each other, something clicked inside me like a puzzle piece snapping into place. I knew in that moment my mind would never be rid of you. And now that you're here with me, free to be who you are? I'm never letting you go. Ever. You're stuck with me—if you want."

"If I want." He snorted, the uncertainty easing from his eyes. "I found the balls to drive all the way up here with less than fifty bucks in my pocket and make myself vulnerable after being turned down. More than once."

"I'm sorry."

"I hate those words."

I didn't apologize again, simply allowed myself to be as open as he did, hoping he would see my feelings for him—but he needed the vocal assurance too. "I know this happened quick, a lightning strike of what I'd thought was an unholy yearning, but I'm falling in love with you, Levi, and there's nothing wrong or evil about it. You light up the darkness, illuminating parts of my life I hadn't realized sat dimmed by wrongful, hurtful teachings. I'm weak as fuck around you—in the best way possible. I've never cursed my inability to say no like I've done in fighting this draw between us, but I wouldn't change one goddamn thing. You make me a better man."

"You love me."

I leaned in and pressed my lips to his in a chaste kiss, the soft pillow of his mouth causing happiness to swirl through my entire body. "Yes."

Levi leaped off the chair and ungraciously tackled me to the floor, and I got lost in the taste of him, unable to keep my hands to myself. And when he begged me to let him into my body again, I ignored the ache in my ass from the day before and agreed to what he wanted—in our bed because I didn't want a bruised spine.

"Zeke," he groaned while sinking into me, his shudder tightening my balls against my groin regardless of the stretching sting. He held my gaze, green eaten away by swelled pupils. "I love you too."

I wrapped my heels around his ass and pulled his torso down to rest on mine. "Say it again."

"I love you."

"Show me."

And he did—with his whole body, with the dirty words falling from his parted lips, with every kiss and shared breath. As expected, he gave me all he had, leaving me aching in the best way possible.

Once spent, he sprawled atop me while I mapped out every inch of his skin I could reach.

"I don't handle rejection or being let down very well—it's my number one trigger," he murmured, his breath hot against my neck.

"I can't promise that won't ever happen," I told him. "But I'll be careful. You're always in my thoughts—I *can* promise you that."

Levi propped up onto an elbow, resting his head in his hand. "What changed your mind about us?"

"Realizing the path I'd set in stone didn't match up with my heart's desire. I didn't want to live without you."

His lips quirked up as though he'd imagined the same thing.

"I'd made the decision to go back to Philly to tell you so, to ask you to come back to New England with me, but you arrived here seconds later."

"Damnit. You mean I could have had my knight-in-shining-armor show up at my parents' door to rescue me from the pits of hell?"

"You didn't need rescuing, Levi." I smoothed a hand down his spine. "But I'll be your knight or your king for life if you'll have me."

"Are you calling me a queen?" He snickered.

"I'd rather just call you mine."

The press of his lips against my mouth tingled clear down to my toes. "Yes," he whispered and kissed me again.

40

ZEKE

FOUR MONTHS LATER

My lover sat across the white-linen tablecloth from me, enjoying his first glass of wine. Soft overhead music caressed the restaurant's sprawling room, the clink of silverware and murmured voices adding to the atmosphere for our celebration dinner.

"So, are you excited for tomorrow?" I asked him.

Levi held his glass of Chardonnay to his lips and smiled around the rim before taking a sip. "Nervous."

"Are you going to keep those scallops down?"

"Gross, Zeke."

I shrugged while smirking. "You know how I was raised."

"Yes, but at the dinner table?"

"I think you're going to be a perfect fit at Benson

& Benson. They're a huge firm, one my dad has worked with for years."

Levi's eyes went misty as he set his glass back on the table. "I'll never be able to repay your dad for helping me land that job."

"You're his son, Levi, same as me. There's nothing either of my parents wouldn't do for you."

"Stop," he muttered, swiping his sleeve across his eyes.

I decided to take pity on the man who got caught up in his emotions whenever reminded about how full his life had become.

"Did I tell you that Chase wants to go back to school for psychology?" My friend and gym partner—as well as Levi's since he started going with me every morning—had decided he didn't just want to stand up for himself. He wanted to take a page from my book and become a counselor at one of the LGBTQ homes in the Boston area too.

I'd been working in my new labor of love at the Humanity House for close to three months, and I'd never known such contentment.

The board in charge of Malden's shelter for homeless LGBTQ persons didn't care if I was a former Christian, a fire and brimstone guy, or that I'd broken up two marriages.

Levi claimed I hadn't broken up anything but saved Lily's uncle from an abusive relationship and himself from a lifetime of discontentment and heartache.

"What?" he asked, peering at me, and I realized I'd been silent while staring at him, processing his words I'd heard before but hadn't internalized.

He spoke truth—and peace over both situations settled inside me.

"I love you," I told him, no trace of doubt in my voice or heart.

Pink flushed his cheeks as it always did whenever I declared my feelings in public without keeping my voice down. "Love you too," he murmured, the want in his eyes twitching life into my dick I'd spent in his ass not an hour earlier.

"Ezekiel?"

Scowling, I turned to see who the fuck would even call me that—

"Pastor Hardy," I stated quietly, all trace of pissiness dissolving at his wide smile.

"John, please."

I nodded, knowing he no longer had his license to preach.

"You remember Jill?" he asked.

My gaze tore off the man who'd once been on a high pedestal, and I recognized the woman on his arm. The one he'd had an affair with, the woman who'd tempted him to sin and leave his son behind —even if his marriage with Braden's mom had been on troubled ground for years.

But Braden had told me he'd forgiven him in his heart when making amends with God, and their past was none of my affair.

Jill wore a wedding band as did John, and I found myself strangely...happy for them.

"Looks like congratulations are in order," I said, offering him my hand.

His smile widened, his shoulders relaxing as he grasped my palm. "Eight years tonight—and four kids later."

"Shit," I muttered and chuckled. "You two didn't waste any time."

"When you meet the one your heart belongs to later in life," Jill said, her tone soft and sweet while leaning into John, "there's no sense in waiting. The years, every day, passes too quickly."

"When two souls connect like ours did, even amidst heartache," John said, glancing at Levi across from me, "there's no denying you're meant to be together."

"Shit," I muttered again. "Sorry. John, Jill, this is my boyfriend Levi." I lifted my chin, waiting for him to prove himself a hypocritical asshole like I'd accused him of being for years.

"Levi." John held out his hand, his smile still firmly in place, not so much as a twitch over the fact I loved a man.

No judgement shone on his or his wife's faces,

and when they walked from the restaurant a few minutes later, my gaze trailed after them.

"Looks like he's a changed man too."

I turned back toward Levi. "He seemed...peaceful."

"Happy," Levi added.

I nodded, filtering through the differing emotions I felt for my old pastor. I'd badmouthed him countless times, uncovered his so-called sins—when all he'd done was fall in love with the woman who fit him like a puzzle piece.

He left Braden behind for love...

But there were so many sides to a story, and I'd been tunnel-visioned by my bitterness.

Levi reached across the table to grasp my hand, pulling me into to the present.

I studied the back of his left hand, dreaming about the silver band I wanted circling his ring finger in the near future.

"What's that growing grin for?" Levi asked, quirking an eyebrow.

"I'm thinking about next weekend."

When Malachi and Isaac, the dynamic duo, would make a surprise appearance at Humanity House for an early mini-Christmas concert.

"I can't believe they agreed to swing by between tour stops."

I lifted Levi's hand and kissed his knuckles. "He didn't even hesitate when I'd asked him to help us celebrate the expansion and opening of the new building."

"I'm dying to meet him."

"He's going to love you. Promise."

"You know how I feel about *that* word too," Levi said and finished off his wine.

"You gave me a chance at true happiness," I reminded my lover. "That's all the reason he needs."

41

LEVI

Malachi and Isaac were everything Zeke had promised. Kind and accepting without a trace of arrogance over their success in the music industry.

They stood on the small makeshift stage set up in Humanity House's new cafeteria, guitars in hand, no flashing lights or booming bass for their part of the celebration.

And the crowd packed into the room around me and Zeke shrieked their love for the couple as Isaac sang.

Beautifully us, worth the sacrifice. I would choose you all over again.

Malachi leaned toward him as though Isaac's soul ensnared him, drew him in—same as that night in Nashville when my whole world had changed.

My light.

My life.

My love.

They shared a brief, chaste kiss and continued singing, staring into each other's eyes as their voices wove in a breathtaking beauty that everyone around me cheered on. Caught up in love, caught up in life... my pulse thrummed, and I grasped Zeke's hand tight, pressing against his side.

I'd thought Lil had filled me with light, but hers didn't compare to how Zeke brightened me from the inside out, creating the type of golden rays that no shroud of depression could smother.

He shared his life with me, every aspect, every emotion.

And our love flourished into an immovable source of happiness I clung to with a thankful, over-flowing heart.

Malachi and Isaac finished the song—the final in their set, and Zeke made for the stage, tugging me along behind him.

Heat rushed through me at the thought of standing in front of the crowd, but he obviously wanted me by his side. I went with willing but shaky footfalls. Ten to the platform, two more steps placing us a head above the crowd.

Zeke hugged Malachi, slapping him on his back. He took the mic and thanked him and Isaac for taking the time out of their busy schedule to support Humanity House.

Isaac stared at Malachi from where he stood with a soft smile on his face, love shining in his eyes.

I no longer felt the envy like I had in Nashville since I'd found the same.

My everything.

Zeke angled toward me, holding out his hand.

I glanced around, realizing the crowd had quieted.

Holy hell...now what?

Face hot, I shuffled forward three steps, placing me beside him. He kissed my temple—and a few hoots raised in the echoing cafeteria.

"You all have heard me talk about Levi—"

"Too much!" someone hollered, causing laughter to rise.

"Never enough!" Zeke shot back with a laugh. "Seriously, though, it was the arrival of this man in my life who helped me see I had worth beyond what I'd been raised to believe was right. He's *my* light, my love, and I want him, *need* him by my side until I breathe my last breath."

Zeke went down on one knee—and my breath ripped from my lungs. He fished a black box from his pocket and flipped the lid while I stared, light-headed and swaying.

"Don't puke," he whispered up at me, his dark blue eyes full of the emotion that made my legs weak. "Or pass out. Please."

"Yes," I choked out and sucked in oxygen to appease my racing heart. "Yes."

His smile sent butterflies to flight in my belly. "I didn't even ask you yet."

The crowd laughed, but I barely heard them. Tears slid down my cheeks, and I bit my lip to keep from losing my shit right there in front of everyone.

Zeke slid the ring on my finger and stood, yanking me into his arms. "I appreciate you. Love you desperately. Need you more than air," he whispered against my ear.

Malachi's voice boomed through the speakers, but I didn't hear a word he said as Zeke laid claim to my mouth, uncaring of the crowd.

"Will you be my number one?" he asked against my lips.

My heart melted. "As in nothing but negative came before me?"

He chuckled and squeezed me tighter. "Be my first positive. Be *mine*."

"I already am."

Malachi and Isaac started another song, but I stayed pressed against Zeke, lost in his kiss.

Found.

THE END

———

ABOUT THE AUTHOR

Lynn Burke is an international bestselling and award-winning author. A stay-at-home mom, she's a lover of coffee and vino, and with three spawn and two fur babies underfoot, noise levels dictate the daily switch-over time. In her few quiet 'me' moments, she can be found hunched over her Mac, trying to type as fast as her muse spews hot stories.

You can find more about Lynn at her website: www.authorlynnburke.com

ALSO BY LYNN BURKE

Abel's Obsession

Divulging Secrets

Healing Storms

In Between

Reluctant Lumberjack

Resisting his Mate

The Playboy Bachelor

Billion Dollar Love Anthology

Blood Born Series

Bonds of Worship Series

Dark Leopards MC

Darkest Desires Series

Devil's Outlaws MC

Elite Escort Series

Fallen Gliders MC

Forbidden Obsession Duet

Found by Fate Series

Midnight Sun Series

Missing Link Series

Risso Family Series

Sandy Ridge Series

Sinful Nature Series

Vicious Vipers MC

www.ingramcontent.com/pod-product-compliance
Lightning Source LLC
Chambersburg PA
CBHW070821190726
48292CB00006B/2071